SAM SISAVATH

Published by Road to Babylon Media LLC
www.roadtobabylon.com

Edited by Jennifer Jensen & Wendy Chan
Cover Art by Deranged Doctor Design

ISBN-10: 0997894660
ISBN-13: 978-0997894660

BOOKS IN THE ROAD TO BABYLON SERIES

Glory Box

Bombtrack

Rooster

Devil's Haircut

ALSO BY SAM SISAVATH

Saint/Sinner

Finders/Keepers

THE RED SKY CONSPIRACY SERIES

Most Wanted

The Devil You Know

ABOUT DEVIL'S HAIRCUT

THE DEVIL ALWAYS GETS HIS DUE.

Keo has tried to stay out of it, but five years in the wild have only led him back to the one place he dreaded most—alongside a woman from his past and fighting someone else's cause. Except this is one war he can't turn his back on. What's a reformed mercenary to do?

Lara didn't want this. Not another war to fight. She's been struggling to bring order to chaos since The Walk Out and doing it with as little bloodshed as possible. But Fenton is forcing her hand, and sometimes you have to get a little bloody, whether you want to or not.

What *is* happening in Fenton? Despite attempts to answer that question, the mystery behind the former collaborator town remains hidden. What is Buck planning, and why has he done the unthinkable and joined forces with a blue-eyed ghoul? What is their ultimate endgame?

Those are questions Lara must answer before she commits forces to putting an end to Fenton's rampage. To do that, she'll need to rely on people she can trust to help her expose the enemy's secrets to the light of the day.

In *Devil's Haircut*, Book 4 in the Road to Babylon series, a mission behind enemy lines will set the stage for a battle that will shape the lives of everyone involved...and beyond.

ONE

The first subsonic round *zipped!* past Keo's head about half a dozen inches from taking off his left ear. It would have gone directly into his forehead had the shooter been aiming for him and not poor Chang, who was walking to Keo's left and had been since they hopped off the helo and inserted into the woods. They were still more than ten miles from Fenton's perimeter, and there shouldn't have been any sentries this far out, never mind a shooter lying in wait.

Except there was, and that mistake cost Chang his life.

Chang was a big man—a beefy six-two, which made him the ideal candidate to carry the belt-fed M249 light machine gun by himself. His buddy, Banner, was carrying the spare ammo for the MG and walking two feet behind Chang when the bullet entered the machine gunner's right temple and exited the back of his skull, his brains spraying the smaller Banner in the face less than half a heartbeat later.

Keo instinctively flicked the fire selector on his MP5SD to

full auto and shouted as loud as he could, "Sniper! Take cover! Take cover!" and pulled the trigger.

In the brief second or two he had turned his head with the incoming sniper bullet, he saw the round go through the front and exit the back of Chang's head at almost the same angle, which meant the shooter was on the ground and somewhere in front of them.

Somewhere in front of them wasn't exactly the most specific target, but it did give Keo a direction to shoot in. This was one of those times when he wished the submachine gun didn't have a built-in suppressor that, true to its purpose, suppressed his shots. He was used to the *pfft-pfft-pfft!* sound, barely louder than the audible cycling of the weapon's parts as it spat one 9mm round after 9mm round, but the loud crackle of gunfire would have been preferable to get everyone moving, moving, *moving.*

Thank God the men Lara had given him weren't total idiots, and he could hear them jumping into action behind him even before he got the final *cover* out. Out of the corner of one eye, he glimpsed them darting for cover behind trees—

Zip!

Jesus! Keo's mind screamed as a silent second round almost took his head off. Like the first one, this shot missed by inches, and Keo spun to his left just in time to see Banner, who had for some reason reached for Chang's fallen MG, stumble as blood spurted out of his chest and sprayed the knee-high grass around him.

Banner had refused to let go of the M249 even after being shot and was somehow still clinging to it, trying to line it up for a return volley despite the fact he was much smaller than Chang and there was no way—

A red mist formed in front of Banner's face—like a mystical puff of cloud appearing from nowhere—and the man dropped the weapon and collapsed over Chang's unmoving form.

Shit shit shit!

Keo spun and ran toward the closest tree. Unfortunately for him, it wasn't nearly close enough.

Five meters.

Four.

Three—

Another subsonic round *buzzed* his head as it missed him —but not Springer, who was running toward Banner and Chang. The bullet caught the blond in the shoulder and spun him like a top while he was still halfway to his target.

Idiot! Keo thought, then, *And so am I!* as he turned and ran back to Springer.

Keo hadn't gotten more than two steps toward the fallen man when someone shouted "Covering fire!" and the forest erupted in thunderous gunfire as seemingly every weapon in existence opened up.

Definitely not total idiots!

Springer had somehow managed to get back up on his knees and was also firing into the trees in front of them. But like Keo earlier, Springer and the others didn't know where to put their rounds and only had a general direction to go by. The truth was, the shooter could have already moved. Assuming there was just *a* shooter and not shoot*ers*.

"We're putting you guys ten miles from the target. That should give you plenty of space to hump your way toward the objective without alerting anyone."

Keo laughed to himself now.

Not "plenty of space" enough, I guess!

But of course there was nothing to laugh at, especially with the hellacious barrage drowning out every single other noise in the woods around him for miles. If there were more than just the shooter out there (*He's trying to nail me right now, isn't he? Of course he is. Why wouldn't he be? I'm the dummy running back into the open when everyone else is already behind cover!*), they would surely be converging on them right now.

More good news! Swell!

Springer saw Keo running back to him and attempted to get up even while fumbling to reload his M4 rifle.

"Stay down, you idiot!" Keo shouted, but he was pretty sure Springer couldn't hear him over the roar of automatic rifle fire. The others were pouring it on, and if Keo could spare a second to glance right toward where the shooter would be, he would see leaves and branches and tree trunks disintegrating against the onslaught. But he didn't have that second to waste, and he didn't have to anyway because he could *smell* all the green burning as hot rounds sliced through them in a sea of spitting lead.

Keo was (somehow!) still alive when he reached Springer, who was desperately trying to find his legs in the midst of reloading. He was failing miserably with the first but did manage to get the magazine in, if just barely. Before he could work the charging handle, Keo grabbed him by the shoulders from behind—Springer screamed in pain, but Keo ignored it— and began dragging him backward as if he were a helpless dummy.

"Over here!" a voice shouted. It was soft, barely audible, but that was just because the others were still shooting, the *pop-pop-pop* of their weapons easily drowning out everything else capable of making noise.

Keo shot a quick glance over his shoulder, in the direction where the voice had come from. An oval-shaped face poked out from behind a massive elm tree while a hand waved him over. Rita, all five-three and one hundred and twenty pounds of her, had slung her MP5 and had her Mk 14 braced against the side of the tree that she was currently well-hidden behind.

Keo pulled Springer, stumbling in front of him like a toddler just learning how to use his legs, over to his team's sniper. Rita had returned her eyes to her scope when Keo dragged Springer behind the tree and dumped him unceremoniously on the ground.

"Jesus!" Springer shouted.

"Stay down!" Keo shouted back before moving over to Rita and leaning against the tree trunk next to her.

The knife!

He reached behind his back to make sure it was still there and hadn't fallen during all the chaos. The rubber handle of the knife fastened to his waist by his belt was slightly warm to the touch. It was nothing special—ten inches long, the five inches that made up the bladed portion composed entirely of silver—but it was supposed to bring him good luck. Right now it was doing a pretty bad job of it.

Any second now, good luck charm. Any second now...

The others had stopped shooting as soon as Keo and Springer made cover. They were now reloading, the *clack-clack* of magazines inserting and charging handles snapping back and letting go ringing around the suddenly very quiet woods.

Rita hadn't said a word since his arrival and was moving

her rifle around, trying to find the shooter. He didn't interrupt her or break her concentration, and instead focused on the others.

Gholston was about ten meters to his right, using a tree half the size of his own. But Gholston could afford the smaller shield since there was just him. The lanky Georgian, the lower half of his face covered by a Lynyrd Skynyrd bandana, glanced over and nodded even as he fiddled with the optic on top of his heavily modified AR rifle.

On the other side of Gholston, and about a meter in front of him, were Rudolph and Wells. They were sharing a tree. Rudolph was calmly chewing gum and loading shells into his M1014 shotgun while the much younger Wells crouched on one knee next to him, wiping at beads of sweat dripping from his face. Like Gholston, neither man looked wounded, but just to be sure, Keo caught Rudolph's and Wells's eyes and got back reassured nods.

There was a haunting silence to the woods around them. Even the animals had ceased moving or making any sounds. Keo swore he could hear every heartbeat at the moment with, possibly, the exception of Rita's. He wouldn't know if the sniper was breathing next to him if he couldn't see her with his eyes.

Keo glanced back at Springer, who had taken out a field first-aid kit and was wrapping up his shoulder. Blood covered the gauze and ran down his sleeve.

"You good?" Keo asked.

"Fuck no," Springer said, clenching his teeth. "But I'll live."

"Good enough." He turned back to Rita. She hadn't taken her eye off her scope. "What do you see?"

"There's just one shooter," Rita said. "I saw him back-tracking."

"Did you get him?"

"I had him in my sights before Springer stood up and blocked my shot."

"What?" Springer said from behind them.

"I lost him after that," Rita said, ignoring Springer. "He's hiding and he's good. I haven't been able to find him again."

"What about Chang and Banner?" Springer asked.

"They're dead," Keo said.

"Are you sure?"

"Yeah, I'm sure," Keo said, but he peeked around the tree and toward the two bodies just in case. He had seen men survive head shots before, but...

Neither Banner nor Chang were moving.

Keo pulled completely back behind cover. "They're dead."

"Shit," Springer said.

"You see him, Rita?" Gholston asked from the next tree over.

Rita shook her head. "I lost him."

"Shit."

"That seems to be the consensus." She kept her eye on the scope while moving the rifle around. Searching, searching... "What now, boss?"

"Boss?" Keo said.

"She put you in charge, didn't she? So what now, boss?"

Keo sighed. He hadn't wanted the position for precisely this reason. He looked around the tree at Chang and Banner again. Then there was Springer behind him, trying to catch his breath and not bleed to death.

An eight-man team on a recon mission. Inserted ten miles

well beyond the range of Fenton's perimeter. The walk over to the town itself should have been tedious and uneventful. Supposedly, anyway.

I guess we weren't "beyond" enough.

Keo glanced over at Wells, with that bulky pack slung behind him, housing the radio. They weren't scheduled to report in to Black Tide for another five hours—exactly at noon. He resisted the urge to make use of the communications device now and call Lara, tell her just how FUBAR everything had gotten, then wait for the order to retreat because the mission was blown. If the pooch wasn't screwed when the sniper put the first bullet through Chang, and it still wasn't when Banner bought the farm, it was now after they'd unloaded a few hundred rounds and alerted just about every Bucky for miles.

Definitely weren't "beyond" enough.

"Well, boss?" Rita asked. "What's the order?"

"He's got us pinned," Keo said. "We're not going forward. By now he'll have radioed in for reinforcements. If there aren't Fenton patrols on their way now, they'll be soon enough." He met Gholston's waiting gaze over the short distance. "Get ready to move."

Gholston nodded over at Springer. "What about him?"

Keo looked over. "Can you walk?"

"Yeah," Springer said, and pushed himself back up to his feet, grimacing the entire way. "I can walk."

"Make sure he doesn't fall down," Keo said to Gholston.

"I'm not gonna fall down," Springer said.

"Yeah, yeah," Gholston said. "Just let out a warning shout first if you're gonna, pretty boy."

Springer grunted back.

Keo turned to Rita. "You got anything yet?"

"Nothing. He's being a very, very small mouse," Rita said.

"Could he be trying to flank us? Get a better angle for a shot?"

"I don't think so. I only lost him for a second. There's no way he could be moving out there." She shook her head, her eye never leaving her rifle's scope. "No. He's hunkered down, boss. All that covering fire would have ripped him apart if he'd tried anything. He's still there. Waiting."

"Hey," Gholston said. Then, when Keo looked over, "You want me to try to draw him out?"

Keo stared at him.

"I'm serious," Gholston said. "You want me to draw him out? Give Rita a shot?"

"Jesus Christ, this redneck idiot," Rita muttered under her breath.

"What did you say?" Gholston said. "I didn't catch that."

"She said that's a stupid idea," Keo said. "He's using a suppressed rifle. You wouldn't even hear the shot when he kills you and we'd still be guessing where he's firing from."

"Oh," Gholston said.

Keo glanced past Gholston and at Rudolph, standing over Wells while giving him a *"So are we going or what?"* look. Then again, Keo could have been reading the man wrong and he was just thinking about a new pack of gum. He did have a thick red beard, and it wasn't always easy to read someone with that much facial hair—

"Keo!" a voice shouted.

What the hell?

It was coming from in front of them.

It was the sniper.

"What the hell?" Rita whispered out loud next to him.

"What the hell?" Springer said behind them.

To the left of them, Gholston mouthed the words in Keo's direction, *"Did he just say your name? What the hell?"*

Keo sighed and thought, *Well, I'm glad we're all on the same wavelength, at least.*

TWO

"Keo! Give me a shout back if you can hear me. I didn't plug you by accident, did I? Now that would be a crying shame!"

It was coming from in front of them. The shooter. It was a he, and his voice sounded firm but also...echoey, like every syllable was being bounced off a tree then ricocheted off another one before they finally reached Keo. He didn't know how that was possible.

"You know this guy?" Rita asked.

"No," Keo said.

"How does he know your name?"

"I have no idea."

"He's talking like he knows you," Springer said.

"Yeah, I noticed that," Keo said.

"So does he or doesn't he?"

"I don't know. I can't tell by the voice."

Keo glanced across the woods and saw the same question on Gholston's and Rudolph's faces. Wells was too busy trying to find the sniper to join in on the fun.

"Can you..." Keo started to ask.

"No," Rita said before he could finish.

"Not at all?"

"Not at all." She paused, then, "Keep him talking."

"Keo!" the sniper shouted. "Can you hear me? Say something, if you're still alive!"

"He knows your name," Springer said behind them. "How does he know your name?"

Keo ignored him and instead tried to match a face to the voice, but nothing popped. It didn't help that he had difficulty placing the origin of the voice. At first he thought it was coming from his left, but every word the man shouted out gave a new location.

"I don't know," Keo finally said.

"You sure?" Springer asked.

"Yeah."

"But he *knows* you."

"I heard you the first three times, Springer. Now shut up." Keo sighed, then, leaning slightly out from behind the tree, shouted back, "Yeah? What do you want?"

"It is you!" the sniper shouted. Was that coming from his left? His right? Or both? "I knew it!"

"Who wants to know?"

"I wasn't sure." The man said, as if Keo hadn't asked a question. He might have also laughed. It was short and died too quickly for Keo to even try to pinpoint it. "But you match the description. Tall. Asian. A big ass ugly scar down one side of your face. And he said you might be coming back here."

"*He said...*"

Keo didn't have to think very hard to know who *he* was.

"I don't think your scar's that ugly," Rita said. "Scars give a man character."

"That's what I keep telling everyone," Keo said.

Rita chuckled but never took her eye away from the scope. She kept moving her Mk 14. Searching, searching... For such a small person, she didn't look at all fatigued from holding the rifle against the tree for long periods.

She must be stronger than she looks, Keo thought. The Mk 14 was over eleven pounds unloaded. Heavier, with a full mag. It wasn't exactly a weapon made for a small man, never mind a small *woman*.

"Keo!" the sniper shouted.

"What?" Keo shouted back.

"I could have killed you, you know."

"Is that right?"

"That first shot? I didn't have to take out the other Asian guy. That wasn't your brother or cousin or anything, was it?"

"No."

"Good. 'Cause I have a hard time telling Asians apart. No offense."

Keo smirked. "None taken."

"You're Chinese, right?" the man shouted.

"You don't know?"

"There was some discussion. Which is why I'm asking. Not that it matters, mind you. Just curious."

Keo glanced over at Gholston and Rudolph. They looked over and shook their heads. They couldn't locate the sniper, either.

"Curiosity killed the cat!" Keo shouted.

The sniper let out another laugh. This one was louder and lasted longer, but it still didn't yield anything that felt like a real location. "I just wanted to let you know that I could have taken you out anytime while you were running around out there in the open, but I didn't."

"How nice of you."

"I could have put a couple of rounds in your legs. Put you down without putting you down, know what I mean?"

"I'll be sure to send you a Christmas card in a few months. Look for it in the mail."

"Will do."

"Who are you?"

"You don't know me, but I know a lot about you."

"Rita?" Keo whispered.

She shook her head. "I don't know how he's doing it, but I can't pin his voice down to any spot. Can you?"

"No. Maybe he's using some kind of machine to throw his voice?"

"Does something like that exist?"

"Hell if I know."

"Well, however he's doing it, he's good. Keep him talking, if you can. Maybe he'll slip up and I can pop him like a zit."

Yeah, that's gonna happen, Keo thought, but he shouted out from behind the tree anyway, "Should I be flattered you know so much about me, but I don't know bupkis about you?"

"That depends," the sniper shouted back.

"On what?"

"About how you feel about me taking you back alive, where you'll no doubt end up wishing I'd killed you out here. You know what I'm talking about, don't you?"

Keo didn't have to think about that question for too long as a voice from the not-too-distant past came rushing back, except instead of a normal voice it was a series of unnatural hisses:

"*I won't turn you. Oh no. You won't get off that easy. We'll bond. And play. And soon, you won't remember what it was like not having me inside, right here.*"

It had touched his forehead with its finger when it had said *right here*, and Keo remembered the wild fluctuations of warm and cold that traveled from that bony finger and onto his skin from the contact. That sense of impossibility, of being close to something so unnatural, filled him with the same dread now as it did then.

Keo flinched unwittingly, then checked to see if the others had noticed. Rita hadn't, because she was too busy staring through her scope, while Springer was dabbing at blood along his arm behind them. Gholston, Wells, and Rudolph had their eyes elsewhere.

"Oh yeah, you know what I'm talking about," the sniper was shouting.

"What's that lunatic talking about?" Rita asked.

"I don't know," Keo lied. Then, throwing his voice forward at the (*Too goddamn well*) hidden Fenton man, "That doesn't sound like fun at all."

The man laughed again. Keo was starting to hate that laughter.

"You got a name?" Keo shouted.

"Calvin!" the sniper shouted back.

"Calvin?" Springer said. "His name is Calvin?"

Keo shrugged. "Hey, let's not start making fun of people's names, okay?"

Rita might have snorted next to him.

"What?" Keo said.

"I didn't say anything," Rita said.

"Uh huh."

He gave Springer a longer look. The young blond hadn't done a very good job of putting a field tourniquet around his wound. Blood oozed around the edges of the gauze, and his face was pale; if he wasn't already sitting on the grass, Keo would have been afraid of him falling down.

"You okay?" Keo asked him.

Springer nodded and gave him a half-hearted attempt at a convincing smile. "Yeah, I'm peachy."

"No, you're not," Gholston said from his tree across from them.

"I'll be fine," Springer said.

Keo and Gholston locked eyes, and the other man nodded his understanding.

"Keo, you still there?" the man named Calvin shouted. "I'm not boring you, am I?"

"Not yet!" Keo shouted back. "You radioed in for help yet, Calvin?"

He didn't expect the man to answer, but he did. "I tried, but I'm either out of range or the trees are blocking my signal. But I'm pretty sure someone heard all that noise your boys made, though, so I don't doubt that I have reinforcements on the way as we speak."

"You think he's lying?" Springer asked.

"Does it matter?" Rita said. "Either way, someone's coming."

"She's right," Keo said. "The fact that they're not here yet just means they're on their way. But they're coming. It's just a matter of time."

"We're gonna have to move soon," Rita said.

"I know."

"What about Chang and Banner?" Springer asked. "We can't just leave them lying out there."

Keo glanced the short distance at the two bodies. There was some poetry to the two men lying on top of one another. They were a two-man machine gun team and were, as far as Keo knew, good friends. They'd joked all the way from the FOB and seemed like they'd known each other long before The Purge.

But they were dead now, and there was nothing he could do about it. All that was left was to tell Lara how he'd lost two men and almost a third. Now that was something he wasn't looking forward to.

See, this is why you should never have agreed to lead this little expedition. Or gotten involved with leading anything in the first place. Nothing good ever comes from it. Nothing good whatsoever.

He looked across at Gholston, then over at Rudolph and Wells, even though only Rudolph caught his gaze.

Two down, six to go.

He hated when the numbers went against him. It was easier (*Okay, maybe not "easier"*) when it was the other guys who were losing men.

So this is how it feels to be on the other side.

He nodded at Rudolph and Gholston, before mouthing, *"Get ready to move on my signal."*

Gholston nodded back, and Rudolph did the same, before tapping Wells on the shoulder to let him know.

Keo put a hand on Rita's arm and squeezed. "Get ready."

"Whenever you are, boss," Rita said.

"Stop calling me that."

"What?"

"You know what."

"Whatever you say, boss."

He sighed. "Danny told me you'd be a handful."

"My legend precedes me."

"That's one way to put it." Keo glanced back at Springer, who had stood up on slightly wobbly legs. "You first. Then Gholston. We'll cover you. Rita—"

"Will shoot the motherfucker when he pops out of whatever hole he's hiding in," Rita finished for him.

"What she said."

"What if he doesn't do that?" Springer said. "He hasn't taken a shot since he took out Chang and Banner. This guy…" Springer shook his head. "He's good. He knows when to shoot and when not to."

"He's not that good," Rita said, and Keo thought she was grinding her teeth.

"You still haven't gotten him," Springer said. "You can't even see him."

"He's using a hide. No telling how long he's been out here getting ready for a group of suckers to walk right into him."

"Suckers like us?"

"I thought that was implied."

"Can it," Keo said. Then, fixing Springer with a hard glare, "You ready?"

"No," Springer said.

"Too bad," Keo said. Then, "*Go!*"

Springer turned and fled into the woods, with Gholston mirroring him a second later. Keo turned and fired into the trees in front of him while Rita remained poised, searching, *searching* through her rifle's scope for a shot.

Farther across from them, Rudolph and Wells unleashed with their own weapons.

Branches snapped, pieces of bark flicked across the air, and leaves disintegrated against the torrent of bullets, the *pop-pop-pop* of fully automatic rifle fire once again filling up the woods.

Keo stopped shooting briefly to check behind him. Gholston was in the process of grabbing Springer, who was stumbling and nearly tripped on his own legs more than once. If the sniper was trying to pick them off, he was failing badly, and both men made it into the thick of the woods unscathed.

"Rita," Keo said.

"I don't see him," Rita said. There was a slight edge to her voice—a mixture of confusion and annoyance.

"Forget about him. Time for you to go."

"Maybe he'll try to take a shot—"

"Do what you're told, woman!"

"Goddammit," Rita said, and pulled up her rifle, turned, and flashed an annoyed glance in his direction, fleeing after Springer and Gholston.

Keo fired off the last few rounds in his magazine, then exchanged a nod with Rudolph before turning and running after Rita.

He heard shooting for another few seconds before the last shots died and there was just the heavy *crunch-crunch* of Rudolph and Wells pounding ground with their boots to the left and slightly behind him.

"Hey, Keo!"

It was the sniper.

Keo stopped on a dime and slid behind a tree to catch his breath. Wells disappeared into the woods after Rita, but Rudolph stayed behind another trunk and reloaded his rifle.

Keo kept waiting for bullets to hit their trees, but they never did. Either the sniper didn't have a shot, or he just didn't feel like it.

Who the hell is this guy?

"You're not saying good-bye already, are you?" Calvin shouted, his voice still as echoey and impossible to locate as they had been all day. "And here I thought we were just getting started!"

"Why don't you come on out, and we'll get this over with!" Keo shouted back.

"Now what would be the fun in that?"

"You scared, Calvin?"

Calvin laughed. "Sticks and stones may break my bones, but names will never hurt me. Bullets, on the other hand, can and will. Especially the kind you don't see *or* hear coming. You know a thing or two about that, don't you?"

Keo exchanged a glance with Rudolph. The look on the older man's face was a clear indication he was sharing a growing dislike for Calvin's stupid voice.

"You sure you don't know this guy?" Rudolph asked.

Keo shook his head. "I don't think so."

"But it's possible."

"Anything's possible. It's also possible I'm dreaming this entire nightmare."

"You and me both." Then, "It's your call, boss."

I wish everyone would stop calling me that, Keo thought, but he said, "Go. I'll cover you."

"What about you?"

"I'll be right behind you."

Rudolph nodded, counted to three, then pushed off the tree and ran after the others.

Keo turned around, looking for something to shoot, but there was nothing. Calvin, if that was even his real name, was giving him nothing.

Not a goddamn thing.

When he couldn't hear Rudolph's footsteps behind him anymore, Keo counted down from five, and on *one* turned and fled after the others.

He kept waiting for the shot—the silent bullet that would prove Calvin was a liar about wanting him alive—but it never came.

He had gotten twenty steps into his retreat when he heard Calvin's voice, booming across the woods. "I'll be seeing you, Keo! I'll be seeing you again real soon, buddy!"

Not unless I see you first, pal. Not unless I see you first!

THREE

"You don't have to do it. You know that. After everything you've told me about what happened at Winding Creek, then Cordine City... It's terrifying, Keo. And I didn't have to live through it. You did. So when I tell you that *you don't have to do it*, you need to understand that I mean it. But I'm asking you anyway, because I think you give us the best chance at success. You're really good at this. You know it, and I know it. Having said that, *you don't have to say yes*. I have people who have experience, who I can send instead."

"You have people with experience in *this*?"

"Well, not *this*, this. But something close to this. I don't think anyone's ever gone through what you have, or has the kind of experience."

"Who are they? Are they any good?"

"They were trained by the best."

"Who's that?"

"Danny."

"When you said 'the best,' I assumed it was someone other than Danny."

She smiled, and Keo thought, *I'll never get tired of seeing that.*

Maybe it was because she rarely smiled in the time he knew her before his undramatic exit from her life. Not that she had a lot of reasons to smile very much back then. They'd just come out of The Purge, and The Battle of Houston had claimed the life of someone very important to her. Beyond those monumental events in her life, she had found herself in command, something he was sure she never saw coming.

In the five years since he last saw her, Lara looked noticeably older, and her face had more lines than he remembered. Her hair was shorter, her skin tanner, and when she looked at him, the crystal blue of her eyes wasn't quite as radiant as the last time he saw her, waving to him as he lifted off in the chopper.

Five years, now, but he always knew he'd be back here one day. Not *here*, here. But here, with her. He hadn't expected— or wanted—it to be like this, under these circumstances. Then again, considering his luck, Keo wasn't too surprised he was still fresh off a bullet wound when it finally happened. That seemed to be how things went for him these days, all a part of the wealth of "experience" she was talking about.

They hadn't talked much since the chopper ride from Cordine City and over to the newly formed forward operating base along the southeast coast of Texas. Keo hadn't kept track of the landmarks underneath them—not that there had been anything of note to keep track of; mostly it was wide-open prairies and abandoned country highways—so he wasn't exactly sure where they were at the moment. Besides, he'd been too busy trying to figure out his next move.

Because he didn't want to be here; he had gone to great pains to avoid it.

But here he was, anyway.

So much for best laid plans.

By the time the chopper slowed, then began hovering for a landing, he had glimpsed a wide-open Gulf of Mexico out the right-side hatch of the Sikorsky UH-60. The left side revealed the rooftops of a small port city. Later, Lara would tell him they were in Darby Bay, a town near East Matagorda Bay, about a hundred or so miles from Houston. The chopper had skirted over the city before touching down on an LZ along the east side, where men and women in similar blue BDUs went to work.

Afterward, Lara had taken him to a room in one of the big brick buildings near all the hustle and bustle of military activity. The noise instantly died as soon as he closed the thick metal door into his quarters and laid down on a cot and went to sleep, all the fatigue and running for his life of the last few days hitting him like a freight train.

He woke up the next morning feeling as good as he ever had, to the sight of Lara already in his room armed with warm food. Real, honest to goodness food. Fish and bread and rice. He wolfed them down while she looked on, the two of them sitting across from each other with sunlight filtering in from a high window to his right. Keo knew he looked like shit but didn't think it was anything she hadn't seen before.

When he was done eating, he chugged down a bottle of ice-cold water. "Ice?" he asked when he was done.

"Ice," she nodded.

"Nice, nice, baby." When she gave him a confused look, he said, "It's an old song."

"'Nice, nice, baby?'"

"Actually, 'Ice Ice Baby,' but I was making a pun."

"Oh."

He grinned and tossed the empty bottle into a nearby bin. "So, what've you been up to since I've been gone?" Before she could answer, "That's another old song, by the way."

"I don't know that one, either."

"Of course you don't. You're just a kid."

She pursed a smile. "I haven't been a kid in a long time, Keo."

He nodded, but Keo couldn't help but remember the first time he saw her six years ago, leading a bunch of survivors on an island as they prepared for an assault from overwhelming forces. He'd seen the steely resolve she could muster then, and he saw it again this morning. She was still the same Lara. But, like him, just older.

"So what's going on?" he asked.

"Where should I start?"

"How about from the beginning. What did Peters and Gaby find out about Fenton, and what do you plan on doing about it?"

She told him, and he listened.

When she was done, Lara said, "You said you wanted Buck for yourself."

"I made him a promise. And I always keep my promises. Well, I try to, anyway."

"What about your friend Emma?"

"I promised her daughter I'd get her out of there, too."

"You should probably stop making promises to too many people. You're bound to disappoint a few of them."

"That goes without saying. But I did it, and there's no going back now." He leaned slightly forward. "So what are we going to do about Fenton?"

"It's...tricky."

"Of course it is. Who wants easy?"

"I do. I always choose easy when it's an option."

She sat back in her chair, and morning sunlight fell over a part of her. She looked odd in the pseudo-BDU that all the Black Tiders wore. Even now, after everything he'd seen her do and everything he'd heard of her doing since Houston, it was still difficult to picture her leading a group of heavily-armed men into battle.

They stared at each other for a moment, neither one saying anything. Keo spent most of that time resisting the urge to lean in closer.

He wanted to. Badly.

"You shouldn't have left," Lara finally said.

"I had to."

"No, you didn't."

"Yes, I did."

"Why?"

"You know why."

"We could have worked it out."

"No, we couldn't have. You couldn't have."

"You're underestimating what I'm capable of."

"No, I'm not. But you had other things to worry about. People were counting on you. A lot of people. If I'd stayed, I would have just been a distraction. You didn't need me around."

"I could have used you."

"I'm expendable. Useful in spurts, sure, but when it comes to long term, not so much."

"You're not giving yourself enough credit."

"We both know that's not true." This time it was his turn to purse a forced smile. "I'm a guy with a gun. That's all I've ever been, and all I'll ever be. You didn't need another guy with a gun five years ago. You had plenty of those, and none of them came with the baggage I was carrying."

"Just a guy with a gun, huh?"

"That's me."

"There were a lot of times when I could have really used a guy with a gun like you out there, Keo."

"Gaby told me."

"What did she tell you, exactly?"

"A lot. And everything she said convinced me I did the right thing. It was better for us that I left. I think you know that, too."

She didn't say anything right away. Then, finally, "And now?"

"And now..." He shrugged. "I don't know. I've never been good at these things. Like I said, I'm just a guy—"

"—with a gun," she finished.

"That's about it."

"Bullshit."

"It's really not."

Lara stared at him in silence again.

Five seconds.

Ten...

"I sent people to look for you, you know," she finally said.

"Did you?"

"Every time I sent someone out there, I told them to keep an eye out for you. Someone matching your description showed up in Kansas, Oklahoma, and as far north as South Dakota."

"I've never been to South Dakota."

"No?"

He shook his head. "At least, I don't think I have."

"You're not sure?"

"There were a couple of months, about two years ago, where I wasn't sure where I was. I mean, state-wise. I guess I was just meandering about and such."

"'Meandering about and such,'" she repeated with a smile. "Good to see you're finally starting to get the lingo. Pretty soon, you'll be a regular good ol' boy."

"Hey, you know what they say: You stay in Texas long enough, you'll start speaking like a Texan. Just wait until I find that perfect belt buckle and complement it with a butt-kicking pair of boots and spurs."

"Ooh, now that's something to look forward to."

They exchanged a smile, and Keo thought, *God, she's beautiful. How the hell did I stay away for five years?*

He thought she might have blushed, but that could have just been the abundance of sunlight casting over her face, making him see things.

"When was the last time you showered?" Lara asked.

Keo sniffed himself. "Do I smell?"

"A little bit."

"It's been a while. Thanks for reminding me."

He got up and walked over to the small sink at the back wall, where he washed his face from a bottle and wiped away some of the grime with a rough hand soap. There was a bathroom, but it was communal and down the hall. He made a mental note to take care of that later.

"Let's get down to the nitty gritty," Keo said while scrubbing at his face. "What are we going to do about Buck and Fenton?"

"I won't make that decision until I find out what's going on in there."

"You haven't done that yet?"

"I've been sending recon teams into the area since Peters and Gaby got back. They've gathered intelligence about one side of Fenton to the other. Everything from manpower to armaments to civilian population."

"So what are you still missing?"

"There's a small island next to their main military compound. There is a large warehouse on it. Newly built, from the looks of it. It's the only structure on the entire island. Gaby got as close to it as anyone I've sent over, but she couldn't tell what was inside."

"What do you think's inside?"

"I don't know. That's the problem. It could be anything."

"Like what?"

"Anything to everything, Keo. From the civilians they've captured from their raids on the surrounding towns to God knows what."

"You still don't know where they're keeping the captives?"

"No. That's the other big question mark." Lara paused and looked as if she wanted to say something more, but didn't.

"What?" Keo pressed.

"We have a spy inside Fenton."

"How'd you manage that?"

"It's a long story. But they've been sending out daily reports."

"Anything about the captured civilians?"

"No, unfortunately. It's like they were never taken to Fenton in the first place."

"That's impossible. I know for a fact that's where they were taken."

"And Gaby agrees with you," Lara said. "But our spy hasn't been able to find a single clue to their whereabouts. But..."

"But what?"

"They've been contained to the civilian section of Fenton. The spy. They haven't been able to access the military half."

"So the captives *could* be there..."

"They could be anywhere, Keo. That's the problem. I have a good idea of what's happening in one half of Fenton, but that's not enough. The military compound, and that island..." She shook her head again. "I need more information before I can act."

"What else has your spy found out?"

"Not nearly enough. But they're limited by where they can go and what they can do without drawing suspicion. For now, the only person who has been inside that fence is Gaby, and she had some disturbing things to tell me about what's going on in there."

He finished drying his face and knocking as much dirt out of his hair as possible with a small towel and walked over to a pile of clothes someone had brought in for him while he slept. A couple of the shirts were too big, some were too small, but eventually he found one that was just right. And best of all, it was cleaner than the one he previously had on.

"Like what?" he asked.

"People caged in shacks like animals, for one," Lara said.

"I wish I could say I'm surprised. Buck seemed like the type capable of something like that."

"You've met him? This Buck person?"

"Not face to face. I've only talked to him over the radio."

"From the way you've talked about him, I would have thought you guys have known each other for a while."

"I've just talked to him, but I've also spoken to people with more inside knowledge of the man."

"What did they tell you?"

"That the world would be a much better place without him around."

"After everything I've seen and heard, I can't say I disagree."

"Great minds think alike." He walked back over and sat down across from her again. "Which brings us all the way back around: What's the plan to deal with Buckaroo?"

"I can't deal with him or Fenton until I know more."

"Exactly what 'more' do you need?"

"Where are the captives? What's inside that warehouse?"

"How big is this warehouse, anyway?"

"One of the recon teams measured it at two hundred meters long and fifty meters wide."

"Jesus Christ. That's big enough for a Jumbo Jet or two."

"Exactly. It could be anything in there. I won't commit lives to attacking Fenton until I know what's in there, Keo. What if it's the captives from the raids? What if it's some kind of weapon Buck is saving to defend Fenton from an attack? God knows there is still military-grade firepower of every imaginable shape and size lying around out there for anyone to pick up. Tanks, planes, killing machines that could raze cities. And Buck's had five years to build that army of his."

Keo thought about Cordine City and how they had essentially rigged the entire city to blow in case of an overwhelming attack. Because Lara was right; there were still a lot of weapons of unimaginable power unaccounted for.

"A full-frontal assault will cost lives," Lara continued. "That's already a given. Ours, theirs...the people of Fenton who are just trying to get through the day. I'm worried about killing people who don't know what's going on. There are a lot of people who just want to be left alone and live in peace. Sometimes they make bad decisions."

"Like letting a former Mercerian into their midst?"

"It's happened before."

"Has it?"

She nodded. "Unfortunately."

"I'll take your word for it." Then, "What *can* you throw at Fenton, if you were so inclined?"

"I can't send in Peele and the tanks, if that's what you're asking. Fenton is surrounded by woods, and Buck's people would hear them coming for miles. That's the other problem..."

"Gee, more problems? Who would have thunk?"

She managed a smile. "Buck was one of Mercer's true believers. The fact that he and his men are running around with that circled *M* on their vests speaks volumes about what the man is capable of."

"But you have a plan to deal with Fenton. You just need clarity. Is that it?"

"That's the long and short of it. Right now, Fenton isn't going anywhere. Buck's recalled most of his people back to the city. They haven't committed another raid since the action with Peters's team. They know we're out here watching them now. As soon as they commit manpower beyond their limited area of control, I have units ready to take them out."

"Does he know that?"

"He'd have to be dumb, blind, and deaf to miss the Thunderbolts buzzing Fenton for the last week or so."

"So he's hunkering down."

"It would appear that way," Lara said before she paused again.

"What?" Keo said.

"The aerial recons are showing a lot of activity around that warehouse. Vehicles and people coming and going along that one-lane road that connects the island to the compound. Trucks with tarps in the back."

"Maybe he knows you're watching, and he's playing mind games. Maybe there's nothing in those trucks. One of his guys in Cordine City told me Buck has been planning this for years."

"Years?"

Keo nodded. "A guy named Greengrass. Buck sent him after me."

"Damn. You really must have pissed him off, Keo."

"Just my natural charm, I guess."

"Uh huh."

"Anyway. I think it's smart that you're approaching this in a cool and calculated manner instead of just rushing in. Me, I would have just gone in guns blazin'."

"And how did that work out for you before?"

He grunted. "I won't lie; it could have gone better."

"This time you won't be alone."

"I guess that means you've already decided what you want me to do."

"Only if you say yes."

"I thought I already did."

"You don't have to do it. But I'd be lying if I said there was someone better equipped for this mission."

"You want me to go into Fenton and get a better look at the compound."

"Yes."

"But that's not all, though, right?"

"No."

"The warehouse."

She nodded. "I need to know what's inside that building, Keo."

"Hey, I don't blame you. I've always been a sucker for mysteries myself."

"Danny and I had a team assembled and ready to go before we heard about what happened in Cordine City."

"Lucky me. I got in on the gig just in time. Where is the Boy Scout, by the way? I noticed he's not around."

"He's busy with something else at the moment."

"Something bigger than this?"

"Unfortunately, there are a lot of fires that I need people I can trust to deal with. Some of them—like the one Danny is fighting at the moment—have the potential to become just as big of a headache as Fenton if they're not dealt with."

"I always knew the Ranger had it in him to become a man one of these days."

"He's all grown up, our Danny. Carly and I couldn't be more proud."

"So the Ranger's out. That leaves the idiot who'll be leading this team I'm joining."

Lara didn't answer him. Instead, she sat patiently looking at him.

"No, don't say it," Keo said.

"You have the most experience."

"There's that word again."

"It's a good word."

"You know I work better alone. It's my thing."

"Not this time."

Keo sighed. "One question, if I'm going to do this."

"What is it?"

"What kind of armory you got in this place?"

She smiled. "I had the quartermaster look for something special while you were sleeping. He let me know he found it this morning."

"Is it German, and is it sexy?" Keo asked.

"Yes to the first, and...I don't know how to answer the second part."

Keo grinned. "That sounds like a yes to me."

FOUR

"You don't have to do it. You know that. After everything you've told me about what happened at Winding Creek, then Cordine City... It's terrifying, Keo. And I didn't have to live through it. You did. So when I tell you that you don't have to do it, you need to understand that I mean it. But I'm asking you anyway, because I think you give us the best chance at success."

Right, Keo thought then, and did again now. *As if I could have said no.*

He'd left the others behind with the wounded Springer and had enough faith in them to keep themselves alive until he could return. Of course, he'd had faith in Chang and Banner, too, and they were lying dead somewhere else in the woods right now. About half a mile to the northwest of Keo's current position, as far as he could tell—

Snap!

He went into a slight crouch, the MP5SD submachine gun rising, ready to fire in front of him. He peered through its scope and looked left, then right, then back left again.

Nothing. There was nothing out there but trees.

And more trees.

Goddamn, there were a lot of trees.

Where am I, in the woods?

He almost chuckled to himself but managed to stop it in time. Even a little bit of noise might be too much right now.

Instead, Keo squeezed out a slow breath before going completely silent.

The noise had come from in front of him, close to the ground—

A rabbit leapt out of a bush and vanished behind a tree.

Keo almost shot it—or tried to pick it off as it was in midair, anyway—but refrained from pulling the trigger when he saw the blur of moving white fur.

Close there, little rabbit. You have no idea how close you came to being someone's stew this morning.

He relaxed and stood up, then moved toward a tree and pressed against it. He had put half a mile between himself and the team and had kept track of his movements and turns. Keo was reasonably certain he could backtrack to the others when the time came. Then again, it was entirely possible he was overestimating his abilities. Wells was their navigator, after all, and he wasn't here, but Keo didn't think so.

Sure, everything looks like everything else in this place, but you're not lost.

Far from it.

Yeah, that's the ticket.

He decided to focus on what had happened this morning instead. There wasn't really much to think about: They had walked right into one of Fenton's snipers. It was bad luck, pure and simple. The chopper had inserted them a full ten miles from their target, for God's sake; what were the chances Buck had widened his security perimeter *that* far out?

He hadn't, was the answer. At least, not really. Instead, Buck had put a single man out here. Who knew how many other one-man patrols were camped this far out from Fenton? Maybe there was even just the one. After all, if there had been more around, they would have converged on them by now, and Keo would have definitely stumbled across a Bucky or two.

But they hadn't, and he hadn't.

Which meant Calvin was out here all by his little lonesome.

"I tried, but I'm either out of range or the trees are blocking my signal."

The problem was that there was no reason for Calvin to be telling the truth. And yet, almost two hours since the ambush, and there were still no signs of any Buckies in the area looking for them. Which was one of the reasons Keo was out here now looking for the man. (*So what are the other reasons, pal?*) If Calvin had no backup, that meant he was still out here all by his little lonesome.

Mano a mano. I like those odds.

Of course, the sniper did have the advantage. Keo didn't delude himself into thinking *he* had the upper hand here. God only knew how long the guy had been out here setting up his kill zones. But Keo didn't think the man had every inch of the woods covered. That was highly unlikely. At least, not with just a single pair of eyeballs and a single pair of legs to work with.

Keo stepped away from the tree and continued forward, mindful of the ambush site somewhere to his left, hidden behind half a mile of woods. Or, at least, it was supposed to be half a mile. Wells had been pretty certain about it when they talked earlier.

"So what are you gonna do, go out there and look for this asshole?" Rita had asked.

"Yeah," Keo had said.

"By yourself?" Gholston had chimed in.

"It's better I do it by myself."

"Says who?"

"Says me."

Gholston hadn't looked convinced, but instead of arguing, he had said, "At least take Rita with you. She can take him out from a distance."

"He's right," Rita said. "That's what I do."

"You couldn't even see him last time," Keo had said, and immediately regretted when Rita flinched noticeably at his words.

"And you're going to see him this time?" she asked.

"Look, he wants me alive. That means he's not going to pop me the first chance he gets. You guys, on the other hand... Look at what he did to Chang and Banner."

"Just because he doesn't want to kill you doesn't mean he won't put a bullet or two in your legs to disable you," Gholston had said.

That was almost the same thing Calvin the sniper had said, but Keo had said anyway, "I'm in charge. So do what the fuck I say, and stay put. Keep trying to reach Black Tide Command. Until then, I'll be back as soon as I can."

They'd had trouble getting in touch with command all morning. Wells thought it might have been because of a storm that was pushing into Darby Bay from the Gulf just before they took off this morning; or maybe it was the thick tree canopies blocking their signal. Either way, Keo was secretly glad they couldn't reach Lara while he was around. He was dreading telling her what had happened.

"Hey, Lara. Thanks for having enough faith in me to put me in charge of my own team, but, uh, I got them killed. Or, at least, two of them. Sorry?"

Yeah, he could imagine how well that was going to go over.

This is shit. Being in charge is for idiots.

So why did I say yes?

Because Lara had asked him to, that was why.

"You don't have to do it... But I'm asking you anyway, because I think you give us the best chance at success."

How was he going to say no to *that?*

He couldn't. No one could. Not Danny or Peters or Gaby or anyone wearing that inguz rune patch on their shoulder. Most of them hadn't been with Mercer five years ago, but had arrived to join the good fight—to join *her.*

She was Lara. The voice on the radio. The woman he couldn't stop thinking about, even though it was driving him nuts that he couldn't. Five years later, and that image of her, that night, was still fixed in his mind's eye—

Zip! as the round sailed past his right ear and embedded in a tree trunk two meters behind him.

Shit!

Keo dove forward and down without thinking—and slammed into the dirt on his chest with the MP5SD clutched in his hands. He was instantly swallowed up by knee-high grass that he used as cover to begin rolling to his right. Thank God he'd had the chance to let all his wounds heal before he jumped onboard that helo and flew back into the fire, or else this would have really hurt.

Pek-pek-pek! as dirt kicked around his head and flicked at his face, each round seemingly getting closer.

Hey! Fenton wants me alive, remember? he wanted to shout at the shooter, but he was too busy rolling, because if he stopped for even a second he might never move again.

Jesus, where was the guy shooting from?

Keo had no chance to figure out that answer, because he was too busy moving moving *moving.*

Finally, he made it behind a tree and scrambled to his feet and pressed his back against the gnarled trunk, the Heckler & Koch still clutched in his hands. He hadn't wasted a shot at the sniper because it would have been exactly that—a waste. And he had a feeling he was going to need every bullet he had on him.

Right now, that was exactly two spare magazines in a pouch on his left hip. Thirty rounds apiece, not counting the additional thirty he already had loaded. Ninety bullets in all for the submachine gun. He had spent two magazines earlier while covering their escape during the first ambush. Another pouch on his right side held two spares for the Glock 19. Fifteen per magazine, for a total of forty-five.

And that was it. Keo had a light load. They all did, with the exception of Chang and Banner, who were carrying the MG. Was that why Calvin had taken them out first? Maybe it didn't even have anything to do with Buck wanting Keo alive; the sniper had simply taken out the most dangerous members of their team because it was the smart thing to do.

Not that the reasons did him any good right now.

Keo made sure the submachine gun's fire selector was on semiauto. It didn't matter how many rounds he could send downrange if he didn't know *where* the man was shooting from. He was somewhere in front of Keo on the other side of the tree, that much was obvious, but where exactly?

Here, there, and everywhere, apparently.

Who is this guy?

"Almost got you!" a voice shouted. *Calvin.* "Again!"

Keo didn't know why he was so surprised that it was the same sniper. Maybe it had something to do with the fifteen hundred meters or so he'd put between him and the last ambush site. How the hell had the guy ended up in front of him, *again?* What was he using, some goddamn satellite that was tracking Keo's every movement?

He glanced up on instinct, maybe hoping to glimpse that secret weapon, but the sky was mostly covered by canopies, and what he could see was a white cloudless day. There could have been a hundred machines orbiting up there for all he knew.

"Consider that a warning shot!" Calvin shouted.

Like the last time, there was something not quite right with the voice. It was too echoey, and it seemed to bounce from one tree to the next, never giving Keo a single source of origin.

How is he doing *that?*

"But it didn't have to be," the sniper continued. "Be grateful my daddy raised me to be the sporting type. I could have just popped you in the legs and dragged you back to Buck without giving you a fighting chance, but I chose not to do that. You can thank me later, buddy."

I'm not your buddy, pal.

But he didn't bother shouting that back. Instead, he tried in vain to put a location to the voice.

"*Maybe he's using some kind of machine to throw his voice?*" he'd said to Rita earlier.

"Does something like that exist?" she had responded.

"Hell if I know," was his not-very-helpful answer.

So how was Calvin camouflaging his position?

"That you, Calvin?" Keo shouted back, even as he slid down along the length of the tree to lower his profile. He glanced left and right, then left and right again. If Calvin already knew which tree he was behind, it wouldn't take him long to try to flank him for a better shot. He hadn't done so earlier because Keo had the others to watch the angles. That, and Keo believed the sniper was too smart to try to pick off more of the team when he'd already done plenty of damage and knew he was outgunned if he exposed himself.

He's deadly, and he's got a strong sense of self-preservation.

Great. That's just great.

"Yeah, it's me!" Calvin shouted back. "You were expecting someone else?"

"Where's your Bucky reinforcements?"

"Bucky?" Then, laughing, "Oh, I get it. That's clever. Bucky, because of Buck!"

Well, it ain't because of your cheery personality, pal.

"Nice one!" Calvin said, and his voice seemed to be coming from Keo's left that time. Or was it?

He's gotta be using some kind of machine. Right?

"Thanks!" Keo said. "I pride myself on being clever."

"How's that working out for ya?"

"Not so good at the moment." Then, "So you're alone, huh?"

"That's right!"

Keo debated if he could believe the sniper. Would Calvin lie?

Yes. A million times over. Why wouldn't he?

"You're not fibbing, are you, Calvin?" Keo asked.

"Nah," the sniper said. "They finally radioed me back, though, but I didn't answer. The only person who knows you're out here is me, Keo, ol' buddy, and it's going to stay that way until I drag you back to Fenton."

"And why would you want to do a fool thing like that?"

"You know how to tell if you're the best at something?"

"I'm sure you'll tell me."

"You put it all on the line against the best. And if you beat him, then you know. That's the only way you'll know for sure."

Keo smirked. "And I suppose hogging all the glory has nothing to do with it?"

Calvin laughed. "Maybe a little. But I assure you, Keo, it's mostly about challenging myself. I haven't had decent competition since the monsters were still in charge. And frankly, I'm getting bored. And then you showed up. The man who killed Mercer himself. Now I'm as happy as a little clam!"

You'll be as happy as a dead clam pretty soon, pal.

"You know what I did to Mercer, but you're still out here by your little lonesome," Keo said. "You must be suicidal."

"Why, should I be scared?" Calvin asked. Keo could tell a mocking voice when he heard one.

"Aren't you?"

"I've been hunting since I could walk, and I'll be hunting long after you're gone."

"You that good?"

"What do you think?"

Keo thought of Chang and Banner.

Yeah. He's that good.

But he shouted instead, "I've seen better."

"Have you now?" Calvin said.

"There was this guy who did this thing with me in Uzbek-istan. Fred-something-or-rather. Now *he* was good."

"So good that you can't remember his name?"

"In my defense, we were using made-up names. So there was really no point in memorizing it."

"Did you entertain poor Mercer with that story before you offed him?"

"Is that what they're calling him now? 'Poor Mercer?'"

"You did blow the man's brains out."

"He had it coming."

Calvin laughed. "Don't we all?"

"Absolutely!" Keo shouted just before he spun and, bent slightly over at the waist, darted out from behind the tree.

He moved right while edging forward at the same time. The MP5SD was ready, and while his eye was not quite looking through the scope, he was fully prepared to shoot anything that might pop up in front of him.

There, slight movement from a bush about thirty meters in front of him!

Keo fired five times—*pfft-pfft-pfft-pfft-pfft!*—by squeezing the trigger as fast as he could, sending every round into the bush as he continued to move, move, *move*. There was no return fire, and Keo made it behind another elm tree two seconds later.

He slid against the rough bark and leaned out the left side to get a better look—

Pek! as a big chunk of tree exploded in his face.

Keo pulled his head back and blinked away the pain. He was pretty sure he had pieces of the tree in his eyes, maybe a splinter or two (or a hundred) sticking out of both eyeballs. But that couldn't have been the case, because he could still see just fine after a few seconds of focusing.

Booming laughter from the other side of the tree. "Hey, Keo, I think you got it! That little bunny isn't going to hurt anyone anymore!"

Instead of being angry about missing Calvin, Keo smiled, because he had figured something out that the sniper probably didn't want him to know.

Keo checked the bullet that had chopped off a generous patch of bark from the tree in front of him a few seconds ago. There, the greatly exaggerated diagonal line made by a bullet firing from a high angle and at a downward trajectory.

Calvin was in a tree.

FIVE

Idiot. You can't dodge bullets. Remember?

He remembered, but it wasn't like he had any choice. He'd committed to this path of action, and he couldn't do anything about it now. The only thing left was to run, and run *fast!*

Thank God his wounds were healed.

Thank God he wasn't still limping around.

Thank God Lara had insisted he was 100 percent—or close enough—before she would let him hop on that helo. She had made sure, too, and even checked his scars herself. Sometimes he forgot that she was once a doctor. Or a medical student, anyway. And she still was, he guessed, but it just wasn't her calling anymore.

What are you doing thinking about her? Do you wanna die? Run!

Run run run run!

He did, picking up speed with every pounding heartbeat, darting left then right, then forward, and using the trees around him for cover when he could. The bullets came hard and fast, sometimes so close that he could *feel the heat* of the subsonic rounds. They were screaming at him from an angle like before, slamming into the ground behind and around and sometimes in front of him as the sniper tried to guess his pattern.

Good luck with that! Keo wanted to tell the guy, because *he* didn't know which direction he was going to take before he actually took them.

Bark flew from every direction, and the air was filled with clouds of dirt as Calvin fired and fired, and Keo figured the man was using a weapon with a generous magazine given how fast and furious the lead was coming. The sniper might have been trying to nail Keo in the legs before in order to take him alive, but with every passing second Keo was still running, the bullets were edging higher until the last one *zipped!* over his scalp and Keo swore it singed a few strands of hair as it passed.

Close one!

He wasn't sure how long he'd been running, but it had to be anywhere from five to ten seconds, even though it had felt more like five to ten *hours*. But that was what happened when you threw yourself into the lion's den and waited for the animal to open its mouth and take a bite. Time slowed down and every heartbeat became a monumental victory, every inch he managed without eating a bullet a minor miracle.

He never stayed behind one tree for very long before moving again. In fact, he rarely stopped at all and was constantly moving, moving, *moving*. It was the only way to throw Calvin off while at the same time keeping track of where the bullets were coming from. He had no chance to see the exact location, but with each round—each chunk of bark that blew loose—he began narrowing down his target.

And narrowing it down even further.

And further still.

There!

It was either the eleventh or fifteenth second (or possibly the twentieth *minute*) since he began his mad dash, but Keo finally glimpsed camouflaged fabrics moving along one of the branches about twenty meters in front of him. It wasn't too high up—seven or eight meters from the ground, give or take—and the man wearing those fabrics was standing.

Keo felt a sting along his left hip (*Shit!*) but he kept moving, knowing that if he stopped for even a second to lick his wounds that he was a dead man. Instead, he lifted the MP5SD into position—it wasn't hard to do since he had the submachine gun in front of him the entire time, and all it took was tilting it slightly in the right direction—and squeezed the trigger, and kept it depressed. He'd switched to full-auto earlier, and he sent every shot toward the tree where the figure was standing—some kind of wooden platform covered with natural colors to help it blend in with its environment. A hunting stand!

Branches and foliage disintegrated against Keo's 9mm rounds. The figure attempted to crouch—or maybe he was trying to somehow spin out of the bullets' way?—but ended up staggering, then falling over the edge and slamming into the ground below with a loud *thwump!*

Keo made a run toward the fallen figure, slinging the almost-empty Heckler & Koch and drawing the Glock as he did so. He checked his left hip as he ran and saw a hole in one of his pouches. When he slowed down to open it, he glimpsed the portable radio inside, along with the hole that had gone through it.

But a destroyed radio was better than a hole in his leg!

Keo picked up his pace, fully expecting the sniper to be dead by the time he reached him. Except the man was alive and lying on the ground where he had fallen. He was on his back and gasping for breath while his rifle—some kind of heavily modified AR covered in camo paint with a big scope on top—rested a few yards from his outstretched right hand. The weapon had a built-in suppressor, much like Keo's own MP5SD, and its magazine had come dislodged in the fall.

Calvin was still alive, but he gave up reaching for the rifle when Keo neared. Instead, the sniper pulled back his hand and rested it on his chest. He looked like a man who had just decided to lie down to rest instead of one that had been shot out of a tree. Keo couldn't tell how old he was with all the paint on his face, but the Bucky was probably in his thirties, maybe early forties. Not exactly a big man, but tall even with his ghillie suit covering most of his body.

The man from Fenton turned his head to look at Keo as he walked the final few meters and stopped. Calvin hadn't bothered to go for the sidearm on his right hip and seemed more concerned with the small puddle of blood forming underneath his legs, coming from a hole in his right thigh. Keo didn't think it was the wound that had made the man give up. No doubt the fall was the real culprit.

"Shit, I think all my bones are broken," Calvin groaned.

"Don't be so melodramatic," Keo said. "I've seen worse. Besides, it's not *that* high up."

Calvin smirked but didn't reply.

Keo snatched the Bucky's handgun—a Beretta 9mm—out of its holster to alleviate him of any temptations of going for it. Now that there was no danger, Keo holstered the Glock and reloaded his MP5SD. Calvin hadn't bothered trying to get up but had both hands on his bleeding thigh. Blood oozed through his fingers and stained his gloved hands.

"Calvin, huh?" Keo said. "Not exactly the most dangerous sounding name, for a sniper."

"This, coming from a guy named Keo," Calvin grunted.

"I'm not a sniper. Snipers should have fearsome names, like Hawk. Or Doom. Or Hawky McDoom."

"You're not a sniper, but you're plenty dangerous."

"Lies. All lies, I tell you."

"That's not what Buck said." Calvin sucked in a deep breath. "Can I pull myself over to a tree and sit up? I gotta tend to this."

"Be my guest."

Keo meandered away to pick up Calvin's rifle while the man crawled over to the tree he'd fallen out of and sat himself up with a pained groan. He took out a handkerchief from one of his pockets and wrapped it around the bullet hole.

"Where's all your equipment?" Keo asked.

"Tree stand."

"Whatcha got up there?"

"Climb up and find out."

Keo glanced up at the stand, barely visible against all the foliage even though he was standing almost directly underneath the hide. The fact that he had seen it at all earlier was a miracle. Maybe it had something to do with a man standing on it that had made it more obvious. You could camouflage something to look as natural you want, but once you put a human being inside it, it becomes unnatural.

"How'd you get up there?" Keo asked.

"Ropes and spikes."

"Where are they now?"

"Still up there." He grinned at Keo. "You want my gear, you'll have to climb up for them."

"I'm a pretty good climber."

"Is that right?"

"Uh huh. My mom used to call me *wonsungi*."

"What's that mean?"

"Monkey."

"So you're what, a Jap?"

"Do I look like a Jap?"

Calvin shrugged. "I don't have a fucking clue."

"You alone?" Keo asked.

"I already told you I was."

"I thought you might be lying."

"Well, I wasn't."

Maybe, Keo thought, looking around the woods. He felt good about reinforcements not showing up anytime soon. If Calvin hadn't gotten any Bucky support before, it was doubtful he'd get them now. Besides, both he and the sniper had been using suppressed weapons, so even if there were people walking around out there, it was doubtful anyone had heard their back and forth.

He turned back to the sniper. "You gonna die on me?"

Calvin looked up from his bloodied rag. "Not yet. But I assume you're going to kill me eventually."

"And why would you assume that?"

"This is war, isn't it?"

"Is it?"

Calvin squinted at him. "Isn't it?"

Keo shrugged. He opened one of his pouches and took out a small bundle of gauze and tossed it over.

Calvin caught it. He stared at it for a moment before looking up at Keo. "What's this?"

"What's it look like?"

"Bandages."

"Looks like bandages to me, too."

"What're they for?"

"To keep you from bleeding to death, genius. Granted, it's unlikely you will even without it, but all that bloodletting won't be very good for you. Take it from someone who knows."

Calvin didn't say anything, and he also didn't do anything with the bandages, either.

"Go ahead," Keo said.

"Why?" Calvin asked.

"I have a proposition for you."

Calvin kept squinting at him, but kept quiet.

"You a Mercerian?" Keo asked.

"A what?"

"A Mercerian."

"I don't know what that is. Is that Chinese?"

"Not as far as I know."

"So what's a Mercerian?"

"The circled *M* that Buck's boys wear on their vests. I assume you have one, too, when you're not all covered up in mud and trees and out here lying in wait for innocent folks like myself."

"Innocent," Calvin snorted. "Right."

"You know what I mean."

Calvin shrugged. "I didn't know that that was what the *M* stood for."

"No?"

"Nah."

"What did you think it stood for?"

"I dunno. I never bothered to ask."

"Never?"

"Well, that's not true. I asked once or twice, but the guys I asked didn't know either, and after a while, I didn't bother to ask again."

"Not the curious type, huh?"

"Not really."

Keo grinned. "Go on. Fix yourself up, and we'll talk."

"About what?"

"Do it first."

Calvin did. Grudgingly.

Keo took the moment to look around the area again, then back up at the tree stand. It wasn't *that* high up, and he'd definitely climbed higher trees. Except those always had things for him to grab onto. He could see indentations along the trunk where Calvin's rope and spikes had cut into the bark as he scaled the big elm tree. Minus the gear, the closest branch was a good three meters up, and Keo wasn't going to be able to jump high enough to reach it.

When Calvin was done dressing his wound, he tossed what remained of the bandages back, and Keo put it away.

"What kind of name is Keo, anyway?" Calvin asked.

"Hey, we can't all be Calvins. Some of us gotta make do with what we're given."

"That's not Japanese, is it?"

"Nope."

"Chinese?"

"Strike two."

"What is it?"

"That's for me to know and for you to find out."

Calvin grunted.

"So you weren't lying," Keo said. "You were trying to capture me alive all by yourself."

"I haven't told you a single lie since our first encounter."

"That's awfully decent of you."

"I can be a pretty decent guy."

Chang and Banner would disagree, Keo thought, but he smiled and said, "Me too."

The sniper's eyes, mostly hidden behind his face paint, really focused on Keo's face. "What exactly do you want with me?"

Keo crouched in front of Calvin. He had kept enough distance that he wasn't afraid the other man might try something stupid that would force Keo to shoot him, but just in case, Keo had the MP5SD draped over one knee as a deterrent. You never knew when someone would get a case of the stupids.

"I need to get into a very specific part of Fenton undetected," Keo said. "Then once inside, I need a way out."

"So? What's that got to do with me?"

"You're going to assist me."

"How the hell am I gonna do that?"

"I'm sure we can figure it out."

"Even better question, *why* the hell would I even entertain the idea of helping you get inside?"

"I already have a way inside. But you can never have too many options, just in case." He pointed at the sniper. "You're my 'just in case.'"

Calvin stared at him but didn't respond right away. Finally, he said, "What if I say no?"

"Then I shoot you and bury you behind a bush so your

friends can't find you, but anything else can, especially when night falls."

"You're going to do that anyway."

"If I were going to do that, it would have been done. You'd be dead, and I'd be on my merry way to Fenton right now. But here we are talking like two grown men. We are two grown men, aren't we?"

"Last time I checked."

"So there you have it."

Keo paused to let his words sink in. He could see it in Calvin's eyes—the man was thinking about it. How close or far Keo was from convincing him, on the other hand, was difficult to really tell.

"You're not a Mercerian," Keo said. "You would have known what that *M* stood for if you were."

"Unless I was lying," Calvin said, smiling.

"You weren't."

"You willing to risk your life on that?"

"Yeah, I am."

"Brave man."

Or a stupid man, Keo thought, but he said, "Look, it's a simple deal: Give me a hand with this job I gotta do, and I let you live. After that, we go our separate ways. You'll be free to go, and no one will ever know you were involved. You have my word."

"Your word?" Calvin said and almost laughed. Almost.

But he didn't. Did that mean something?

Maybe...

"You're not going to get a better deal than that," Keo said.

"Buck would kill me."

"Only if he finds out. You have my word that he won't."

"And what's your word worth?"

"A lot more than the alternative." Keo stood up and held his hand out to Calvin. "We got a deal?"

Calvin stared at Keo, then at his proffered hand. "Do I have a choice?"

"Of course you do. We all have choices. The question is, will you make the right one?"

"I guess we'll find out." The sniper extended his own hand and shook Keo's. "You're crazy."

"I've been called worse," Keo said, pulling Calvin up—

When Calvin *grabbed at the Glock in Keo's holster with his other hand.*

For a man moving on one gimpy leg, the sniper was surprisingly fast, and he had his hand on the pistol and was trying to yank it free even before Keo could react—when there was a single, thunderous *crack!*

Calvin spun and dropped to the ground, leaving behind a puff of red mist in the space he had been occupied mere seconds ago.

Keo twisted around, unslinging his submachine gun.

Rita was standing next to a tree, her rifle pressed against it as she pulled her eye away from its scope and smirked across the distance at him.

Keo looked back at Calvin, a thin trail of blood dripping from his left temple while his brains and chunks of skull had splattered the tree trunk that he'd been sitting against earlier. He was as dead as dead could be.

Rita walked over to Keo while glancing around alertly at their surroundings, the Mk 14 gripped tightly in front of her. The weapon still looked way too big for someone who was so small.

"What did you think you were doing?" she asked.

"I was trying to make a deal with him," Keo said. "Increase our odds of success once we're inside Fenton."

"It didn't work."

"Obviously," Keo said, and let out a frustrated sigh.

SIX

"She's safe and sound and was exactly where you told me she'd be. The first thing she asked when we found her was, 'Did you save my mom?' The second thing was to demand to know where you were."

"She demanded?"

"That's what the guys said."

Keo smiled. "Yeah, that sounds like Megan, all right."

"Did you adopt her or something?" Gaby asked.

"No. Nothing like that."

"You just spent a lot of time with her and her mom at Winding Creek."

"Yes."

"How long are we talking about here?"

Keo thought about it before answering. "A while."

"That's not very specific, Keo."

"I wasn't exactly marking the days off on a calendar, Gaby. It was one of those things that happened, and I went with the flow."

"And I'm sure the fact that her mom was a full-blown babe didn't hurt."

He chuckled. "'Full-blown babe?'"

"Something I heard some of the guys say. Supposed to mean she's a real beauty."

"I guess so."

"So was she?"

"What?"

"Megan's mom. Was she a full-blown babe?"

"She wasn't ugly."

"Don't worry, I won't tell Lara."

"Gee, thanks."

"You're welcome." She grinned. "So, after five years of avoiding us, here you are. Funny how things work out, huh?"

"*Funny* wouldn't be the word I would have used."

"How does it feel?"

"It's...weird."

"What's weird about it?"

"What's *not* weird about it?"

They stood on the rooftop of the building where the Black Tiders were quartered, watching as an A-10 took off from the makeshift tarmac about two hundred meters away. If Keo squinted, he could just make out a clown's face on the front of the Thunderbolt.

"Mayfield?" Keo asked.

Gaby nodded. "The clown gives it away." She sipped her coffee, one hand inside her jacket pocket. "She's doing aerial reconnaissance over Fenton. Lara wants them to know that we're watching them day and night."

"She told me."

He sipped his own coffee, but the cafeteria lady had put in too much sugar, and it was way too sweet. He grimaced it down anyway and made a mental note to pour his own cup next time. Coffee wasn't something you turned away these days, even if the taste wasn't to your liking. The croissant he'd enjoyed at breakfast was settling nicely in his stomach, as were the bacon and scrambled eggs. Keo had forgotten what it was like to be back among civilization. Winding Creek had been close, but it wasn't Darby Bay.

He turned away from the airfield and sat on the ledge and looked toward the civilian side of the port city. Instead of Jeeps and aircraft, there were fishing boats moored to docks while others moved steadily up and down the coastline with their large sails flapping in the wind. The townspeople relied on horseback and wagons, but most of them were on foot. He wondered if any of the people down there knew what was happening around Fenton or even why Black Tide had taken over a large chunk of their town.

What's that saying? Ignorance is bliss?

Until guys in technicals show up in your streets, anyway.

"How're your wounds?" Gaby asked as she sat down next to him.

"Healing," Keo said. "Yours?"

"Getting there."

"Are you coming with me?"

"Lara won't let me."

"Why not?"

"She thinks I need more time to heal up."

"You look fine to me," Keo said, which wasn't completely true. Gaby was still limping noticeably when she first showed up in his room that morning, but he didn't think she wanted to hear that.

"Tell Lara that," Gaby said. "She won't believe me."

"Maybe she'll come around by the time I leave."

"From your lips to God's ears."

Keo grinned. "Is that what Lara is now? God?"

Gaby chuckled. "Depends on who you ask. But don't tell her I said that. She hates the idea that people think she's more than just a failed medical student."

"In her defense, she's only a failed medical student because the world ended before she could finish."

"Excuses, excuses."

They both smiled and said nothing for a while. Instead, they drank their coffee in silence and watched the civilians of Darby Bay going about their lives. Nearly half of the town was engaged in fishing, which meant the marinas were a constant hub of activity. The smell of seafood—fresh, rotting, and every-thing else in-between—was thick in the air, and it clung to people's clothes, especially the ones that had been here awhile.

Most of the boats he was looking at were using sails to get around, but wind power wasn't going to cut it for the planes and other heavy machinery moving around loudly behind him. When he'd asked Gaby where they were getting all the jet fuel and gasoline, she had smiled and said, "Five years, Keo. You can get a lot of things if you put in the effort to make friends. And Lara's been making a lot of friends the last five years. She's practically rebuilt the trade routes in the south all by herself."

Keo took another sip from his too-sweet coffee. "She wouldn't come back with you? Megan?"

Gaby shook her head. "The guys tried to convince her, but

she wouldn't budge. I think it was because you weren't there. I got the feeling she didn't entirely trust us."

"She's a smart kid, and she's been through a lot."

"We all have."

"Who did you send?"

"Margie, Ronald, and Johnson."

"I don't know who any of those people are."

"You wouldn't. They showed up after you left. I would have gone myself, but..."

"Your leg."

"Yeah. Anyway, they said she was with some guy named Jonah. You know him?"

"We met. Nice enough chap."

"He a Brit?"

"No. Why?"

"I dunno. You called him a 'chap.' I thought only Brits use that word."

"Now you know a non-Brit who also does."

"You're weird."

Keo grunted and finished off the coffee with some effort before putting the cup down next to him. It was heavy ceramic and wasn't in any danger of blowing off the rooftop and smashing the heads of the Black Tiders walking around underneath them.

"Margie said this Jonah guy seemed to be doing a good job keeping everyone together and safe," Gaby was saying. "Megan wouldn't come back with the team, but about a dozen others did. Some from your town, in fact."

"I wouldn't exactly call it *my* town. I spent some time around Winding Creek, that's all."

"With Megan and her mom. Her very attractive mom."

"I'm not fixated on looks, Gaby. I try to see the beauty inside of everyone."

"Oh, I totally believe you, Keo. Totally."

He grinned before glancing up at the sudden *whup-whup-whup* coming from above. A helicopter on approach, skimming over the rooftops of Darby Bay.

"That's a Little Bird," Keo said. "When did you guys get that?"

"Three years ago," Gaby said. "Equipment is never the problem. Finding people who can use them without killing themselves—or the people around them—has always been the real trick. Fortunately, Mercer left us with a lot of good people."

"At least he did something decent in his life."

The morning sunlight gleamed off the black hull of the MH-6 Little Bird as it swooped by overhead. Keo followed its path, locking eyes with two guys in blue BDUs sitting on the bench alongside the chopper, legs dangling off the sides while they cradled rifles. Or Keo would have locked eyes with them if they weren't both wearing black goggles. There were two more on the other side, but Keo only saw their legs.

"Where are they coming from?" Keo asked as the attack helicopter headed for an available LZ in the airfield behind them.

"Looks like they're just getting back from a night mission," Gaby said. "I don't know the specifics. You'll have to ask Lara or Danny for those. Have you talked to Danny yet since you came back?"

"I was told he's out of state."

"He's in Louisiana."

"What's he doing in Louisiana?"

"Cleaning up some problems that we thought we'd dealt with already, but apparently we were too optimistic. He's handling that in person while providing support through the radio. Lara rarely does anything this big without his input. She relies on him."

"She should. Bad jokes aside, Danny knows what he's doing out there. He's got experience out the ass."

"So do you."

"Unfortunately."

Keo took a moment to look around him at the organized chaos taking place within the Black Tide section of Darby Bay. The more he saw of the FOB, the more impressed he was. Lara and Danny had done a hell of a job forming an army, even if neither one of them would come right out and call it that. But that's what it was: an army. Keo had seen enough of them to recognize one.

"You're impressed," Gaby was saying next to him. She was also smiling.

"Yeah, I am."

"This isn't even the biggest FOB we have. You should see the one outside Boulder City that we put together about four years ago."

"Colorado?"

"Uh huh. The one commanded by Beecher. It dwarfs everything we have down here in Texas."

"So why isn't Beecher down here lending a hand?"

"Lara didn't ask for it. And besides, he's got his own hands full. You were up there, weren't you? Colorado?"

"Once or twice. But I didn't stay for very long."

"You need to get out more, Keo. There's a big world you

haven't seen. A lot of things are happening you don't know about."

"So people keep telling me."

"The Purge might be over, but that didn't stop the bad guys from doing bad guy stuff." She finished her coffee and set it down on the ledge next to his. "Goddammit, I wish I was going out there with you."

Keo sighed. "You and me both, kid. You and me both..."

Keo changed his clothes for the second time, but only after the first hot shower he'd had in more than five years. Or, at least, he thought it had been over five years. It was hard to keep track of those kinds of things. Cleanliness was what Gaby called a First World problem when they were walking down from their long morning coffee on the rooftop.

He was pulling on a new shirt and cargo pants when someone knocked on his door.

"It's not locked."

A woman he hadn't seen before stood in the open doorway but didn't come in. About five-five in combat boots, shorter without, with dark hair. Late twenties, but she could have been younger. *Ortega* was stenciled across the name tag on her BDU.

"You busy?" she asked.

Keo shook his head and finished drying his hair with a towel. He'd gotten a fresh cut before the shower and was feeling less like a hippy. "Do I know you?"

"Ortega. You can call me Rita."

"Come in."

She stepped inside and closed the door behind her. "I've been assigned to your team."

"Already?"

"They didn't tell you?"

"No. I don't even know when we're going out there."

"As early as two days from now, as late as five, depending on what the eyes in the sky are seeing around Fenton. And Lara's here to call the shots, which means this is a pretty big deal."

"Is that what that means?"

"She's usually not around. She's a busy woman."

"So I hear." Then, "So what else do you know that I don't, Rita?"

"That's about it."

"What about who else is on my team?"

"I think it's just me so far."

"I guess we'll find out together, then." Keo tossed the towel while Rita leaned against the wall next to the door and watched him curiously. "Was there something else?"

"I just wanted to introduce myself." She paused, before adding, "And get an up close and personal look at the famous Keo."

Keo chuckled. "Famous or infamous?"

"Same difference."

"Is it?"

"You're the one who put Mercer out of his misery. The guy who ended a war that could have killed thousands of people. The way I hear it, you snuck onto Black Tide Island, found him asleep in his room, and blew his brains out."

"It wasn't quite *that* simple."

"But you did do all of those things."

"Yeah, I guess I did."

"Well, damn. You da man."

Keo smiled, though he wasn't sure if he should feel flattered or a little (or maybe even a lot) alarmed that people were going around talking about the things he had done. He'd killed Mercer for personal reasons, not because of some desire to end the man's bloody rampage.

He grabbed his old clothes from the floor and tossed them into a bag to be destroyed. "Were you one of Mercer's people?"

"God, no," Rita said. "I was living in one of the towns his people nearly wiped off the map. I barely got out of there alive."

"So I guess you weren't shedding any tears when you heard he died."

"I might have even thanked God once or twice. That was before I learned about this guy with *cojones* the size of Mount Rushmore named Keo."

Keo raised both eyebrows. "Mount Rushmore?"

"Or bigger."

When he looked over at her, Rita was staring at him with a big smile on her face. He couldn't decide if she was just messing with him or... Yeah, she was probably just messing with him.

"So you're on my team, huh?" he asked.

"Uh huh."

"What's your specialty?"

"I'm your sniper."

"No shit?"

"You sound surprised."

"You're a little small to be a sniper."

"I'm bigger out of my clothes."

"Are you, now?"

"Just say the word, and I'll show you."

Keo grabbed a jacket from the pile. "Ever hear the phrase 'Don't shit where you work?'"

"That sounds...disgusting."

"It means not to get involved with someone you work with."

"Who said anything about getting involved?" Rita grinned, and Keo thought she was having a ball making him uncomfortable.

"So, you're a sniper. Any good?"

"I was trained by the best."

Keo gave her a wry look. "Don't say Danny."

"Peters. That was before he decided to give up the warmth and safety of the gun range for the cold and mud of field work."

"Okay, that makes me feel better. But you still haven't told me if you're any good."

She shrugged. "I'm okay."

"If you're going to go out there with me, I'm going to need more than just 'okay,' Rita Ortega."

"I was trying to be humble," the sniper said. "I'm actually pretty good."

"Pretty good is good." He sat down across from her, and they locked eyes. "Let's get down to it, then."

"Let's."

"Were you assigned, or did you volunteer for this?"

"I volunteered."

"Why?"

"Because I didn't sign up to mop floors or make breakfast."

"Fair enough. Have you ever killed anyone?"

"A few."

"How many is 'a few?'"

"Enough that when you need me to pull that trigger, it'll get pulled," Rita said.

Keo grinned, because he believed her.

SEVEN

It took Keo five minutes to look for a bush big enough to hide Calvin's body, then ten more to carry him over and make sure he couldn't be spotted unless someone took a really close look. It helped that the sniper's ghillie suit allowed him to blend in. It wasn't perfect, but was as ideal as it was going to get under the circumstances.

Rita stood guard the entire time while he worked, sometimes moving around to get a better look at their surroundings. She was back when Keo finished up with the Bucky, and he wiped the man's blood off his fingers using Calvin's already bloodstained handkerchief before tossing it into the bush to be reunited with its owner.

"Did you ever find out how he was doing it?" Rita asked.

"Doing what?"

"Throwing his voice around like that."

Keo shook his head. "It didn't come up. I'm assuming whatever he used"—he glanced toward the tree stand nearby

—"is still up there somewhere. You in the mood to do some climbing?"

"I'll pass."

"Suit yourself."

"You think he had another one of those things back at the other place or if he was just carrying it around with him?"

"I don't know. But he had plenty of time to set them up."

Rita glanced over at the tree stand. "How the hell did he get up there, anyway?"

"He said he had ropes and gear."

"Let me guess. Those are still up there, too?"

"Uh huh."

"And you literally shot him out of the tree?"

"I shot *at* him, but he fell down on his own."

"How did he survive the fall?"

"I dunno."

"He could still walk?"

"Apparently."

She looked back at him. "I heard stories you're a pretty good climber."

"People need to stop telling stories about me."

"If it makes any difference, they were all impressive stories. Especially the one about how you dodged a bullet and head-butted a man to death."

"Who said I dodged a bullet?"

"Didn't you?"

"People can't dodge bullets, Rita."

"They said you did."

"I got shot in the head."

"Really?"

"Yes. If you look closely, you can still see the scar."

"But you're still alive."

"You can survive getting shot in the head."

"Hunh," Rita said.

"That's what I said." Keo snatched up Calvin's rifle and tossed it into a nearby thicket. "You didn't want that, did you?"

"I got mine," Rita said, patting the buttstock of her Mk 14.

"Did the others finally make contact with Command?"

"I don't know. They were still trying when I took off after you."

He gave her a wry look. "You shouldn't have done that. I gave you orders."

"They were lousy orders," Rita said. She met his stare and didn't look away.

"Doesn't matter. Orders are orders. Soldiers are supposed to follow orders."

"Not when they're lousy orders."

"So is this going to be a pattern? You're only going to do what you feel like doing, my orders be damned?"

"No. But I'm not following a dumbass order. You shouldn't have left by yourself. You almost got killed."

"I didn't."

"You'd be dead if I wasn't watching the whole thing and took him out."

"I had it handled."

She smirked. "He got your gun."

She's got a point, he thought, but didn't feel like letting her know that. She was already too full of herself.

He said instead, "Getting his hands on my gun and using it are two different things."

"Uh huh."

Keo started walking back in the direction they'd come, and Rita followed.

"We're heading back?" she asked.

"I need to let Lara know what happened."

"What if she tells us to abandon the mission?"

"Then we abandon it."

"But the mission's not done."

"That's not my call to make."

"You're the boss, boss."

"She's the bigger boss. Besides, we made a lot of noise out here. There could be a platoon of Buckies on their way right now."

"They're not, or they would have been here already. The fact that they aren't means they're not coming. We're still too far away from Fenton for them to risk precious manpower they don't have."

She wasn't wrong, but again, Keo didn't let her know that.

He said, "Either way, it's not my call. It's above my pay grade."

"So why did you come back here on your own, then?"

Keo didn't answer her and kept walking.

"You knew the sniper was out here," Rita said. "You wanted to get back at him for Chang and Banner. Admit it."

"What if I did?"

"You're not going to get any arguments from me. Anyway, I wouldn't expect less from the guy who blew Mercer's brains out."

Keo sighed. He wondered how long that act was going to follow him. It was five years ago, but to hear people keep talking about it, it might as well be last month.

"I'm surprised you felt the need to, though," Rita continued. "You didn't even know they existed until three days ago. I bet you don't even know their first names."

"Ronald and Jeff."

"Yeah, but which one is which?"

Damn, she got me, he thought, but said quickly, "It's not about names. It's about who they were. They were a part of my team. *My* team. And Calvin took them out. I'm responsible for that."

"I know. Not that it was your fault. That's not what I'm saying. But that they were on our team. What happened to them was on all of us."

"Maybe," Keo said, but he thought, *But it's mostly on me. That's what happens when you do something stupid like agree to lead a bunch of people.*

God, what was I thinking? How did I ever let her talk me into it?

They walked in silence for a few minutes. Keo was pretty sure he knew where he was going; there were a lot of trees, and they all looked identical, but he recognized the path. Or, at least, he thought he did.

"So what are we going to do now?" Rita finally asked.

"The same thing as when you last asked that question. Radio Command, let Lara know what's happened, then proceed from there."

"Even if she tells us to head back?"

"She's the boss. Isn't that why you joined up? Because of her? You're going to disregard her orders, too?"

Rita didn't answer.

Keo glanced back at her. "Cat got your tongue, Ortega?"

The Latina shrugged. "I didn't join up because of her." She paused briefly, before adding, "Not completely, I mean.

Partly, but not completely." Then she smiled at him. "I don't have to ask why *you* came back."

"Truth, justice, and the American way, of course," Keo said, turning around before she could read the lie on his face.

Apparently, it hadn't been fast enough, because he heard her saying, "Riiight."

Keo wondered how much Rita actually knew about his relationship with Lara. How much did any of the others know, if anything, beyond gossip? It wasn't as if what happened five years ago between them was common knowledge. Maybe Danny had a clue, but he knew for a fact the ex-Ranger's wife definitely did. Carly and Lara were as close as sisters, and sisters tended to talk. A lot. About everything.

"I don't think you're her type, anyway," Rita was saying behind him.

He smiled, but only because he knew she couldn't see it. "You don't think so?"

"She's into guys in suits."

"And how do you know that?"

"I saw the guy she was dating a few years ago. I don't think he could lift a rifle, never mind actually use one."

"Is that right?"

"I can see why she'd prefer the type. She's around gung-ho soldier boys all day, so a regular civvie in a suit makes for a nice change of pace."

"'Regular' guys, huh?"

"You know what I mean."

"How long ago did she date one of these regular guys?"

"The last one? I heard a few years back." Then, with more than a little humor in her voice, "What's with all the questions? You planning on taking your shot at the ring, Keo?"

"Just curious, that's all."

"You'll have to get in line. I know a lot of guys who signed up because they wanted to meet her in person. Know a lot of girls, too."

"But not you."

"Maybe a little, but it was mostly for the nice duds."

Keo was going to say something, but he stopped and dropped to one knee, lifting the submachine gun to aim first.

"Don't shoot!" a familiar voice called from behind the tree that Keo was aiming the MP5SD at.

"Goddammit," Keo said under his breath. He relaxed his grip on the weapon and stood back up. "I almost shot you."

Rudolph appeared from behind the tree, while Gholston did likewise from another one nearby.

"Good thing you didn't," Rudolph said. "That must have been the quick instincts that got Mercer."

"Must be," Gholston chimed in.

"Make more noise, why don't you," Rita grunted.

"Hey, you guys were making plenty of noise yourselves with all that chatter," Gholston said as he and Rudolph walked over to them.

"Where's Wells and Springer?" Keo asked.

"They're being evac'd to Darby Bay as we speak," Rudolph said. "Helo swooped by and grabbed them about an hour ago after Rita took off after you."

"You made contact with Command?"

Gholston nodded. "Skies finally cleared up. The chopper was making a supply run from Cordine City and detoured to pick up Springer."

"I told Wells to go with them," Rudolph said.

Keo didn't have to ask why; he remembered the sight of

Wells, sweating profusely in the aftermath of Calvin's ambush this morning. Apparently Rudolph felt the same way about their navigator that Keo did—the kid wasn't ready for primetime.

"What did Command say?" Rita asked.

"When I told them that Keo ran off by himself, the response was, and I quote, 'Why the hell would he do something stupid like that?'" Gholston said.

Keo sighed, and thought, *Sounds about right.*

"She wants to talk to you," Gholston said. "She didn't sound very happy."

"Of course she's not," Keo said.

Rudolph, meanwhile, was glancing from Keo to Rita, before finally asking, "So. Anything fun happen while you two were traipsing around out here?"

"Tell me the truth," Lara said over the radio. Her voice sounded a lot stronger than the last time they spoke, but that could have just been wishful thinking on his part. "Is the mission over?"

"No," Keo said into the microphone attached to the radio sitting on the ground next to him.

"Is that the truth, Keo?"

"Yes."

"Are you lying?"

"No."

"I can't tell if you're lying."

"I'm not."

"Keo..."

"Lara," Keo said with as much conviction as he could send over the radio waves. "The mission's hit a bump in the road, but it's not compromised. The plan was to insert into Fenton through the spy. That part is still very much intact."

"What about all the other parts?"

"That will depend on how much freelancing Calvin was doing out here."

"Calvin. That's the Bucky sniper."

"Yeah, that's him."

"He told you his name?"

"He did."

"Why did he do that?"

"He was...chatty."

"And you think Chatty Calvin was all alone out there?"

"I *know* he was all alone out here. We kicked up a hell of a ruckus this morning when we stumbled across him. If there were any of Buck's boys around, they would have been all over our asses by now. But it's been hours since that gunfight, and we haven't seen a peek from them. Calvin pretty much confirmed to me that he was out here alone before he died."

"So our surveillance hasn't been completely useless," Lara said. "There's that, at least."

Keo sat against the tree with the receiver to his ear. Gholston stood about ten meters in front of him, but there were no signs of Rita or Rudolph. They were somewhere out there keeping an eye out for those missing Buckies that should have been all over them by now, but weren't.

"You know how to tell if you're the best at something?" Calvin had said. *"You put it all on the line against the best. And if you beat him, then you know. That's the only way you'll know for sure."*

You better not be telling fibs, Calvin, you piece of shit.

"Did you know them well?" Keo said into the radio. "Chang and Banner?"

"I knew Chang well," Lara said. "He was one of Mercer's men. And one of the first to join me after Black Tide. Banner came a few years later."

"The way they were around one another, I'd assumed they were old friends."

"I guess they hit it off. Which was strange, because they really didn't have a lot in common." Lara paused briefly, before continuing. "Chang had a wife and a son, but Banner wasn't married."

"I'm sorry."

"It wasn't your fault."

"I mean, I'm sorry that you're going to have to tell Chang's wife about what happened to him."

"She's a good woman. The kid looks just like him."

"Can you get someone else to do it?"

"I can, but I won't. I sent him and Banner out there."

And I led them to their death...

"That's part of the job," Lara continued. "I hate it, but I can't avoid it."

"You have an excuse this time," Keo said.

"It's not a good one."

"Are you kidding me? It's a pretty good excuse, if you ask me."

"Not for me." She paused again. "Were you telling me the truth? About the mission?"

"Yes. We can still make this work. We have plenty of daylight left to reach Fenton and make contact with the inside man. The plan itself is still intact."

"Can you do it carefully? That's the question, Keo. Can you get there while avoiding further trouble? According to aerial reconnaissance from the last few days, Fenton's been constricting their forces, bringing those Buckies of yours closer to the city. It's only going to get harder."

"Only if they know we're coming, which they still don't." Keo glanced down at his watch. "I think we can still do this, Lara. You sent me out here for a reason." *And Chang and Banner died because of it*, he thought, but he said, "Let me finish it. Let me make today count."

Lara didn't answer him right away, and Keo took the opportunity to glance over at Gholston nearby. Keo couldn't tell if the Georgian had been listening to his conversation with Lara this entire time or not.

Finally, Lara said, "You have to promise me one thing..."

"Which is?"

"That you won't take any unnecessary risks. Do your best to make the rendezvous point and get inside Fenton, but if it doesn't happen, then it doesn't happen."

"I can do that."

"Keo..."

"I won't take any unnecessary risks."

She sighed. It was heavy, and it came through the radio as if she were sitting next to him. "I know you. You're not the type to just give up. But this isn't personal. You can't make it personal. If it's not there—if you can't complete the mission without risking yourself or the others—I need you to abandon it. Tell me you understand."

"I understand."

"Say it."

"I'll drop it if it's not there."

"Why don't I believe you?"

"I don't want to die out here, Lara. Not if I can help it."

"I just wanted to make sure you weren't going to do something stupid."

"Again?" he smiled, then remembered she couldn't see and felt a little stupid.

"I wasn't going to say it, but yes. Again."

He thought back to the last time they had a conversation similar to this one. They were on an oil rig back then...

"So do I have your okay to proceed with the mission, boss lady?" Keo asked.

This time, the sigh from her end was all exasperation. "I hate it when Danny and Gaby call me that. So you need to cut it out, too."

"I thought you'd be used to it by now."

"From other people, yes. But not from you or Danny or Gaby. You guys aren't like everyone else." Then, before he could say anything, "Keo..."

"Yeah?"

"The mission is important, but it's not *everything*. Do you understand what I'm trying to say?"

"Yes," he said, and checked to see if Gholston was watching, but the man still had his back turned to him.

"Okay," Lara said. "I just wanted you to know that. Be careful."

"I'll see you when I get back. Keo out."

"Oh no, you don't."

"What are you talking about?"

"That's not your call sign."

He groaned. "Don't make me say it. It's stupid. Just like Danny's stupid for coming up with it."

"It's protocol, mister. So you have to say it."

He wouldn't have indulged her—protocols be damned!—if he didn't think it would put a smile on her face. And that was the only reason he did it.

He pressed the transmit lever and said into the microphone, "KY One, out."

EIGHT

They moved cautiously back to Chang and Banner, taking their time and listening for evidence that Calvin was lying after all, and that there were Buckies in the area. But there was no one around the ambush site when they arrived, and no signs there had been except for some animal footprints. Rudolph and Gholston retrieved the bodies of their dead comrades, then carried them about fifty meters to give them proper burials.

Keo and Rita stood guard as the other two did the hard work behind them.

"Did you know them well?" Keo asked her.

"Banner," Rita said. "We joined up about the same time. Chang was already here. But no, I didn't really know either one of them that well."

"Lara told me Chang had a family, but Banner didn't. Did he have a girlfriend?"

"I don't know. Maybe." She shook her head. "We weren't really that close." She glanced back at Gholston and Rudolph as they dug shallow graves with collapsible shovels. "They knew them better than I did."

Keo nodded. He didn't know what else to say. His questions had just been to pass the time, to push the *crunch-crunch* of shovels out of his mind.

The woods were lively around them, with activity above and at ground level, which Keo took to be a good sign. The animals tended to go quiet when they sensed imminent danger in the vicinity. The fact that the chirpings had remained loud since they trekked their way back for Chang's and Banner's bodies was a good sign.

It should have been cold around him given the month, but Keo had become acquainted with the unpredictable nature of Texas weather. It was cold this morning when they touched down, but noticeably warmer now.

Don't like the cold? Wait ten minutes.

Don't like the heat? Blah blah blah.

When Gholston and Rudolph were done, they walked back over, bringing with them the letters both men had written to give to their respective loved ones. Afterward, they continued with the mission, choosing a different path toward the objective. There was no rush, and the last thing Keo wanted was to run across a Fenton patrol unexpectedly. All it would take was one contact and they were done. The closer they got to the city, the harder it was going to be to extricate themselves from a full-blown gunfight if they had to retreat a second time.

"What happens if the contact's not there?" Rita asked about a mile into the resumed mission.

She walked next to him, with Rudolph to Keo's right about

ten meters away and Gholston to Rita's left at about the same distance. Close enough to stay within each other's lines of sight at all times, but far enough that a shooter couldn't pick them off all at once with a well-lobbed grenade. The simple maneuver had proven effective this morning.

Well, mostly.

"We'll improvise," Keo said.

"You good at that? Improvising?" Rita asked.

"I've been known to come up with a plan on the fly once or twice. But we won't have to this time. Our contact will be there."

"Why are you so sure?" Then, looking over at him, "You know who it is, don't you?"

"Yes."

"Who is it?"

"An old friend."

"This old friend got a name?"

"Yes, but I'm not going to tell you, so you can stop asking."

"Why not?"

"Operational security."

Rita might have smirked, but he didn't glance over to make sure. "What if something happens to you?"

"Then you and the boys are to follow orders and retreat back to the evac site."

"What about the mission?"

"There is no mission if I'm dead. The contact won't recognize any of you, so they won't proceed with the plan if I'm not there."

"I guess we better make sure you don't kick the bucket, then," Rita said. "If that happens, Chang's and Banner's deaths will have been for nothing."

They didn't run across a Bucky patrol until nearly five miles later, and that was only a two-man team that looked to be in a hurry to move on. They waited as the pair—a man and a woman, both wearing camouflage hunting clothes instead of the familiar black assault vests with circled *M*'s—passed before they continued on.

"I expected to see more of them earlier," Rita said when they were back on their feet again.

"Fenton's got limited manpower," Keo said. "The bulk of their forces will stay closer to home. They know an attack's coming. That patrol was just part of an early warning system."

"If they're so hard up for manpower, why are they picking a fight with us?"

That's a good question, Keo thought, remembering what Greengrass had told him not all that long ago:

"*I think you'd appreciate the scope—the complexity—of it. Buck's been working hard to put it all together. Years of work, getting it ready.*"

Greengrass had been talking about Buck. Lara's intel didn't know the status of the man named Copenhagen, who was supposedly running things in Fenton before Buck showed up. Was Copenhagen overthrown? Or was he a silent partner, yielding to Buck's authority?

Too many questions, not enough answers.

I guess that's why I'm here.

And there was that other thing Greengrass had said:

"*I'm talking about the big picture. You don't have a clue. Not a whit. There's a grand plan happening that you don't even know exists. It's kind of sad, really.*"

That kind of talk reminded Keo of someone else, whose name was the inspiration for the *M* that Buck's men wore on their clothes these days. That man had come up with a grand plan, too; a "big picture" that he was determined to push through even if it killed a lot of innocent people.

Everyone's got big plans, Keo thought as they passed the sixth mile mark, *until they eat a bullet.*

They stumbled across two more Bucky patrols—including one that had a four-man team, all of them wearing assault vests with circled *M*'s—before reaching the seventh-mile mark. They were now close enough to Fenton that Keo's scar along the right side of his face began tingling out of the blue.

During the trip, they heard the occasional roar of aircrafts flying by overhead. He couldn't tell if they were A-10s, because the canopies were always in the way. But it had to be Black Tide's air force, because Fenton didn't have one of its own. Maybe even Mayfield was up there doing recon over the city, getting updates on the movements of Buck's troops.

What are you doing in there, Buck? Why are you taking on an army without an air force of your own? Are you crazy? Is that it? Everyone knows you can't win a war without air power. Everyone knows that.

"*I'm talking about the big picture,*" Greengrass had said. "*You don't have a clue. Not a whit. There's a grand plan happening that you don't even know exists. It's kind of sad, really.*"

It didn't make any sense. What kind of idiot would tug at

Superman's cape? And that was exactly what Black Tide was at the moment. Granted, Keo had only talked to Buck over the radio, and only once at that, but he didn't think a man like Greengrass would fall in line with an idiot. Greengrass was too experienced and too smart for that.

So what the hell was going on in Fenton that Buck thought he could take on Black Tide? Did it have anything to do with what had happened at Darby Bay three days ago? Was that it? Was all of this just an excuse for *that*?

"There's a grand plan happening..."

Keo shook the questions away. The answers weren't going to do him a lick of sense right now.

Rudolph had disappeared temporarily to his right before reappearing on the other side of a tree. Gholston did the same on Rita's left. Both men walked with purpose, careful of every step they took to lessen their noise pollution. Keo and Rita were doing the same, even though he hadn't had to tell her to do so.

This part of the woods was new to Keo, even if every wooded area up and down the state of Texas tended to look the same. The tree species may change the farther north he traveled up the continental United States, but when you got right down to it, it was still just a wall of brown and gnarled trunks and green leaves, right?

A tree was a tree, was a tree, was a tree...

After another twenty or so minutes, they stopped and gathered in a semicircle while Rudolph pulled out a map. The big man with the bushy beard had taken over navigational duties from Wells and was keeping track of their movements. Looking at the map that Rudolph put on the ground, Keo was surprised by how close they already were to Fenton. No wonder his scar was really tingling now.

"We're here," Rudolph said, pointing. Then, moving his forefinger slightly, "That's Fenton."

Keo nodded before giving all three of them a good, hard look. "There's no turning back now, boys and girl. I know all of you volunteered for this, so if you wanna unvolunteer, now's the time to do it." He glanced at his watch. "You can still make one of the evac sites before nightfall if you go now."

The three of them exchanged a look with one another, but it was Rita who said, "Not a chance. I mean, there was never a chance before, but now there's not even a sliver of one after what happened."

"What she said," Gholston added.

"Yeah, let's get this done," Rudolph said as he folded the map and put it back into one of his pockets. "I didn't come all the way out here just to turn tail now."

"All right," Keo said, standing up. "Let's get this done. I don't wanna still be out here when night falls."

After about ten more minutes of carefully plodding through the woods, they finally reached the rendezvous point. It was an old trailer park about half a mile from a river that flowed from the main Lake Mansfield that gave Fenton its water. The place was overgrown, the road that connected its grounds to a highway somewhere beyond the trees already reclaimed by the woods that surrounded it. Three or so dozen structures, most of them old single and double-wide mobile homes, were lined up in three surprisingly orderly rows.

There were no signs of people, and no voices, move-ments, or anything that even gave the impression someone had been using the area as a home recently. The park had been scavenged and gutted of anything useful years ago, from the looks of it. Given its current condition—dirty and moss-covered, the buildings rotting and falling apart at the seams—it wouldn't have made a very good place to seek shelter.

Which, Keo guessed, made it a perfect spot to meet up in secret.

Not that they ran out there and started calling out the contact's name right away. Instead, they spent thirty minutes hidden in the tree line and watched the park. It had a name, once upon a time, but vines had swallowed up whatever was written on the sign a while ago.

Keo checked his watch. They were cutting it close, and he could already see small hints that the bright sky, now fully exposed above the clearing that housed the park, wasn't going to stay that way for very long.

Rita was crouched next to him, with Gholston and Rudolph farther back. She was looking through her Mk 14's scope while Keo used his binoculars to scan the buildings, going from one former dilapidated home to another. The houses were built from cheap material, designed to temporarily house people, and he wasn't too surprised by their current condition. Time and the elements had taken their toll, and it wouldn't be long now before the whole lot disappeared completely.

"How much longer are we gonna wait out here?" Rudolph whispered behind him.

Keo lowered his binoculars. "Thirty more minutes."

"What if they're not here?" Gholston asked. "It can't be easy to get out of the city unnoticed while it's locked down."

"Thirty more minutes."

"Then what?"

"Then we call it a day and head back."

"We'll be cutting it close," Rudolph said. "Real close."

"Shaving my balls close," Gholston added.

Nice imagery, Keo thought, when Rita pulled her eye away from her scope and gave him a quick look before peering back through her device.

"Where?" Keo asked.

"Third building in the middle row," Rita said.

Keo lifted the glasses back up and looked through them, moving slightly to the right. Fortunately they had approached the trailer park at the right angle, with the three rows spread out evenly in front of them. They couldn't see every single building in the clearing, but it was probably the best view—

There.

The white curtains behind a broken window in the third mobile home in the middle row. Keo couldn't make out a face looking out at them but the fabric was clearly being held back by a hand—for a couple of seconds—before they fell back into place, covering up the window once again.

"Someone's definitely in there," Keo said. He put the binoculars away and unslung his MP5SD. "Gholston, you're with me. Rudolph, watch our six with Rita."

"Gotcha," Rudolph said.

"Good luck, boss," Rita said.

Keo nodded at Gholston, who moved over. Then, together, they jogged out of the tree line and into the clearing.

They kept low, but even with the grass slapping at their

knees—some reaching up as high as their waists—they were still more exposed than Keo would have liked. But they'd been watching the grounds for over thirty minutes and no one had even made a peep (*Until now*), and Keo only felt like he was about to get shot dead by another Calvin-like sniper every three or four steps instead of every single one.

Yeah, that's better.

He wasn't sure how Gholston was doing as the man followed close behind him, but the Georgian didn't slow down as they moved steadily across the field, covering the thirty or so meters of open space as fast as humanly possible. Keo was at least reassured that Rita was watching their backs, and that even if a sniper took them out she'd get them in return.

Unless, of course, this guy was as good as Calvin had been.

That's it, pal. Positive thoughts. Think positive thoughts!

He almost laughed. It said something about how low his expectations had gotten that his best-case scenario involved Rita avenging his murder by sniper fire.

Remember the days when good news was you living through a gunfight?

Ah, good times, good times.

He didn't have time to look at or inside any of the mobile homes as he passed them, and kept his sights squarely focused on the third building up ahead. The path got rocky as soon as he entered the main housing area, with pebbles sliding underneath his boots. He imagined he was making just as much noise as Gholston behind him, and Gholston was making a *lot* of noise as he ran after Keo.

Too much noise. Way too much noise.

The target was directly in front of him, and Keo tightened his grip on the submachine gun as they approached it. The windows were still covered by curtains, and there were no signs anyone was inside or outside.

He was about to slow down when the single-wide's door snapped open on its own.

Now that's an invitation if I ever saw one!

Keo slid to a stop and pointed his MP5SD, Gholston doing the same next to him and aiming with his camouflaged AR. The other man was breathing hard, and Keo assumed he was, too, except it was too difficult to hear anything over the pounding in his ears.

"Well?" a voice said from inside the house. "You guys going to stand out there all day, or come in?"

Keo exchanged a look with Gholston before lowering his weapon and hurrying forward. The steps up to the mobile home squeaked way too loud and threatened to buckle underneath him and Gholston.

There weren't any artificial lights inside the structure and very few natural ones, but Keo could make out a figure leaning against the counter in the kitchen area looking back at him and Gholston as they stepped inside. The figure had long blonde hair tied back in a ponytail and was wearing a long-sleeved sweater. Blue eyes watched Keo and Gholston with just a hint of amusement as they took a moment to catch their breaths.

"You guys really took your time," their contact said. "I was this close to taking off."

"Glad you didn't," Keo said. He walked over and smiled at her. "Damn, you got tall, kid."

She laughed and came out from behind the counter. "And you got ugly."

"Hey, come on."

"I meant *handsome*."

"There you go."

Keo smiled as she hugged him. The fourteen-year-old kid he remembered had grown up to become a tall and fine-looking woman, even though she was probably still just nine-teen. A teenager, even if she had always been much older than her age, and nineteen for her might as well be twenty-nine, or older.

"So where's the rest of your posse, KY One?" she asked.

"Don't go there," Keo said.

She grinned. "Why? Still tough sledding? I thought it'd already be heavily lubricated by now."

Keo groaned, then muttered, "Fucking Danny."

Gholston cleared his throat behind them. "Have we met?"

"Gholston, this is Claire," Keo said. "She's our inside man."

"Some 'man,'" Gholston said, and walked over to shake Claire's hand. He had a big, stupid grin on his face.

"Watch it," Keo said.

"What?" Gholston said.

"Just watch it." He turned back to Claire. "I hear you can get us into Fenton?"

Claire nodded. "That's the plan." She glanced out the window. "Speaking of which, we should get going. It'll be dark soon, and you know what happens when it gets dark."

"Don't remind me," Keo said as memories of a pair of bright blue eyes flashed across his mind's eye.

Jesus. I can't believe I'm walking right back into that.

Keo managed to hide the slight shiver from both Claire and Gholston by turning toward the door and walking back to it. Or at least he hoped he had done it in time.

"How's everyone?" Claire asked as she fell in beside him.

"You don't know?" Keo said.

"I've been in daily communications, but I've had to keep everything straight and to the point to limit the risks of being discovered. There was never really any time for 'Hey, how's it hanging.'" She watched his face closely when she added, "Everything's okay over there? Everyone's fine?"

"Yeah, everything's okay and everyone's fine," Keo lied.

NINE

"Claire? The kid? That's your spy inside Fenton?"

"She's hardly a kid anymore," Lara said.

"What is she, seventeen?"

"Nineteen," Gaby said. She took a slightly frayed Polaroid out from her back pocket and handed it to Keo. "We took this at the last Christmas party."

Keo took the picture. "You guys had a Christmas party?"

"Every year."

"Didn't you?" Lara asked.

"Uh, no," Keo said.

He looked at the picture—Claire standing with Gaby, the two women almost exactly the same height, while holding see-through plastic cups filled with dark liquid. He wouldn't have been able to tell them apart from a distance. He also wouldn't have recognized the fourteen-year-old he had spent months with after Houston teaching how to fight and shoot alongside Danny and the others if he'd met her out there in the wilds.

"She's almost as tall as you," Keo said, handing the picture back.

"Taller," Gaby said. "I was wearing boots in the picture."

They were inside a room in a building next to the one Keo had been staying in for the past few days. There was just the three of them standing in front of a large and heavily anno- tated map of Texas taped to a blackboard. Overhead surveillance photos of Fenton covered the walls and were laid out on tables around them. To look at the city, it didn't stand out as anything different from the hundreds of towns he'd walked through since The Purge—rooftops, streets, and acres of agriculture, usually with a nearby water source. The only thing that made it different were the recent additions next to the lake, separated from the rest of Fenton by hurricane fenc- ing. And there, surrounded by water, was a small island with one lone building in the middle.

What's in that warehouse, Buck? What are you trying to hide?

The briefing room was really just a classroom minus the desks, which were stacked in a pile in the back. One of many inside what was once the Darby Bay High School, since repur- posed for Black Tide Command. Instead of desks, there were big flat tables, and instead of ABCs on the walls there were black and white surveillance pictures of Fenton. Black Tide had been busy watching Buck's every move, even if the man himself didn't show up in any of the pictures.

"She was outside a town called Penn Hall about a week ago when it came under attack," Lara was saying. "It was one of the places I sent men to help them defend it in case it came under attack. There was a fight, but our guys were able to repel

Buck's men. While they were retreating, they found Claire along the road and captured her."

"'Found' her?" Keo said.

"More like she let them capture her," Gaby said. She sighed and shook her head. "That girl..."

"She knew we needed intel on Fenton, and she was in a position to get what we needed," Lara said. "I'm not saying I would have approved if she'd told me what she was going to do and asked for permission, but, well..."

"What did she do, exactly?" Keo asked.

"She took off her uniform, put on civilian clothes, and when the Buckies were running with their tails between their legs, flagged them down."

"And they took her back to Fenton with them, just like that?"

"Keo, did you get a good look at nineteen-year-old Claire in that picture?"

Keo chuckled. "Of course they took her back with them."

"When she was in Fenton, she got her hands on a radio—don't ask me how, she didn't say—and made contact. She's been sending us daily intel ever since."

"So she knows about the warehouse?"

Lara shook her head. "She hasn't been able to get close to it. The military area is closed off from the civilian side." She nodded at Gaby. "She saw the same thing when she was there. They don't let anyone past the fence who isn't supposed to be there."

"She couldn't get to the island, but she asked around," Gaby said. "Bottom line, the civilians have no idea what's really going on inside the compound. Or, more importantly to us, what's in that warehouse."

"I hope she asked around carefully," Keo said.

"Don't worry about Claire. She got through basic training like everyone else, and everything Danny and you couldn't teach her, I did."

Keo gave her a curious look. "Which is what?"

"Everything Danny and you *couldn't* teach her because the two of you don't have titties. Do you really need me to elaborate?"

"Ah, not necessary."

"She's your inside man, but keep that just between us," Lara said. "You're the only one she'll respond to. If you're not there, I gave her explicit orders not to make contact."

"Is she even going to recognize me? It's been a few years."

"She's changed a lot, Keo, but you haven't."

"Plus, that ugly scar," Gaby said.

"Scars give a man character," Lara said.

Keo grunted.

Gaby chuckled before continuing. "Claire's been working on this plan for a while now, and she's assured me it's almost there."

"'Almost there?'"

"Don't worry, I'm not sending anyone out there until it's completely there," Lara said.

"That makes me feel better," Keo said. "A little."

There was a knock on the door behind them.

Lara looked over. "Come in."

A man stepped inside. Early thirties with short blond hair. He wore the same blue-themed BDUs as Lara and Gaby, with a gun identical to Gaby's. Lara was unarmed, and Keo hadn't bothered to arm himself since arriving at Darby Bay. That sudden revelation surprised him—more so that he hadn't noticed until now—and he couldn't remember the last time he had walked around without a gun for so long.

The man—the name *Biden* was stenciled across his name tag—immediately searched out Lara. "Commander Hartford's on the radio, ma'am. He's waiting for you."

"He's early," Lara said.

"Yes, ma'am."

Lara turned to Keo. "Come on. You'll want to hear this, too."

Keo followed her and Gaby out of the room, with Biden in the lead. There was a second man waiting for them outside in the hallway. *Loman* was written on his name tag.

"Ma'am," Loman said to Lara. Keo and Gaby might as well not have existed to the man. Or to Biden, for that matter.

They walked down a brick hallway lined with lockers. Worn-out school banners hung from the walls, and there was a glass case housing dust-covered trophies inside. Most of the rooms they walked past were empty, but a few had been put to use for other tasks. Black Tiders in BDUs moved around them, almost all of them nodding acknowledgements in Lara's direction as they passed. Keo thought he saw a few eyes widening at the sight of her, as if they had never seen her in person before.

I guess we know who's getting the votes for Homecoming Queen this year.

"Who's Hartford?" Keo asked.

"Danny," Gaby said.

"His last name's Hartford?"

"You didn't know?"

"Um, no."

Keo checked her name tag. *Gaby*. Lara's was just *Lara*.

"We're special," Gaby said, answering his unasked question.

"I can see that," Keo said.

"You never told us your last name," Lara said.

"You never asked."

"I'm asking now."

"You really wanna know?"

"Why? Is it a big secret?"

He shrugged. "It's pretty generic."

"It's not Smith, is it?" Gaby said. "Because if it is, God, that would just be so lame. And almost cliché."

"No, it's not Smith," Keo said. "What's yours?"

"Peterson."

"Like Peters?"

"No. Peterson. Did you miss the 'son' at the end?"

"Close enough."

"Not really."

"Why isn't that on your name tag?" Keo asked.

"Because everyone already knows me as Gaby."

"What if another Gaby shows up?"

"Five hundred more Gabys can show up, but I'm still going to be the only one with *Gaby* on her name tag."

"Song Island privileges," Lara said.

"For real?" Keo said.

"Damn straight," Gaby said.

Keo chuckled. When they finally reached their destination at the very end of the hallway, Keo didn't see anyone else around except them.

"Right here, ma'am," Biden said as he stopped in front of a door and opened it for them. "We moved some of the communications equipment in here to give you more privacy."

"And no one bothered to tell me this before they did it?" Lara asked.

"Sorry, ma'am. Someone must have forgotten."

Lara flashed a slightly annoyed look back at Gaby and Keo —and Keo thought, *That's a first*—before she stepped inside the room.

Gaby was right behind her, with Biden following—but not before he looked past Keo and back at Loman, standing in the hallway behind Keo. Loman had kept so silent during the entire trip over that Keo had forgotten the second half of their escort was even back there.

Keo followed Biden's gaze to Loman, even as Biden himself disappeared into the room behind Gaby.

Loman, like his buddy Biden, was in his early thirties, with short dark hair that might have been a buzz cut about a week ago but had grown out since. He had light brown eyes and was a few inches shorter than Keo, and when they stared at each other, the other man smiled.

Except it was forced.

Too forced.

There was no reason for it to be *that* forced.

What...

There was also no reason for Loman to be sweating, either, because the temperature inside the building was just right at around seventy degrees.

...the...

Keo's eyes dropped down at the same time Loman's right hand stabbed toward his holstered sidearm.

...fuck!

"It's a trap!" Keo shouted, even as he lunged forward and shoved his right forearm into Loman's throat and used the surprise and leverage to drive the man back, back, *back* into one of the lockers.

The *bam!* of Loman crashing against the metal box rang up and down the empty hallway, but it was quickly dwarfed by the gunshots coming from behind him.

There were two shots—*bang! bang!*—before they were quickly joined by a third and a fourth—*bang! bang!*

All four shots had come from inside the classroom.

Lara! Keo's mind screamed, but there was no way he could run into the room to check on her, because Loman's right hand was lifting the Beretta into firing position.

Keo grabbed the man's wrist with his own left hand and pinned it against another locker. Loman pulled the trigger, either accidentally or on purpose, and a fifth *bang!* sent a round into the ceiling above them.

Lara! Keo's mind screamed again as he pulled back slightly, just enough to disengage his right arm from Loman's throat. Loman took advantage and started pushing off the locker even as they continued to grapple for control of the gun.

Keo drove his right arm forward, this time driving with everything he had, and he swore he heard the *crack!* as Loman's windpipe snapped.

Loman's right hand became jelly as his body went limp, and Keo wrestled the 9mm out of his suddenly weak grip. He spun around and practically dove into the open door that Lara and Gaby—and Biden, that fuck!—had gone through just seconds ago.

He burst into the classroom and almost slipped on a puddle of wet blood on the floor. He somehow maintained control, and glanced down and back to find Biden sitting against the wall next to the open door gasping for breath as blood poured out of two holes in his chest. His hands were splayed open next to him, a Glock resting inside his open right palm.

Biden couldn't care less that Keo was there and was staring forward at something else. Keo followed his gaze.

There was nothing in the room that even looked remotely like communications gear. There was a pile of desks in the back and chairs stacked in rows in a corner, but Keo only cared about Gaby, crouched next to Lara, who lay on the floor clutching her left side.

Keo ran over.

"The other one," Gaby said to him. She had her SIG Sauer in her hand, her other one pressed over Lara's own hands. There was something that clearly looked like a fresh bullet hole in the wall just over her right shoulder.

Keo shook his head before putting his gun down. He took a quick glance at Lara's waist, at where her and Gaby's hands were clutching. There was a thick pool of blood around Lara and a lot more swelling underneath her.

He focused on the wound. "It's good, it's good. Looks like a through and through. She's bleeding out of both sides, but it's not bad."

"It's not bad?" Gaby asked, but Keo couldn't tell if that was doubt in her voice or hope.

"Yeah, it's not bad," he said, hoping it was convincing, because although he was sure it wasn't bad, it really did *look* bad. "What happened?"

"She pushed me out of the way. The first shot. He was trying to take me out first."

Pounding footsteps as people poured into the room behind

them. Keo glanced back at a wall of shocked faces, most of them holding weapons.

"Get a medic!" he shouted. "Now!"

A couple of the newcomers hurried away, but some stayed behind. He wasn't even sure if the ones that didn't move had even heard him.

"Clear the fucking room!" Gaby shouted, her voice as angry as Keo had ever heard it.

It did the trick, and the room emptied except for the three of them and Biden—

Keo looked over his shoulder to make sure. Biden was dead. His eyes were closed, and his head was lolled to one side.

He refocused on Lara. She was grimacing, her lips quivering. She was hurt—maybe in the worst pain she'd ever felt—but there was nothing like shock to act as a natural anesthesia. He knew a little bit about that.

"What's taking them so long?" Gaby asked.

Keo pulled off his sweater and looked across at her. "Never mind them. We gotta plug up the holes until they get here. It's not bad, but we don't want it getting worse. You're going to have to move her hands when I give the signal, then turn her slightly so I can get to the other side."

Gaby nodded and gritted her teeth. "Say the word."

"Now," Keo said, and Gaby pried Lara's hands away. Lara held on instinctively, and it took a lot of effort for Gaby to get them free.

When Gaby finally succeeded, blood bubbled to the surface of Lara's shirt. But it looked worse than it really was. Another inch to one side, and she would never recover. Then again, another inch to the other side, and the bullet would have missed her completely.

Keo shoved his clothes against the wound, heard Lara grunt with pain, then waited another two seconds for Gaby to lift Lara slightly off the blood-slicked classroom floor so Keo could get at the other bullet hole. His hands were instantly covered in blood, but Keo could barely muster up the energy to care. He was too busy looking at Lara, trying to catch her eyes.

There. Those crystal blues were staring back at him even as the rest of her trembled against his and Gaby's hands.

He grinned down at her. "You should have seen the other guy."

She responded with something that might have been a grin of her own, but that was impossible to know for sure with the intense mask of pain on her face.

"Keo," Gaby said.

"She'll be fine," he said.

"Are you sure?"

"I've seen a hell of a lot worse."

Gaby looked toward the door. "They're here. Keo, the medics are here."

Keo nodded as figures slid to the floor next to him. Someone said something to him, but Keo didn't take his hands off Lara until two other pairs, both wearing surgical gloves, were fighting for space along her midsection.

He staggered up to his feet and took a couple of steps back to give the medics space before looking across at Gaby. Her lips were quivering, the anger flushing across her face as clear as day. Her hands and clothes were covered in Lara's blood, and Keo wondered if he looked that bloody or pissed off, too.

TEN

"You sure you know where you're going?"

"Yes."

"You're sure, sure?"

"Yes, yes."

"Just wanted to make sure."

Claire threw a quick smirk over her shoulder at him. "Relax, Keo."

Yeah. Relax. Right.

Why shouldn't I be relaxed? I'm just walking into the teeth of the enemy when I should be running the other way and not stopping until the Gulf of Mexico is underneath me.

But noooooooo.

"I've gone back and forth along this area for the last few days while waiting for you guys," Claire was saying. "I know every inch of it. Trust me."

She sounded so convincing that Keo found himself convinced. At least, more than he had been a few minutes ago.

You're right, Gaby, she is all grown up, Keo thought as he followed Claire through the woods, with Rita bringing up the rear of their small three-man group.

It was just the three of them, with Claire up front, because Rudolph and Gholston were back at the abandoned trailer park where they would wait until Keo needed them. The hope was that he wouldn't, but as someone was fond of telling him, *"just in case."* Of course, there was supposed to be a five-man team ready to help him exfiltrate from Fenton when the shit hit the fan, but he guessed two combat-weary guys were better than none.

It wasn't about Black Tide being limited by available manpower. It was the exact opposite—Black Tide had plenty of men and arms to bring to bear on Fenton. Lara could have flattened the city a thousand times over since Buck drew her back to Texas. It was about intelligence, and a two-person team (three, if he counted Claire) had a better shot at stealth.

They had been moving steadily east for the last ten minutes or so, and Keo spent as much time listening and watching for Buckies as he did glancing up at the fading sunlight above them. Nightfall was coming. Soon. The idea of being caught out here in the woods at night left him slightly chilled.

Keo still remembered its words. Even now, days after being stuck underneath Cordine City with that thing, he couldn't shake what it had said to him:

"Everything you are, everything you were, everything you wish to be; they'll be open to me. Your secrets, all your secrets..."

It wasn't just what it had said, but how it had said them. Its words were dripping with venom, and at the same time, unbridled ecstasy at what it was planning to do to him.

He shivered and glanced back to see if Rita had noticed.

She was too busy looking to their right, her rifle cradled in front of her. When she turned back around—maybe sensing his attention—he saw the uneasy look on her face.

"You okay?" he asked.

She nodded. "You?"

"I'm walking into Fenton—*voluntarily*—knowing what I know." He shook his head. "Nothing about this is even remotely okay."

Rita smiled. "So what are you doing here, then?"

"What can I say? I'm a sucker for good causes. Also, being a big dumbass probably has something to do with it."

Claire chuckled in front of him. "And I'm sure being asked by Lara to do this had nothing to do with it, either."

"Wait. *Lara* asked you do this?" Rita said.

"I volunteered, just like you did," Keo said.

"But did Lara ask you to?"

"She might have."

"You don't remember?"

Keo ignored her and turned back to Claire. "How much farther?"

The teenager (*God, she's so grown up; can I still call her a "teenager," really?*) flashed him an amused look. "Thirty minutes, give or take. We should be catching them getting ready to head back into the city. Even the Mercerians don't want to be out here at night."

"I don't think they're as afraid of the dark as you think, kid."

"What do you mean?"

Keo thought about telling her what he had learned at Axton and beyond. Greengrass's team working with the blue-eyed ghoul, along with their lengthy and at times extremely revealing talks underneath Cordine City while being held captive.

Instead, he shook his head. "Plenty of time to talk. Let's just get in there first."

Claire nodded and picked up speed through the woods.

Jesus, did I just say 'Let's just get in there first?' Into Fenton? Right into Buck's waiting arms?

Yes, you did. Yes, you just did.

I really am the world's biggest dumbass.

Keo sighed and turned slightly right, following closely behind Claire. The young girl was wearing civilian clothes—loose cargo pants, T-shirt and jacket, and boots—and it would have been easy for her to claim any excuse if she were caught out here. She didn't have any weapons on her—at least none that Keo could see—and he tried to imagine her running into the open road as Buck's men were retreating from Penn Hall.

He grinned to himself. Keo had done a lot of dumb things in his life (*This is one of them, you dummy*), but *that* took guts.

Keo and Rita had swapped their dark camo gear for cargo pants, shirts, and jackets that Claire had smuggled out of the city in preparation for their arrival days earlier. Keo's clothes were a decent fit, but Rita's were slightly baggy. It wasn't Claire's fault, as she had brought as many sized articles of clothing as she could get her hands on, but she hadn't counted on one of Keo's team being a short woman.

Both he and Rita could have passed for Fenton civilians in their current state. That is, if their captors could ignore their weapons and all the extra items in their packs and pockets.

"Down!" Claire hissed, even as she dropped to one knee, before scampering behind a large bush. She moved incredibly fast and silent, like she'd been doing it all her life.

Keo mimicked her movements and hurried next to her. He changed up his grip on the MP5SD as Rita appeared next to him. He wasn't sure if the sniper was breathing louder than usual or if his hearing was just overly sensitive as the two women flanked him.

Rita's noises were quickly replaced by the purposeful *crunch-crunch* of boots on soft soil moving about ten meters on the other side of the bush. Claire, so close to Keo that her shoulder rubbed against his, lowered herself further to the ground. Keo did likewise, and Rita, to Keo's left, followed suit. By the time the *crunch-crunch* began to noticeably fade, the three of them were almost hugging the dirt.

They didn't move or get up or even say a word until they couldn't hear the footsteps any longer. That took about two minutes, though it felt more like five.

Either that, or two hours.

Finally, Claire raised herself up first and peeked over the hedge, before giving him a nod. "They're gone."

"Stray patrol?" Keo asked.

"Maybe. They usually don't cross through here on their way back into town." She seemed to think about it for a moment, maybe going over everything she thought she knew. Then, "Come on, let's hurry before we run into more surprises."

Keo stood up and brushed dirt off his clothes before once again following Claire through the woods. She was moving noticeably faster now, not quite panicking, but the sense of urgency was there even if she didn't know it. But she probably did by the way she kept checking their surroundings.

He glanced back at Rita and found her already looking at him. They exchanged a quick, wordless nod.

"Be ready for anything."

It turned out they didn't have to do anything or shoot anyone. Claire had chosen their path into Fenton wisely.

Keo wasn't expecting security perimeters in the form of fencing or anything physical anyway. Black Tide's aerial recons had already told them that there were no such things around the city's borders. Instead of a wall or a fence—both of which would have taken months and too much manpower to erect—Fenton was relying exclusively on manned patrols.

They crouched near a tree line and looked out at a seemingly endless field of cornstalks moving against the breeze. Keo glimpsed buildings in the background to the right, but there didn't seem to be anything on the left. But of course he knew better. The left was his real target: the military half of Fenton. The right, where he could see apartment buildings, would be the civilian section.

A powerful gust of wind came out of nowhere and swamped them, followed by the gray belly of an A-10 Warthog as it flew by overhead. Keo followed its trajectory as the aircraft swooped over the cornfields, flying low enough that it would have been tempting for someone to try to shoot it down. Whether they would actually hit it was another matter. But there was no gunfire and soon the plane disappeared into the distance, becoming little more than a black dot against the darkening skies.

"Come on," Claire said, and got up and jogged across the

twenty or so meters of open field between the woods and the first row of corn.

Keo was right on her heels, the submachine gun at the ready. He listened to Rita's footsteps but didn't glance back to check on her. As long as he could hear her...

He expected Buckies to pop out of the wall of corn in front of them and shout out, *"Boo! Tricked ya!"* but no one did. They didn't come out of hiding in front of them and not from their sides or behind them. There was no one anywhere to greet or interfere or even notice their dash from the trees.

Keo didn't breathe easier until he was surrounded by swaying stalks—and only because the plants stretched well above his head, hiding them from curious eyes. Claire never stopped moving, and neither did Keo. The kid definitely knew where to go, despite everything looking identical to Keo.

"Damn, there's a lot of corn," Rita said behind him.

"There are acres and acres of it," Claire said. "They had me working the apple orchards when I first got here before I got them to switch me over to corn. I've managed to stay away from the wheat fields, though."

"What else do they have growing around here?" Keo asked.

"Just about everything they need to survive. Fish, too. A lot of fish from the lake."

"How close have you gotten to the restricted area?"

"You're looking at it. They don't let anyone through the gate who doesn't have clearance to be there. And there's only one gate in and out."

"You haven't been able to step foot inside at all?"

"Not yet."

"So how are you getting us in there?"

"I said I haven't been able to get in there yet, but that doesn't mean I haven't been working on it," Claire said as she began angling right.

They moved in the new direction for a few more minutes, with Keo checking the paling horizon every three steps or so. The quiet around them—with only the whistling of wind moving through the corn—was disconcerting. Keo had never gotten this far into Fenton, and even though Black Tide reconnaissance already told him where Buck's main forces were, he expected *some* hints of Mercerian activity nearby. Or, at the very least, something to indicate the place was getting ready for a war.

But there was nothing of the kind, and it bugged him.

"So you have a plan to get us in there," Keo said.

"You wouldn't be here otherwise," Claire said. "Trust me, Keo."

"I do trust you, kid."

Claire finally slowed down as they came to the end of the cornfield, and the teenager glanced around them. He was going to ask her what she was looking for when she crouched and snatched up a grungy duffel bag buried in the ground. As she was searching through its contents, Keo took a quick peek out at the city of Fenton.

Fenton was a good-sized city, with apartment buildings, strip malls, and paved roads that stretched well beyond what he could see with the naked eye from his current position. He glimpsed a few dozen people in the streets and on the side-walks; they were starting to file into nearby housings. Not a lot of people, but enough to confirm that Fenton wasn't abandoned. And he was looking at just one very limited part of the place, so there would be even more people and activity elsewhere.

"Here," Claire said, taking out a couple of Texas Rangers ball caps and handing them to him and Rita. "You'll have to put your weapons in here. Gun belts, too. Civilians aren't allowed to carry guns in the city, so you can't be seen with yours out in the open."

Keo was prepared for that and took the bag, then placed his submachine gun inside. Rita did the same with her rifle, even if she did hesitate for just a brief second or so. They unbuckled their gun belts, but Keo took out his Glock and slid it behind his back where it was hidden by his jacket (*Just in case*). Rita did likewise with her SIG.

"If the civilians can't have weapons, how do they fight off ghouls?" Keo asked.

"They don't," Claire said. The teenager shook her head. "I don't know how they're doing it, but ghouls rarely come into the city. At least, not since I've been here. From the people I've talked to, Fenton used to have problems with the occasional strays, but they haven't had the kind of pack attacks that most cities with a thriving population still get."

Keo zipped up the duffel bag with their weapons inside and slung it over his shoulder. "So no ghouls?"

"There are ghouls out there. I mean, there are ghouls out there everywhere, but in small numbers. People have told me they've seen active packs in the area at nights, but they never attack. It's like it was back during The Purge, when there were still collaborator towns, and the creatures stayed beyond the city limits because they were told to." She paused for a moment, before continuing. "Does that make sense?"

He nodded, and thought, *Yeah, it makes sense. Too much sense.*

After everything he had learned—about Buck and Blue Eyes, about their unholy partnership—Keo didn't doubt that everything Claire was telling him made perfect sense.

"You know why, don't you?" Claire asked. She was eyeing him curiously.

"I'll tell you later, when we're not standing around out here waiting for nightfall," Keo said.

"Sounds like a plan," Claire said. She peered out at the city before looking back and grinning at him. "Try to keep up, old man!"

The teenager jogged out of the cornfields and into the open.

Keo exchanged a quick look with Rita.

"Old man?" Keo said.

"Well, you are pretty old," Rita said, grinning back at him before she charged out after Claire.

Keo sighed and ran after them, the thoughts, *I can't believe I volunteered for this. I must be crazy*, running through his mind.

ELEVEN

"Will we be safe here?" Rita asked.

"For now," Claire said. "You won't have to stay here for very long, though."

"The plan you're working on?" Keo said.

"It'll happen tonight."

"Assuming it works."

"It'll work," Claire said, and she sounded completely convinced. "I can be very, very convincing."

Keo raised both eyebrows, wondering what she meant by that, but held his tongue. He guessed he'd find out. After all, Claire had told Lara everything was a "go," which was the only reason they were in Fenton in the first place. The kid wouldn't have given them the green light if she had any doubts. Or, at least, Keo hoped she wouldn't do something so reckless.

You mean something reckless, like take off her uniform and voluntarily let herself be captured?

Oh, right.

He decided to focus on the positive instead. Like how they

had managed to make their way into Fenton without being caught. Calvin, of course, notwithstanding. The fact that the Buckies weren't everywhere searching for them in the aftermath of their run-in with Calvin further cemented Keo's belief the sniper hadn't squealed on them.

"You know how to tell if you're the best at something? You put it all on the line against the best. And if you beat him, then you know. That's the only way you'll know for sure."

Thank God for big egos, Keo thought now as they walked around a small clinic squeezed between two much larger buildings. They had entered through the back and moved to the front, where Keo gazed out at the darkening streets from behind the curtainless windows. That had concerned him, but Claire said the windows didn't have curtains when she found it, and she hadn't added any because it could draw unwanted attention from those familiar with the area.

The lights directly outside their door remained turned off, but he could already see solar-powered lamps attached to strategically chosen poles up and down the streets starting to come on. There weren't nearly enough lights to brighten every part of the city, from what he could see, but enough to keep Fenton from going completely dark during nights. The same couldn't be said for the buildings in front of and around him. There were at least thirty more minutes before complete nightfall, but the apartments were already dark and quiet, as were the other structures he could see from his limited angle. But that didn't mean everyone was already indoors. A few stragglers were still hurrying up the sidewalks.

Five years later, and we're still afraid of the dark.

Keo watched a couple knock, then enter a red brick four-story building across from the clinic. There were rebars over windows on the first and second floor, but none on the third and fourth. The presence of extra security seemed to be random, as far as Keo could tell. He wondered if that was something new or if it had always been like this. The window in front of him, for instance, had protection, though it was clear some of the bars had been removed and repurposed elsewhere, leaving gaping holes that were big enough for a child to squeeze through. A child, or something resembling one.

Rita and Claire appeared next to him and looked outside. There were no lights inside their building, though there were half-used candles on the counters and an LED lamp gathering dust on a table in the reception area behind them.

"How many people are living in this place?" Rita asked Claire.

"A couple thousand," Claire said. "Maybe more. I didn't exactly do a head count, but most people I've talked to seemed to agree on a couple thousand civvies."

"That's a lot of people. I mean, I've seen bigger, but still, a couple thousand's a lot."

"How did you think I was able to move around so freely? They don't actually have records of anything, including who comes and goes. All I had to do to move between jobs was to ask the right guy."

"All you had to do was ask, huh?" Keo said.

"Ask nicely, yeah," Claire said.

"How nicely?"

She smiled across the window at him. "I have my ways."

"I'm sure you do." Then, "Are you sure we're okay in here?"

"We should be fine."

"'Should?'"

Claire shrugged. "Hey, if you want 100 percent anything, try knitting."

"You've been spending way too much time with Danny."

"That's what Gaby says, too. And Lara. And Carly..."

"So what's the plan?" Rita asked. "How do we get from here to inside the compound?"

"The only way in without leaving a trace is through the front gate," Claire said.

"There are woods on the other side of the warehouse," Keo said.

"You could definitely swim from the woods to the island, sure, but that's a long swim."

"I'm a pretty good swimmer."

"I know. You're half-dolphin."

"Say what?" Rita said.

"Long story," Claire grinned.

"One better left never told," Keo said. "I'm assuming a late-night swim to the target is out of the question, then?"

"I wouldn't say that, exactly."

"What would you say, exactly?"

"It would be difficult. They know the warehouse is vulnerable from that side. That's why they have patrols in the woods in the day and snipers in the guard towers 24/7. I'm assuming —though I don't know for sure—that they also have guards on the grounds of the island. I could be wrong, though."

"You're probably not."

"Besides, it'll be safer through the front gate."

"'Safer?'" Rita said doubtfully.

"This plan of yours?" Keo asked.

Claire nodded. "Have faith, Keo."

"I do, kid. Otherwise we wouldn't have humped ten miles

to get here." *And lost Banner and Chang in the process,* he thought, but Claire didn't know about that, and Keo didn't think it would do anyone any good if she did.

He looked back out the window at the empty streets and the darkening buildings. If he didn't know any better, he would think Fenton was expecting a ghoul attack anytime soon.

Rita must have been thinking the same thing, because she asked Claire, "If Fenton hasn't had any ghoul problems in a while, why's everyone locking themselves in at night?"

"I don't know. Habit, I guess?" Claire said. "Besides, it's not like Fenton has a thriving nightlife. The people here are like people everywhere. They work their asses off in the day and rest at night so they can wake up and do it all over again."

"You sound like you admire them."

"I just understand them."

"Where are you supposed to be staying?" Keo asked Claire.

She pointed out the window and at a two-floor about five buildings farther down the street. "There's a bed-and-breakfast above a restaurant. Or what used to be a restaurant. I have three roommates. All women."

"Are they going to miss you?"

"Nah. I told them I had plans for tonight. We're not on lockdown out here. People are free to come and go as they please, but most don't because it's safer indoors at night."

"They're free to come and go, just not into the military section."

"Except that, yeah. Fenton is very clearly separated between the workers and the security forces. The civvies feed Buck's people and Buck's people protect them."

"Is that what they call themselves?" Keo asked, even as images of the bloodbath in Winding Creek rushed back to him. "Security forces?"

"Uh huh. I doubt if most of them know what Buck and his people are doing out there."

"You didn't tell them?" Rita asked.

Claire shook her head. "That wouldn't have done anything for us except give me away. Besides, they're survivors. In a lot of ways, they're still existing like The Purge is ongoing, that they *need* protection."

"They're not entirely wrong," Keo said. "The problem is, the protection they need is against the people supposedly protecting them."

"But they don't know that. In here, hidden by these woods, the only thing that matters is the people around you, the one working beside you. You can't really blame them after everything they've been through. After everything all of us have been through."

Keo nodded, because he did understand, and because he knew about Claire's own losses. "You did good not to draw too much attention to yourself. They don't know what they don't know, and it's not our job to change that."

He paused for a moment, thinking about the right away to ask the question that had been on his mind ever since he saw Fenton from a distance.

"What?" Claire said, looking at him closely. "What is it, Keo?"

"Did you find her?" he asked. "Emma?"

The teenager shook her head. "I'm sorry. I asked about her by name, even mentioned the town where she was from, but no one's heard of her. Most of them have never even heard of Winding Creek."

"Do you believe them?"

"I do. Like I said, these people don't know what's going on out there. To them, Buck and his men really are just a security force keeping them safe from the big bad world. Even Buck himself..."

"What about him?"

"Most of the people I've talked to have never seen him in person. It's the system—only a few guys in town actually communicate with the Mercerians in person. There's a big wall separating everyone else."

"And they're good with that?" Rita asked.

"Good?" Claire said. "I think they prefer it that way. It keeps their hands clean."

"What about you?" Keo asked. "Have you seen Buck since you've been here?"

"Not once. Honestly? If you hadn't spoken to the man and Gaby hadn't chatted with him face-to-face, I'd almost think the guy was some kind of bogeyman adults made up to scare little kids."

Keo believed her. Everything Claire was telling him jived with Black Tide's recon reports. Not that it was easy to spot a face on the ground from an airplane even using telephoto lens, but no one fitting Buck's description had shown up in any of the photos. Even the ground teams that had gotten close enough to the town in the early days had not seen anyone resembling the Mercerian leader.

"What about the other captives?" Keo asked. "The women and children they took from the towns?"

"Like I told Lara in my reports, I came up empty on that

front, too," Claire said. "If Buck's people brought them here, then they have to be inside the compound somewhere. It's the only other place to put them where they wouldn't be seen."

"Or they might not even be here."

"Or they might not even be here," Claire nodded. "I wish I had better answers for you, Keo, but I just don't know what's happening on the other side of those fields. Or what's in that warehouse."

"I guess that's why we're here," Rita said.

"Somcone has to do it," Keo said.

"Hurray for us, I guess."

Claire looked at him, then over at Rita. "They told me you guys volunteered for this mission?"

Keo and Rita exchanged a look.

"Wow," Claire said. "And I thought getting myself captured on purpose was the dumbest thing someone has done this year."

Rita grinned at him. "Well, can't really say she's wrong."

"This plan of yours," Keo said to Claire. "Tell us about it."

"Not it, but who. His name's Jeremy," Claire said, "and he should be on his way here soon."

Beams of light flashed across the window, silhouetting the iron bars that still covered them, followed by the *tap-tap-tap* of footsteps on the street outside.

Keo remained where he was and had been for the last two hours, sitting on the floor with one of the windows over his right shoulder and the door to his left. The lights from the flashlights were fleeting—appearing and disappearing seconds later—as the men on horseback moved up the road without bothering to stop.

He glanced over at Rita, sitting on the floor on the other side of the door from him. She had her Mk 14 rifle in her lap, her head slightly lolled to one side, and if he listened closely enough, he could hear her snoring softly. Claire was on the floor in front of them, lying on her back with a pillow from one of the back rooms underneath her head. She had gone to sleep an hour ago and was snoring louder than Rita.

He was amazed at how easily Claire had clocked out. He envied her because he couldn't do more than grab a few minutes of sleep at a time before his internal alarm kept going off. He didn't fight it; he was, after all, behind enemy lines even if the people in the immediate buildings around him weren't a threat. Not yet, anyway. In Keo's experience, non-threats could become one in the blink of an eye.

It was different with the guards on horseback. Those would be Buck's men. Buckies. Mercerians. Whatever you wanted to call them, they were the "sanctionable" ones. The ones Lara wouldn't give him too much grief over if he had to kill. "Self-defense" went a long way these days.

The patrol that had just passed them by was the second one in the last hour, but he couldn't tell if they were the same ones or a completely different team. According to Claire, the bulk of Buck's men would be sheltered behind the fence on the other side of the agriculture field. Which was also where he had to be. That was the whole point of coming here, after all.

Get in, get out. No muss, no fuss.
Yeah, should be easy enough.

He might have unwittingly chuckled out loud, because Claire sat up on the floor in front of him.

She looked around before locating him in the semidarkness. "Everything okay?"

"Everything's fine," Keo said. He glanced down at his watch's glowing hands. "It's almost midnight, and still no signs of Plan Jeremy."

Claire looked down at her own watch. "He'll be here soon."

"How do you know him?"

"I introduced myself."

"You 'introduced' yourself?"

"Let's just say I haven't been farming the entire time I've been here."

Keo smiled. "Is this part of what Gaby taught you?"

"Among other things." She stood up and walked over to the other side of the window next to him and peered out at the streets. "How many patrols so far?"

"Two. Is that normal?"

She nodded. "They take their time. Not exactly a lot going on at night. Especially now that they don't even have to deal with ghoul strays."

"You really have been paying attention."

"Hey, that's my job—" She stopped short and hurried away from the window, flattening her back against the wall next to it.

Keo snatched up the MP5SD lying across his lap and hurried to his feet just as flashlight beams hit the curtainless window between him and Claire and lingered on the far wall across the reception area. Keo glanced over at Rita to check on her—

Rita's eyes snapped open, her hands clutching at her rifle. They locked eyes, and Keo put a finger to his lips. The sniper stood up and flattened her back against the wall. It didn't take her long to see the beams coming in through Keo's window and hitting the back wall. The lights moved gradually along framed paintings and old pictures of the clinic's former staff like a pair of eyes searching for something.

Keo glimpsed a shadowed face peering into the window on the other side while the flashlight in the man's hand continued to move around the interior of the building. It went every-where, including—

Goddammit.

Claire saw it at the same time he did—one of the flashlight beams had found and stopped on the pillow on the floor where she had been sleeping. Claire looked over at Keo and shook her head as if to say sorry.

Keo snapped a quick glance back at Rita, who had slung her rifle and drawn her SIG Sauer. There was a long suppressor attached to the end of the barrel, and she clutched the pistol and nodded back at him.

And things were going so well, too.

One of the beams had vanished, leaving just one to scour the parts of the reception area that it could reach from outside.

Searching, searching...

Footsteps immediately behind Keo, on the other side of the wall, just before the doorknob next to him jiggled—softly at first, then louder and harder as the man on the sidewalk put some muscle into it.

But the door was locked, and it wouldn't budge.

The lingering flashlight beam finally left the window, but Keo didn't breathe any easier or loosen his grip on the submachine gun, because someone was knocking urgently on the door next to him now. The rapping was like firecrackers in the deathly quiet Fenton night.

Knock-knock-knock!

Keo exchanged another look with Claire, then with Rita. He saw steely determination from both women.

Knock-knock-knock!

Then silence.

"Well?" a voice asked.

The door rattled for a few more seconds.

"It's locked," a second voice said. The speakers were both male, as far as Keo could tell.

"Why wouldn't it be?" the first one said.

"There's someone inside," the second one said.

"You don't know that."

"Someone put that pillow there. It wasn't there last night."

"So?"

"So?"

"It's probably just kids looking for a place to hook up. They still do that, you know."

"I wanna make sure."

"It's just a pillow, man. Who cares?"

"I care."

"Why do you care?"

"Gee, I dunno, because it's my job?" the second one answered.

Great, Keo thought, *I had to run into the one guy in Fenton who takes his job seriously.*

He softly *clicked* the fire selector on his MP5SD to semi-auto. The switch barely made any sound, but it made enough of one that Rita could hear it. The sniper looked across the door at him, and they exchanged a brief nod. Claire, standing unarmed on the other side of the window from Keo, stood perfectly still.

Bam! as something slammed into the door on the other side. The slab of wood trembled slightly, but never came close to breaking.

Someone laughed.

"Not funny," the second man said. "You try it."

"Hell no," the first one said. "You're the one with the hard-on to get inside."

A second *bam!* from outside. The door quivered like the first time, but again, easily held.

"Okay, okay," the first man said. "Go easy there, Tarzan. If you absolutely have to get inside, I'll go wake up Benson. He's the one with keys to all these buildings over here."

"Why didn't you say so before?" the second one asked.

"I dunno. Maybe because it's funny watching you try to break down a solid oak door?"

"Fuck off."

Another round of laughter before the two men left, taking their bickering voices with them.

Keo sought out Claire in the darkness. "How long before this Jeremy shows up?"

"He should be here soon," Claire said.

"Not soon enough," Rita said. "Those guys are coming back. If we're still here when they do…"

Keo focused on Claire. "Can Jeremy really get us where we need to be?"

"Yes," Claire said.

"Are you sure?"

"Yes."

"I mean it, Claire. Are you *sure.*"

This time, Claire didn't answer right away. She seemed to think about it—for a second or two too long for Keo's liking—before finally nodding. "Yes. He can get us inside."

"All right, then we'll wait for Jeremy."

"What about the patrol?" Rita asked.

"That's what the suppressors and dark closets are for," Keo said.

TWELVE

"Who were they?"

"Loman and Biden."

"Are those their real names?"

"Your guess is as good as mine. Is Keo your real name?"

"Unfortunately, yes. Did you know them?"

Gaby shook her head. "I've never seen them before. But that's not unusual. We were getting huge influxes of recruits in the first two years after Houston, and they've been coming in at a steady stream ever since." She glanced over her shoulder at the guards standing outside the room; only two of the four were visible through the security glass. "I don't know most of these people by name unless I look at their name tags. Some of them came here with Lara when she returned to Texas to deal with Fenton, but not everyone."

"Did you guys ever start keeping records?" Keo asked.

"Of course. Everyone who joins up has to go through Black Tide's basic training. We don't just give everyone a gun and send them out here, Keo. So yeah, there are records. I have

Carly going through them now, but it might take a while for her to get everything together. We have a lot of people out there, stationed in a lot of places."

"Paperwork."

"Yeah, paperwork. That's the problem with civilization. The paperwork."

They stared at each other in silence for a moment. He was standing, leaning against the brick wall while she sat on a chair. Lara lay on the bed between them, tucked underneath a duvet. She had been heavily sedated after the surgery and hadn't woken up since. This was, ironically, her first full night's sleep, and all it took was an attempted assassination.

"Too bad we can't question them," Gaby finally said. "Who they were, how they got here..."

"Yeah, too bad," Keo said.

"Of course, we could have, if you hadn't crushed Loman's neck."

"He didn't exactly give me a choice."

"Couldn't you have just broken a couple of bones?"

"Couldn't you have just wounded Biden?"

"Fair enough," Gaby said, and smiled.

He returned it.

It was quiet inside and outside the room, as if the entire city of Darby Bay had learned what had happened and no one was quite sure how to proceed. Of course, that was unlikely. The Black Tiders definitely all knew, but the civilian population probably didn't have a clue. At least, not yet. But news like this wouldn't stay secret for very long. Sooner or later, it would leak.

"Thank God you were here," Gaby said. "Lara and I'd be dead right now if you were still running around out there doing your own thing. It must be fate, bringing you back here just when we needed you most."

"That's one way to look at it."

"You don't believe in fate?"

"I believe in a lot of things. Most of them, I can't put into words."

"For a guy who's survived so much, I'm shocked you're still such a Doubting Thomas."

"That's my secret to staying alive this long. Doubting everything."

"Seems to be working."

"Seems to be." Then, "What else did you find out about the partners in crime?"

"Nothing that'll help us figure out who they really are, but I should have more soon. Malone and a few others are asking everyone about them now. If I'm being honest, I'm not very confident they'll find anything useful. Whoever they were, they were really good."

Not good enough, Keo thought, looking at Lara's sleeping form. *But* almost *good enough*.

"What kind of sedatives did they give her?" he asked.

"I don't know; I didn't ask. They said she should be awake later today and that she's not in any danger."

There was a knock on the door, and Keo instinctively brushed against the butt of the Glock in his hip holster with a couple of fingers. He'd found a gun belt after what had happened, just in case.

"Come in," Gaby said.

A young man with a blond buzz cut opened the door and leaned inside. There was light in the hallway behind him, but it wasn't bright enough in the room for Keo to read the kid's name tag, though he assumed it was Malone when the man said, "I'm done with the interviews, Gaby."

"I'll be right there," Gaby said.

Malone slipped back outside, closing the door after him.

Gaby stood up. "You gonna stay a while?"

"I got nowhere else to go," Keo said.

"Good. I'd like one of us to be with her at all times."

"I got this covered."

Gaby left, and Keo walked around the bed and took her spot in the vacated chair. It was wooden and uncomfortable, and he couldn't understand how Gaby could sit in it for so long. His butt was already starting to rebel, and it had only been a few seconds—

"You guys really know how to ruin someone's nap."

He smiled at Lara as she turned her head to look at him. She managed a small smile back, but it clearly took a lot out of her.

He leaned forward. "You're looking pretty good for someone who almost died last night."

"What can I say? I come from good genes." She paused, then, "Last night?"

He nodded.

"What time is it now?" she asked.

"Six in the morning. You've been out for about ten hours."

"No wonder I feel so good. Well, as good as you can feel after getting shot, I mean." She tried moving but gave up after a few seconds of wincing. She lifted the duvet and peeked down at her bandages for a moment before covering herself back up. "Why is it so dark in here?"

"Mood lighting."

"What's the mood we're going for?"

"The 'our fearless leader is hurt and everyone's sad about it' mood."

Lara gave him a wry smirk. "At least it's not Dear Leader. I'd be really worried if people started calling me that." She sighed and closed her eyes for a moment, gathering her strength. She opened them again after a few seconds. "Where did Gaby go? I thought I heard her voice."

"She went to talk to Malone. He's been asking around about Loman and Biden."

"Who?"

"Loman and Biden. Biden's the one who shot you. Loman was his partner in crime. You didn't recognize either one of them?"

Lara shook her head and stared up at the dark ceiling. "Too many new faces every day to keep track of them all. I spend a lot of time with the operational teams, but the support guys... There are a lot of new faces."

"That's what Gaby said."

Lara looked over at him. "You guys okay?"

"We're fine. You're the only one who got tagged."

"Is that what you call getting shot? 'Tagged?'"

"You should hear what this guy I did a job with in the Balkans called it. Something to do with a mule's ass."

"Pass."

"Smart."

They exchanged another brief smile.

"So what's the working theory?" Lara asked.

"We can talk about that later, when you're better."

"Might as well talk about it now. Give me something to do."

"Lara..."

"Tell me," she said, with as much conviction as she could muster. "Please. It'll give me something to do instead of just lying here like an invalid."

"We don't know all the facts yet. Gaby's trying to figure them out. She'll come back and fill us in when she knows more."

"No guesses so far?"

"There's a chance they could be Mercerians. You, me, and Gaby aren't exactly very popular with them these days. Especially me and you. And if they were Mercerians, then they could have been sent by Buck."

"You think they could be from Fenton..."

"It's possible Buck saw an opportunity with you being here and acted on it. Like you guys said, people are joining and putting on those fancy blue BDUs all the time. There are too many faces to keep track of, and it's not like you guys were IDing people before letting them in the door. Does anyone even still carry around their driver's license anymore? Loman and Biden could have been called something else a week ago. Even a day ago."

She closed her eyes and let out a tired sigh. "Everything's been moving so fast since Houston. We expanded too quickly. In turn, we needed more and more resources. That meant more and more manpower."

"And round and round it goes."

"Exactly." She paused again. "This was bound to happen. We've become a bureaucracy, Keo. Too many people, too many things happening at once, and not enough control. This is my fault. I should have seen it coming, but I was too preoccupied. I'm always too preoccupied with something. If it's not Fenton, it's something—or someone—else."

"Maybe it's time to rein it in."

She looked over at him. "How?"

"After we deal with Fenton, maybe it's time to focus on one mission at a time. You've done enough out there. They should be able to take care of themselves for a while without you having to hold their hands."

"You think I've been wasting my time, don't you?"

He shook his head. "No. I don't."

"It sounded like you were."

"I wasn't. I think you've been doing a hell of a good job. But..."

"I knew there was a *but* coming."

"You're only one person, Lara. And one person can't save the world by herself."

"But I can try. Who else is going to if I don't?"

"You can't do it alone."

"You left me."

And there it was. He'd been waiting for it since he came back. They'd been skirting around the issue all this time, approaching it from angles but never tackling it head-on. But he knew it wouldn't last. He knew that sooner or later they would have to confront it.

Lara sighed and looked away. "I didn't mean it like that. It was your life. I didn't have any right to make you commit to something that would have taken years of your life. That would have been selfish. You had every right to leave when you did. I shouldn't have said what I said."

He sat back in the uncomfortable chair and didn't say anything. He didn't know what to say. He'd never been especially good at this.

"I'm sorry, Keo," she said softly.

"Me, too," Keo said, and let the silence fall between them.

"No one knows who they were," Gaby said. "They showed up about four days ago, and as far as anyone knows, Darby Bay was the first time anyone had ever seen them."

"How is that possible?" Keo asked.

"We have too many people and not enough oversight," Lara said. "I saw it coming. Years ago, when the first wave of recruits showed up. Carly and I had to scramble to put together clerks to deal with it." She looked over at Keo. "But like you said, people could call themselves anything they want these days. They could invent entire backstories, and no one would know the difference."

"And we didn't care, either," Gaby said.

Gaby stood on one side of Lara's bed, while Keo stood on the other. Morning sunlight had brightened the room as well as the hallway outside, and last night's assassination attempt seemed a distant memory. It helped that Lara looked noticeably stronger than the first time she woke up.

"What does that mean? You didn't care?" Keo asked.

"Everyone was getting a second chance," Lara said. "It didn't matter what you did during The Purge or what you were. Everyone got a second chance. That was the whole point, Keo."

"I can see how that would attract a lot of people..."

"And 99 percent of them were good people," Gaby said. "For five years, we never had a problem."

"Then Loman and Biden came along."

"I have Malone and a team making sure everyone who is

here with us now is supposed to be here. They'll be cross-checking everyone with Carly back at Black Tide. If no one else is supposed to be here, we'll know it."

"What else did you find out about them?" Lara asked.

"Besides the fact that no one knows where they came from or when they got here? Not much else. They did odd assignments around the base, and Loman helped out with the refueling and rearming of the aircraft for a few days. Biden, meanwhile, joined the security rotation. The Darby Bay FOB didn't exist until two weeks ago, and we had personnel shuffling back and forth between bases and the island. A lot of people came from out of state with Lara. It was a mishmash of old and new people, and everyone was too busy doing their jobs to worry about a couple of new faces. They had the right uniforms—which they could have gotten anywhere—and they seemed to know what they were doing and didn't attract attention to themselves. Everyone just assumed they were new recruits who were settling into their roles, like they themselves were not long ago."

"They were good," Keo said.

"Yeah, they were really good."

"You still think Buck sent them?" Lara asked him.

"I think Buck would have seen a perfect opportunity to cripple Black Tide," Keo said. "Taking you out would be one hell of a crippling move."

"He's definitely capable of this," Gaby said. "A man like that would jump at an opportunity to send Biden and Loman on a kamikaze mission to take you out."

Lara's face paled noticeably. Keo didn't blame her. He knew from firsthand experience that knowing someone had your name at the top of their shit list and was willing to do whatever it took to cross it off was not a very good feeling.

"What about you?" Lara asked, looking over at him.

"What about me?" Keo said.

"He's not exactly your biggest fan, either. You don't think Biden and Loman could have been here for you?"

"Loman didn't seem very shy about trying to kill me. If Buck knew I was here, he would have told them to take me alive. That...wouldn't have been easy, but they didn't even try. They went right for you."

"Buck wants you alive because of Blue Eyes," Gaby said.

Keo nodded. "Yeah, unfortunately." He looked back at Lara. "I'm pretty sure this was all about you."

Lara sighed. "Great. I feel so honored."

"Did you find out if they were communicating with Fenton?" Keo asked Gaby.

Gaby shook her head. "We went through all their belongings in the room they were sharing with four other people. If they had a radio that could make contact with Fenton, they found a damn good hiding spot for it."

"What are the chances this was Buck's endgame all along?" Lara asked. "What if all those town raids were just to bring me here so I could be assassinated? Is that possible?"

"Anything's possible with a guy like Buck. He's capable of just about anything."

"The asshole did make an alliance with a blue-eyed ghoul, for Christ's sake," Gaby said. "I'd say he's capable of just about anything if he can do that. But there is one way to find out for sure. You can ask the man yourself if the opportunity presents itself."

"I'll be sure to add that to my To Do list," Keo said. "Right before I put a bullet through his head."

Lara exchanged a look with Gaby.

"What?" Keo said.

"I tried to convince Lara to tell you to sanction Buck if you get the chance," Gaby said. "But she refused to do it."

"'Sanction?'"

"It sounded like something you would say."

"I told her I'd never tell you to do something like that," Lara said to him. "That kind of order..." She paused and shook her head, before continuing. "It doesn't matter what anyone calls it; it's not something I'll ever do or ask anyone else to do in my name."

"Maybe it has to be done," Keo said.

"No, it doesn't. There are other ways to achieve the same ends. Ways that won't compromise our principles."

"It would be justified."

"No," Lara said. There was finality in her voice. "We'll find another way to beat him, because we're better than him. We have to be, if we want to keep being the good guys."

Keo nodded before exchanging a silent look with Gaby.

"Now, let's talk about ways to increase security on the base here and elsewhere," Lara said. "I want to make sure this can't ever happen again."

"I'm working with Malone to draw up some new protocols..." Gaby began.

THIRTEEN

Mr. Nosy and his partner came back exactly twenty-three minutes later. Keo knew it was exactly twenty-three minutes because he had been keeping track on his watch, literally counting the seconds.

He had already taken up position on the right side of the door while Rita and Claire retreated to the back. Rita had her SIG Sauer with the suppressor attached to the barrel while Claire clutched the Glock he had given her. The 9mm didn't have a suppressor so if she had to use it, he would know they were in trouble.

Not that they weren't in trouble already, but Keo liked to think he could deal with two stray patrolmen operating off the books. At least according to everything Claire had told him. With his MP5SD at his side, Keo pressed his back against the smooth (and slightly cold) wall, and waited. The only bright side was that he was only dealing with two human threats. So things weren't completely FUBAR just yet, but of course it could get there pretty damn fast.

Captain Optimism, as Danny would say.

The only reason he could see the two women in the pitch-black hallway almost directly across from him was because he knew they were there. Anyone else—even looking through the windows—wouldn't have been able to make them out. They were far enough in the corridor that any moonlight coming into the building wouldn't reach them.

Twenty-three minutes and about fifty seconds later (*give or take*), the doorknob moved at the same time that the dead-bolt slid out of position with an echoey *clack!* It was probably not nearly as loud in reality, but with the absence of any other noises save for his calm heartbeat and the slightly accelerated breathing of Claire and Rita reaching out to him from the shadows, any sound at all was magnified.

Keo turned slightly so that his right shoulder was now leaning against the wall instead of his back, and lifted the submachine gun into firing position. Depending on how tall the first man was, Keo would either have to lower the weapon slightly or tilt it up just a tad. Either way, it wasn't going to take very much to splatter the clinic's walls with brain matter.

"Well?" a voice said from outside. Keo couldn't tell if that was the first one—Mr. Nosy—or his partner. From the mocking tone, it was probably Mr. Nosy's partner. "You gonna go inside or not?"

Definitely Mr. Nosy's partner.

"Give me a sec," Mr. Nosy said.

"What for?"

"Just give me a sec, will you?"

"Hey, you wanted to check the place out, so go in and check the place out."

"I am."

"Then do it."

"I *am*."

"So what's the holdup?"

Keo could hear it in the partner's voice. He was egging Mr. Nosy on, having fun at his buddy's expense.

Some buddy.

"We didn't get the key for nothing, did we?" the partner said. "Well, did we?"

"Would you shut up?" Mr. Nosy snapped. "You're making too much noise."

A chuckle. "You afraid of the dark all of a sudden? There's nothing out here but us. Speaking of which, I'm freezing."

"Don't be a pussy. It's not that cold."

"I'm warm-blooded. I get cold easily."

"If only you could shut your mouth as easily."

Another chuckle. "Go on, take a peep so we can get on with it. This is starting to get boring. And you know I hate it when things get boring."

The doorknob turned fully, followed by the door beginning to open. Slowly, like Mr. Nosy was having second thoughts. Either that, or Mr. Nosy liked to take his damn time with everything.

Keo slipped his forefinger into the trigger guard of the H&K and rested it against the trigger. Across the room from him, he heard the slight ruffling of clothes as either Rita or Claire prepared themselves. He hadn't mentioned to Claire that she probably shouldn't use the Glock unless absolutely necessary, but he assumed she already knew that.

That girl's too smart not to know that without being told. I hope.

The door was still opening, so slowly that it began to creak like something out of a bad horror movie.

Hurry up, you putz, let's get this show on the road!

"Oh geez, get on with it already," Mr. Nosy's partner said, echoing Keo's thoughts.

Brilliant minds think alike!

"Shut *up*," Mr. Nosy said.

"I will, if you hurry the hell up," his partner said.

"Man, you're really getting on my nerves."

"Good. Because you're already on mine."

There was a loud sigh before the door opened wide enough that a splash of moonlight entered the room and fell over the pillow that Claire had put on the floor. Keo had told her to leave it there, because removing it now would have only put Mr. Nosy on even higher alert.

Keo sniffed the aroma of beef in the air, either coming from Mr. Nosy's breath or clinging to his clothes. A burst of white cloud filtered between the ajar door as the mouth that breathed it approached, followed by the smooth, long black barrel of a rifle leading the way.

Can't let him use that. Too much noise. Way too much noise.

"Nervous?" Mr. Nosy's partner said from somewhere outside the building.

"Would you *shut up*," Mr. Nosy snapped again.

"You're making me fall behind schedule, man. You know that, right?"

Mr. Nosy stopped moving, and the door stopped opening any farther. The barrel of the rifle lowered, the muzzle pointing at the floor as its owner turned around slightly to look back at his partner. "What schedule? There is no schedule."

"Sure there is," the partner said. "*My* schedule. And we're way behind because of you."

"Give me a sec," Mr. Nosy said.

"That's what you said before."

Great. Behind enemy lines, and I'm being treated to an Abbott and Costello routine. What an entertaining development!

Keo changed up his grip on the MP5SD and briefly considered stepping away from the wall and exposing himself to the two patrolmen and ending it. One way or another, he was going to have to hide some bodies anyway, so he might as well start the show early—

"What the hell are you guys doing?"

The question had come from a new voice—a third person that Keo hadn't heard from before. It was male and had been spoken with an obvious air of authority.

"Whoa, you scared the shit out of me," Mr. Nosy's partner said.

"I asked you a question," the newcomer said. Again with that slight annoyed edge that let Mr. Nosy and his partner know he had power over them. "Don't you have somewhere else to be right now?"

"We're just checking out this building," Mr. Nosy said, and his rifle slipped back through the ajar door.

"What's so special about it?"

"Genius here thought he saw a pillow inside," the partner said. He sounded like he was trying to keep back another chuckle.

"I didn't *think* I saw a pillow, I saw it," Mr. Nosy said. "It's still there. Take a look."

Keo glanced across the room at where Rita and Claire

were hiding. He could just barely make out Rita's outline in the shadows, along with the smooth barrel of her gun's suppressor, but Claire was too well hidden.

"What the fuck for? You should be on the other side of town by now," the newcomer was saying from the street.

"That's what I told him," the partner said.

"What about the pillow?" Mr. Nosy said, and Keo could have been wrong, but the man almost sounded unsure of himself that time.

"That's why you stopped doing your job?" the newcomer said. "Because you saw a goddamn *pillow?*"

"Well, yeah."

"Get back on duty and stop fucking around."

"We weren't fucking around—"

"*Now.*"

"Yes, sir," the partner said, and Keo turned to the window next to him just in time to see a silhouetted figure walking quickly past.

Behind him, the door closed back up with a soft *click.*

"Sir—" Mr. Nosy started to say.

"Go do your goddamn job," the newcomer said. Then, in a less angry voice, "Leave the key."

"Yes, sir," Mr. Nosy said, before a second figure moved down the sidewalk on the other side of the window Keo was stealing looks through.

Didn't see that coming, Keo thought as he turned to face the door.

If the third man was still out there, he wasn't making a lot of noise. In fact, he wasn't making any sounds at all.

A full minute went by.

Two...

Keo glanced over at the back hallway and caught Rita's eyes. If he could read her face at all, he'd probably see the unasked question: *What the hell is going on?*

He couldn't answer that, and he wasn't going to be able to while standing still, so Keo tiptoed across the closed door until he was on the other side and leaned sideways to get a peek out the window.

A lone figure stood on the sidewalk looking down the street in the direction that Mr. Nosy and his partner had gone. He was mostly covered in shadows except for some short blond hair and the long barrel of a rifle jutting out from behind his back. He was wearing a uniform, and Keo could easily make out the white *M* on the front of his assault vest.

A Bucky, but not any Bucky. One with authority. Maybe even one of Buck's lieutenants? If so, what was the man doing out here in the middle of the night? From Keo's experience, COs didn't do grunt work if they could help it.

Who are you, buddy? And what are you doing out here all by your little lonesome?

Three minutes had gone by since the patrol left, and about ten seconds after that, the lone figure finally turned toward the door.

Keo pulled his head back, then slung his submachine gun and reached back for the knife behind his back and pulled it out. The blade gleamed in the moonlight. Five inches of razor-sharp silver. The built-in suppressor on the Heckler & Koch was good for close-up kills that needed to stay silent, but there was always the chance of a freak accident causing too much noise. A knife, on the other hand, would guarantee absolute silence if used correctly, and Keo was good at using one correctly.

He turned around just as the door began opening, except this time it did so at a reasonable pace. A tall, lanky frame came into view as a man stepped inside—

Keo grabbed the figure by his right arm with one hand and jerked as hard as he could. The Bucky stumbled the rest of the way inside, lost his balance halfway, and went spilling to the floor. The man had the presence of mind to stick both arms out just in time to save himself some pain, but not completely if the loud *oomph!* he let out was any indication.

Before the man could gather himself, Keo pushed the door closed—but *didn't slam it shut*—and turned around, clutching the knife in one hand. But as it turned out, he didn't have to do anything else because Rita was already there and standing a few feet from the Bucky with her SIG pointed at his head. The man remained on the floor on his stomach, his head craned up and his eyes locked on the muzzle of Rita's pistol.

The sniper looked fearsome—all gun and shadows and spread-eagled legs. Keo couldn't imagine how much more dangerous she looked from the perspective of someone lying on the floor looking up at her.

Rita didn't take her eyes off the Bucky when she said, "Good?"

"Good," Keo said. He put the knife away and hurried over to relieve the blond of his rifle and sidearm.

"Don't hurt him," Claire said as she came out of the hallway behind Rita.

"What?" Rita said while still never taking her eyes away from her captive.

"It's Jeremy," Claire said. "He's the friend I told you about." She hurried over and crouched next to the man and smiled at him. "You okay?"

The man named Jeremy looked from Claire to Rita and back again. "I don't know. Am I?"

"He looks okay to me," Keo said. He walked back to the windows and looked out just in case Jeremy hadn't come alone, or the two patrolmen decided to disobey orders and had returned to finish the job.

Because of one random pillow. Jesus Christ, that was close.

But there was no one out there except shadows and darkness and soft halos of solar-powered lights that could have used more juice. Fenton was sound asleep and would be for another eight hours or so, depending on how early these people got up to work the fields each day.

Behind him, Claire was helping Jeremy up from the floor. Rita glanced over at him with another unasked question, and Keo nodded back. She lowered her gun and came out of her shooting stance, but she didn't put the SIG away.

"You're bleeding," Claire said, and took out a rag and dabbed it against Jeremy's forehead. It wasn't much of a wound—more like a scratch—but the way Claire was treating it, it could have been a gaping bullet hole.

"I hit my head on the floor," Jeremy said, almost as if he were embarrassed. He might have also blushed, but the room was too dark for Keo to be certain.

What's going on here?

Keo watched them closely: the way she was acting toward him and Jeremy's responses, and even the way they kept staring at each other like Keo and Rita were no longer in the room with them. Mostly, though, he paid attention to Claire—the soft way she spoke to him, the way her hands always found ways to make contact with various parts of him, and how close their faces were at all times.

Gaby's words, about Claire's training, came back to Keo:

"Don't worry about Claire. She got through basic training like everyone else, and everything Danny and you couldn't teach her, I did."

And Gaby had done some impressive stuff since the last time he saw her, with escaping from Fenton being just one of them. What other skills had she imparted on the kid in the years since Keo had seen her?

A lot, apparently.

"He didn't mean to do it," Claire was saying to Jeremy.

"It felt like he did," Jeremy said, glancing back at Keo.

He was younger than Keo had initially thought—mid-twenties, maybe—and the sandy blond hair only made him look more youthful. He reminded Keo of Danny; he was just as tall and lanky. He couldn't quite reconcile this young kid with the same one that had barked orders at Mr. Nosy and his partner minutes ago. If he had sneaked a peek during the exchange outside, Keo was sure he would have seen the two patrolmen quaking in their boots.

But here, standing in front of him, Jeremy looked practically harmless. Or maybe that had a lot more to do with Claire's presence.

The teenager looked over at Keo now, and though she didn't say anything, it wasn't difficult for him to read what she wanted him to say.

Keo obliged, smiling at Jeremy. "Sorry about that, kid. I didn't know who you were, and we were on edge after, well, you know." He walked over and stuck out his hand. "I'm Keo."

"Jeremy," the man said, shaking his hand.

"How's the head?"

"Just a scratch."

No shit, Keo thought, but he said, "Claire says you're going to help us get into that compound."

"Is that what she said?" Jeremy asked, looking back at Claire.

"I told them you were the only one who could do it," Claire said.

"That's true, but..."

"Jeremy, I told you what's going on out there. What's at stake. I thought you understood."

"I do, but what you're asking... They'll kill me if they catch us."

"They won't catch you," Keo said.

"You don't know that. You can't promise something like that."

Kid's got a point, Keo thought, but he nodded and said, with as much conviction as he could fake, "You didn't think we came here unprepared, did you? This isn't a suicide mission, kid. We have a plan to get out of here once the mission's finished. Trust me, we don't intend on being captured. You won't, either."

"Jeremy," Claire said, cupping his face in her hands and turning him back to face her. "Please."

At that moment, she looked taller than the Bucky when it was actually the other way around. Keo only had a couple of inches on Jeremy himself.

"We have to do this," Claire said, dropping her voice to almost a whisper, like her words were only meant for him. "There are so many lives at stake, not just ours. A lot of innocent people need our help. Please, help me to help them."

"I know, but..." Jeremy said.

"Please, Jeremy. You're the only one who can do this. There's no one else."

"But what you're asking..."

"We need your help, Jeremy. *I* need you."

Jeremy sighed but didn't say anything.

And he didn't have to, because Keo could see the way his body sagged against Claire's.

Damn, she's good. What else did you teach her, Gaby?

FOURTEEN

"Claire's right," Jeremy said. "The only way into the compound without setting off alarms is through the front gate. There's no way around that."

"What about the water?" Keo asked. "On the other side of the island?"

"You mean, like swim to the island?"

"That's exactly what I mean."

"She's right about that, too. There are guards watching the island 24/7, not to mention the snipers in the towers. There are four of them on the four points of the island. Plus the foot patrols."

"Are they good?"

"Who?"

"The ones in the towers."

"I dunno. No one's ever tried to go onto the island without permission."

"How many guards per tower?"

"Two at night and one in the daytime, at all times."

"Why only one in the daytime?"

"Because you don't fall asleep in the daytime. You do at night, so there's always one alert guard up there. Or that's the idea, anyway."

Keo went silent for a moment, replaying all the recon images he'd studied of the compound back in his head. Finally, he said, "So it's the front gate or nothing."

"Yes." Jeremy nodded.

They were inside one of the clinic's rooms in the back. The door was closed, and the only light came from the green glow stick resting on a counter. Keo stood on one side of the door with Rita on the other, and Claire and Jeremy sitting on an examination reclining table, their legs dangling off the side. They sat very close together, like two lovers wasting away a boring Sunday. A blue dentist chair, partially covered in tarp, glowed a sickly aqua color in one corner.

"What's in the warehouse?" Keo asked.

Jeremy looked back at him. "I don't know."

"Not even a clue?"

The young man shook his head. "My part of security doesn't extend onto the island. But you can say that about a lot of us. I can count on one hand the number of people with access to that warehouse."

Great. Why didn't Claire seduce one of those guys instead?

"But you can get us in there?" Keo asked.

"Into the compound," Jeremy said. "But not onto the island. You'll have to do that by yourselves." He looked over at Rita before returning to him. "There's just the two of you?"

"The smaller the number, the less risks," Keo said. "But we have friends waiting outside to lend a hand, if we need it."

Keo thought about adding, *And an air force waiting to*

bomb the shit out of your friends in the compound if necessary, but decided that was probably not something that would help his cause with the Bucky.

"How are you going to get us inside?" Rita was asking Jeremy.

"Things are fluid these days," Jeremy said. "Personnel is constantly being reassigned, rotations changing on a daily basis depending on need. No one really knows where they'll be the next day or how long they'll stay there. Everyone's on their toes, and I think you know why."

Keo nodded but didn't say anything.

"I can get you clothes," Jeremy continued, "and walk you through the front gates. After that..."

"We'll be on our own," Keo finished for him.

"Yes." Jeremy glanced over at Claire. "You're staying out here. I don't want you going inside with us."

"I have to," Claire said. "They might need my help."

"No. That's the deal. You have to stay out here." He softened his voice. "I don't want to lose you."

Rita looked over at Keo, a mild smirk on her face as if to say, *I guess he doesn't care about losing us, though.*

Keo grinned back, before saying to Jeremy, "Claire will stay out here." Then, before Claire could protest, "We're going to need her free in case things don't go well or we need a way out *pronto.*"

Claire narrowed her eyes at him but didn't argue. Instead, she put her hand over Jeremy's and squeezed, and the two exchanged a smile. Keo could almost believe he was looking at two lovebirds that were deeply, deeply in love.

Almost.

"We need to get in there before morning," Keo said.

Jeremy looked back at him. "So soon?"

"The longer we're here, the more chances of being discovered. Like what happened earlier. Will it make any difference if you bring us through the front gate now? This late?"

Jeremy glanced down at his watch. "There'll be a shift change at the front gates in two more hours. The one in charge is Tanner. He's young and I know him, and he'll be easier to convince that you guys are new recruits that he hasn't seen before."

Keo nodded. "Two more hours it is. Until then..."

"I'll have to go back and bring you clothes," Jeremy said.

"All right. We won't go anywhere until you get back."

Claire sneaked a look at Keo, and he made a slight nodding motion back.

"Rita," Keo said, "give me a hand outside."

Keo stepped out into the hallway, closing the door after Rita.

Once outside, Rita was about to say something, but Keo shook his head and led her out to the reception area, where they took up positions next to the door and windows. It was just as dark and quiet outside as it had been when they were last out here. Fenton slept peacefully, safe and sound from everything that could hurt them.

"I'm worried about killing people who don't know what's going on," Lara had said back at Darby Bay. *"There are a lot of people who just want to be left alone and live in peace. Sometimes they make bad decisions."*

Keo wondered how many of Fenton's citizens were ever going to know just how close they came to being flattened. If Black Tide were still being run by someone else, someone with Mercer's temperament and less-evolved sensibilities about civilian casualties, this "fight" with Fenton would have been over before it even started.

"They're sleeping like babies," Rita said softly. "Must be nice."

"Must be," Keo said.

Rita glanced over at the back hallway. "What do you think they're doing in there?"

"She's probably convincing him that this is the right thing to do. He still sounded a little hesitant."

"She's good. The kid. I almost believed she was in love with him."

Keo smiled. "Maybe she is."

"You think so?"

"Anything's possible..."

"How did you convince him to help us in the first place?" Keo asked as he watched Jeremy jogging up the sidewalk before disappearing into the darkness.

"I told him about what's been happening out there, about what Buck's people have been doing," Claire said. She stood next to him at the window, looking after Jeremy.

"The truth, the whole truth, and nothing but the truth?"

"You'd be surprised how well that works."

"And he believed you?" Rita asked. She was at the other window across from them. "I mean, he had no firsthand knowledge, and you're new here."

"Not at first, but I convinced him to look into it," Claire said. "He asked some of the guys who have been out there.

Friends of his from The Purge days that he could trust not to go reporting him for asking questions."

"So he didn't know," Keo said.

Claire shook her head. "He's never left town with Buck's soldiers. He was part of Fenton's original security force. That seniority is why he was able to order those two guys around earlier. They're new. He's not."

"You said he asked around. So he knows about everything? He's totally convinced?"

"He was convinced enough to come back and hear me out, and then keep listening."

"What if he hadn't? What if he'd reported you?"

"It wouldn't have mattered."

"Why not?"

"I didn't tell him who I was. I only...intimated that I'd seen what was going on out there. I'm pretty sure I could have talked myself out of it. Failing that, I did go through Danny-approved basic. I didn't reveal everything—including who I was—until I was 100 percent sure he wasn't going to turn me in." Claire gave him a wry look. "And no, in case you were wondering."

"I didn't say anything."

"You didn't have to. And the answer is no, I didn't have to sleep with him in order to convince him to help us."

He smiled. "So you just batted your eyelashes?"

"Not quite."

"What did you promise him?"

"That he can come with us when this is over."

"He wants that?"

"He doesn't have family here. No girlfriend or wife. Just friends, but they're not enough to keep him here."

"I guess he doesn't subscribe to the Bros Before Hoes Club."

"Hey, she got the job done, so I'm not complaining," Rita said.

"Thanks, Rita," Claire said.

"No problem, kid."

Claire looked back at Keo. "So why did you want me to stay back when Jeremy takes you inside the compound?"

"Because the chances of everything going smoothly and our managing to stay under the radar during this whole thing is...slim. That's where you come in. We're going to need you out here to save us."

"You? In need of saving?" Claire grinned. "Has that ever happened before?"

"More times than I'd like to admit."

"I don't believe that."

"It's true. Contrary to popular opinion, I'm not Superman. I only wear my underwear on the outside on special occasions."

"When was the last time you needed saving?"

"We'd need more than tonight for me to list all of them."

"I'm not going anywhere. You going anywhere, Rita?"

"Nope," Rita said. "I'm not going anywhere."

Keo sighed. "Let's keep our eyes on the prize, girls. As I was saying... *If* things don't go as planned, we're going to need rescuing."

"That's what Rudolph and Gholston are for," Claire said. "Isn't that why they're still out there, standing by with a radio?"

"Exactly. They're out there, and you're in here. If anything happens to Rita and me, it'll be up to you to make contact and save our bacons. Just in case."

"Just in case," Claire repeated.

Jeremy returned thirty minutes later than he said it would take him. He was carrying a duffel bag when he knocked on the door, and Keo let him in. Rita stood nearby with her suppressed SIG, which she only put away after scanning the empty dark streets outside.

"Thank God you're back, I was so worried," Claire said as she came out of the hallway and walked over to give Jeremy a hug.

Damn, she's good, Keo thought as he watched Claire embracing the young man and winking at him over Jeremy's shoulder at the same time.

"I'm fine, I'm fine," Jeremy said.

"Did you get the clothes?" Claire asked.

"I got them," he said, dumping the bag on the floor. "There was a little hiccup that I had to deal with before I could come back."

"What kind of hiccup?" Keo asked.

"Nothing to worry about. Just some last-minute security personnel being shifted around. It always happens when Buck shows back up at the compound."

"Buck?"

"Yeah."

"You said he was 'back.' Where was he before?"

"I don't know," Jeremy said. "We don't usually know his itinerary. That's the kind of thing only his inner circle knows.

The guys who have been with him even before he showed up in Fenton."

"But you say he's here now, in the compound?"

"Yeah. Why?"

"You know *exactly* where he is? At this very moment?"

"The conference building. He's in there with some of his people. I'm not sure why they're holding a meeting so late; I guess he just got back from somewhere and called them out of bed."

"How long do these meetings usually last?"

"Could be anywhere from minutes to hours, depending on what's being discussed. This one..."

"What about it?"

"I got the sense that it might take a while. Like I said, he usually doesn't call meetings in the middle of the night. But I guess things are different these days, with everything that's going on."

Keo looked over at Rita, who was staring back at him. It was easy to read what she was thinking, because he was pretty sure it was identical to his own thoughts.

"What?" Jeremy said when he saw the quick glances between Keo and Rita. "What's going on?"

Keo didn't answer him. Instead, he looked past Jeremy and at Claire, and she nodded back at him. It wasn't a big nod—in fact, it was almost imperceptible, and he only noticed because he was looking straight at her when she did it.

"Jeremy," Claire said, focusing on the young man, "can you get them near the conference building?"

"What?" Jeremy said. "Why?"

"Can you do it?"

"Yes, of course. Just getting inside the compound is the real challenge. Once you're inside, you can pretty much go anywhere, because you're supposed to be there. Getting into the conference building itself is another matter. There are guards outside." He looked back at Keo. "What's going on? What are you asking me to do?"

"Buck is the key," Claire said.

Jeremy turned back to her. "The key to what?"

"To stopping the war that's coming, Jeremy."

"I don't understand..."

Keo nodded at Rita, and she followed him into the hallway without a word as Claire began talking to Jeremy.

"We have to stop this," Claire was saying, her voice dropping to almost a conspiratorial whisper. "You want to save lives, don't you? If we can do that. Together. We can stop this and save a lot of people, Jeremy. This is our chance..."

Keo and Rita moved farther into the corridor, until they could barely hear what Claire was saying to Jeremy in the reception area.

"You think she can convince him?" Rita whispered.

"If she can't, there's no chance we're going to," Keo whispered back.

"What's she saying?"

"I don't know."

"I hope it's good, whatever it is."

"Me too."

They looked over at the two young people in the connecting room. Claire was doing most of the talking, cupping Jeremy's face in her hands and looking deep into his eyes as she talked.

"So we're definitely doing this," Rita whispered to him. "We're going to Mercer this fucker?"

Keo looked over at her and raised both eyebrows. "'Mercer this fucker?'"

"You know what I mean."

"When did Mercer's name become a verb?"

"Ever since you blew his brains out."

"Jesus."

"I bet that's what he was saying when the bullet was going through his brains."

Keo chuckled softly. "Damn, girl."

Rita grinned back before putting on her serious face. "So, we're really going to do this?"

Keo nodded. "Before, we didn't know where he would be— or if the man was even still in the city. He's been like a ghost since Black Tide started flying reconnaissance over Fenton. It's a golden opportunity, and it'd be a shame to pass it up."

"And she gave you the okay? Lara. She said we could change the mission and take Buck out if we had the chance?"

"Yeah, she did," Keo lied.

FIFTEEN

"You're going to kill him. I didn't get that wrong, did I?"

"Yes, and no."

"Will that stop it? What he's doing out there?"

"It stopped Mercer's war. It can stop Buck's, too."

"And Lara's okay with this?"

"Yes," Keo lied for the second time that night.

"You guys have actually discussed this?" Claire asked.

Keo nodded. "We did. Gaby was there, too."

"I don't have to ask what Gaby said," the teenager said with a slight smile. "I know her too well."

"She's the one who brought it up, actually."

"I don't have any trouble believing that, either."

Claire glanced out the hallway at Jeremy and Rita in the reception area as Jeremy made sure Rita's clothing fit her. It mostly did, though the pant legs were a bit too long. That wasn't going to work, so Rita was rolling them up. In the semi-darkness, it wouldn't be noticeable unless someone decided to take a very close look. She had already put on a black assault vest—a circled *M* was prominently displayed on one of the pouches—over her black long-sleeved sweater. Keo was wearing an identical vest, but his clothes had fit right away.

The teenager looked back over at him. "Lara, on the other hand, I wouldn't think she would approve something like this."

"She did," Keo said. "We had a very long talk about it. But in the end, she came around."

"If you say so," Claire said, even if Keo didn't think she completely bought it. Maybe she *wanted* to believe it.

"We all good?" Keo asked Rita.

The sniper looked over and nodded. "A bit long in the legs, but it'll do."

"What about you?" he asked Jeremy.

The Bucky nodded, too. "As long as no one asks too many questions, we should be okay."

"Will they? Ask too many questions?"

"I don't know. I don't think so, but..." He shook his head. "I don't know. I guess we'll find out when we find out."

Not exactly brimming with confidence there, Jeremy ol' pal, Keo thought, but he smiled and said instead, "Let's get going, then." He turned to Claire. "Rita gave you her radio?"

"It's in the back room," the teenager said.

"Rudolph and Gholston are waiting to hear from us. Let them know what's happening and what the new plan is."

"Will do." She looked over at Jeremy and Rita, then back at Keo. "Good luck."

"You too."

"You need it more."

"I can't disagree with that."

He walked into the reception room and nodded at Rita, who understood and followed him outside the building.

As soon as they stepped in the cold, chilly night, Keo shivered and quickly pulled on his gloves to tighten them. Rita did the same next to him, her Mk 14 rifle slung over her shoulder. The circled *M*, in white permanent marker, seemed to almost glow on her chest. It was the same with his.

Soft voices from behind them as Jeremy and Claire said their good-byes. Their temporary good-byes, if everything went according to plan.

Captain Optimism, Keo thought, and chuckled.

"What's so funny?" Rita asked.

Her voice was low to keep from being overheard, not that Keo thought there was anyone still awake in any of the darkened buildings around them to eavesdrop. Still, you could never be too careful, especially when you were behind enemy lines and surrounded by a few hundred men with guns.

Damn. How did this happen?

Oh, right. You volunteered.

"Nothing," Keo said.

"No, no, what's so funny? Share with the rest of the class."

"I was just thinking about how quickly things changed."

"The mission?"

"Yeah."

"What's that Danny liked to say? No plan survives first contact with the enemy. Or something along those lines."

"Sounds about right," Keo said, and took out the Texas Rangers ball cap and slipped it on. He adjusted the brim before turning to Rita. "How do I look?"

"I can barely make out your scar. Just make sure to stand away from the light."

"I was never one to hog the spotlight, anyway."

"Funny."

Keo grinned. The cap was to keep him anonymous, now that he knew some of the Buckies had a good idea of what he looked like. Calvin the sniper had proved that when he intentionally killed Chang instead of taking Keo out when he had the chance back in the woods this morning. But Jeremy had also confirmed that he didn't know who Keo was, which meant Buck was only telling certain individuals.

Rita glanced back at the clinic behind them. "They're taking their time."

"Leave the lovebirds alone."

"Do they qualify as lovebirds when only one of the birds is in love?"

"I guess it depends on which one of the birds you asked."

As if on cue, the door opened and Jeremy came outside, with Claire lingering in the doorway behind them. She nodded at Keo and Rita, then exchanged a smile with Jeremy.

"Good luck," the teenager said.

Keo nodded back at her before turning to Jeremy. "It's your plan. Take the lead."

Jeremy pursed his lips and seemed to gather himself before stepping off the sidewalk and onto the street. Keo and Rita followed behind him, even as Keo's eyes roamed the empty roads and the shadowed buildings around them.

Behind enemy lines and looking for more trouble. What more could a guy with a gun ask for?

He smiled to himself and thought of Lara, and how much dancing he was going to have to do when he tried to explain this to her.

Assuming, of course, that he survived tonight...

Jeremy led them out of the city and toward the fields before turning right and continuing down a two-lane asphalt road that had been there long before most—if not all—of the people calling Fenton home showed up. They took their time and walked at an unhurried pace. It was a façade to convince anyone who crossed their path that they belonged and weren't afraid of being seen. Just in case, though, Keo made sure his slung MP5SD was within easy reach. When he sneaked a look at Rita walking next to him, he saw that she was doing the same with her rifle.

Just in case...

Fortunately, neither one of them had to go for their weapons. The three two-man patrols that they met on the road since leaving Claire behind only bothered to exchange nods with them and a few brief *Heys* and *How's it goings* with Jeremy. If any of the Buckies were suspicious of Keo and Rita, it didn't stop them from continuing on their way.

So far, so good.

The compound on the west side of Fenton came into view in all its well-lit glory once they circled around the cornfields and started up another two-lane road toward its front gate. Even before he saw the heavily guarded perimeter, Keo had heard the *buzz* of electricity that ebbed and flowed from the long wall of hurricane fencing that separated Buck's soldiers from the civilians. The area was as obvious as Gaby had told them, with no attempts to camouflage it or make it stand out less from the rest of Fenton.

They passed two more patrols, both on horseback, when they were walking up a road flanked by walls of cornstalks to their left and acres of wheat to their right. As with the foot patrolmen, the mounted Buckies stopped momentarily to exchange a quick word with Jeremy but ignored Keo and Rita.

"Does everyone know you?" Rita asked after the second two-man patrol was well out of earshot.

"I was here before Buck showed up," Jeremy said. "I was one of the people overseeing the town back when it was just T31 and Copenhagen was in charge."

"I heard that name before," Keo said. "Copenhagen. What happened to him?"

Jeremy shook his head. "No one knows. One day he just... disappeared. No one knows what happened. Where he went. Or if he went anywhere at all."

"What does that mean? 'If he went anywhere at all?'"

"We don't talk about it. Buck's in charge now. That's all there is to it."

"When did this happen? When did Copenhagen disappear?"

"Honestly, I can't be sure. One day he was just gone."

"When did you first notice?"

"About seven months ago."

"But he could have been gone long before then?"

"Anything's possible. He and I don't exactly mix in the same company, you know?"

Keo nodded and didn't ask any more questions. He did, though, recall the first (and only) time he'd talked to Buck. That was over the radio, and Copenhagen's name had come up:

"He didn't like that," Buck had said. "Copenhagen, I mean. He got kind of annoyed, actually. Here's this guy he's never met, threatening his life."

"You didn't tell him about me?" Keo had asked.

"I did, actually."

"What did he say?"

"He was like me—he didn't know whether to hunt you down or offer you a position on his staff."

The conversation had been from a few weeks back, long after Jeremy noticed that Copenhagen was no longer seen in Fenton. Was it possible Jeremy had gotten the timetable wrong? Or was it more likely that Buck was lying out of his ass when he told Keo about Copenhagen's nonexistent reaction?

And there was that conversation with Greengrass in Cordine City:

"Buck's been working hard to put it all together. Years of work, getting it ready," Greengrass had said.

"Buck and Copenhagen?" Keo had asked.

"Mostly Buck. He's always been the real brains of the operation."

Greengrass hadn't come right out and said Copenhagen was gone, that Buck was the lone man at the top now. But then, there was no reason for Greengrass to come clean and tell Keo everything. They hadn't exactly been buddies at the time.

Did it really matter who was running things in Fenton now? No, not really. As far as Keo could tell, Buck was the top dog, the alpha running the show. If Copenhagen was even still alive, he was doing a hell of a good job hiding in the background.

Keo pushed all those questions aside (Copenhagen was the last person on his mind right now) as they approached the gate into the compound.

It was as heavily guarded up close as it had looked from

above in the aerial photos. A half-dozen men stood guard while a dozen more walked the perimeter to the left and right of it. More in the background that he couldn't see, but could come running at any second. Keo could hear the engines of multiple vehicles nearby, occasionally moving along the length of the fence, and he glimpsed a white truck parked under one of the lights.

And then there were the two Buckies standing behind a machine gun nest about ten meters from the entrance, surrounded in a half circle by sandbags. When he glanced right, he saw another MG setup; a quick look left revealed yet another one. Three in all, ready to unload on anyone who tried to enter the gate without permission.

There were plenty of lights to illuminate the final thirty meters of the road on this side of the compound, and it took Keo a while for his eyes to adjust to the brightness before he could make out the buildings on the other side of the fencing. There were a lot of them, most one story tall with a few taller structures in the background. They were spread out from end to end, and even more that he couldn't see from the road. Even though he had seen plenty of photos of the place, the combination of darkness and bright lights blasting in his face made it difficult to see exactly how big the place was from ground level.

"It's huge," Gaby had told him. "I would have gotten lost and would probably still be trying to find my way out if I hadn't found a guide."

Her "guide" hadn't assisted willingly, but Gaby could be pretty convincing when she needed to be.

The gate was starting to open before they were within fifteen meters of it. It was Jeremy. The guards recognized him right away, even if a few of them were staring at Keo and Rita as they neared.

One of the guards got up and walked directly to Jeremy.

"There'll be a shift change at the front gates in two more hours," Jeremy had told them earlier. *"The one in charge is Tanner. He's young and I know him, and he'll be easier to convince that you guys are new recruits that he hasn't seen before."*

Keo guessed the Bucky walking over and nodding at Jeremy now was the Tanner guy.

"Back already?" the man said to Jeremy.

"It's freezing out here," Jeremy said.

"It's not that cold."

"You try patrolling."

"Pass!"

The closest machine gun station was to Keo's right when he followed Jeremy into the compound, but the men behind the old model M60 were too busy chatting with another guard to notice them. The gate began to roll close behind them as soon as they stepped past it, with Rita behind Jeremy and Keo bringing up the rear.

Keo made sure to avoid the couple of curious looks directed at him, even if they were fleeting. Most of Buck's men were too busy ogling Rita. She smirked back at them—just like someone who wasn't afraid of being stared at but didn't appreciate it, either, would react.

"Who're they?" the one named Tanner was asking Jeremy.

"Bonney and Cruz," Jeremy said. "I went out with them before the shift change to show them their patrol sector."

"They new?"

"New recruits, yeah. They're being added to the regular rotation tomorrow night."

"Better them than me." Tanner turned to Rita and smiled. "Hey, how's it going?"

"Take a picture," Rita said.

The Bucky chuckled, before miming "snapping" a picture with an invisible camera.

"Jackass," Rita said under her breath as she followed Jeremy farther into the compound.

"Cruz is fucking hot," Tanner said to Keo as he walked past the man.

"She's single," Keo said.

"Oh yeah?"

"Uh huh."

"Good to know, good to know," the man said from somewhere behind Keo.

And then they were inside, and no one had fired a single shot.

Jesus, I think I might have peed my pants a little...

There were no official roads for them to walk along, just paths that had been carved into the dirt ground by vehicles and a few thousand footsteps that had come before them. The trail they were on now snaked around buildings, including two big ones that Keo recognized as barracks. Both were dark and silent, and likely filled with sleeping Buckies.

All I'd need is one grenade to fix that...

They walked past more patrols, but no one gave them more than a cursory nod before moving on.

That's right, boys. We belong here, just like you. So just keep on, keeping on.

There were lights outside most of the newish-looking structures around them and darkness inside. It was, after all, well past midnight. Not quite the Hour of the Wolf, but it would have to do. Fenton didn't look at all like a place gearing up for a war that could decimate them. There was nothing to indicate to Keo that these people were worried about the hell Black Tide could marshal against them. Certainly nothing visible to the naked eye, and there should have been evidence of it, even at night.

Either they don't know what's coming, or they know and they don't care.

Neither possibility made any sense. Buck already knew; the increased security around the town was proof of that. So why did Fenton look so...normal? It wasn't just in the bored ways the guards watching the front gate acted, or in the disinterested patrols they'd encountered. No. It was the whole place. It was so damn *calm*.

For a brief—very brief—moment, Keo entertained the idea of dropping the current mission and returning to the *real* mission, the reason he was here in the first place.

The warehouse. What are you hiding in that warehouse, Buck?

But the moment faded quickly, and he was back on track:

Kill Buck, and Fenton would be without a leader.

Kill Buck, and the raids would stop.

Kill Buck, and the war would be won.

Kill Buck, and Lara would be safe.

And he could achieve all of that while keeping Lara's hands bloodless. He was, after all, Keo. He was the guy who had splattered Mercer's brains on Black Tide Island five years ago and ended his murderous crusade. It would be an easy story to sell: He decided on his own and lied to Lara's people— which were all true, even if he did suspect that Claire might already know the truth.

Cut the head off the snake, and the body dies.

It's the only way, Lara. It's the only way.

Jeremy was still in the lead, walking at the same unhurried pace since they left Claire. Keo had to admit, the kid was impressive. Claire couldn't have chosen a better "convert."

"You did good back there," Keo said to Jeremy now.

"I almost shit my pants," Jeremy said. "I think I might actually have."

"Which part?" Rita asked.

"All of it."

"Oh."

Keo smiled and thought, *At least it wasn't just me.*

He said, "You're doing fine."

"Thanks," Jeremy said.

"Where's that conference building?"

"It's not far," Jeremy said, before turning left and abandoning the path they'd been on, only to start on another one a few seconds later.

They passed more buildings, each one clearly recently constructed. Keo didn't think most of the structures in the compound were here even just a year ago, just like the warehouse.

"Buck's been working hard to put it all together. Years of work, getting it ready," Greengrass had said.

"Years of work, getting ready..."

Getting ready for what? That was the question. What was

Buck's ultimate endgame? What was he trying to accomplish that made him form an unholy alliance with Blue Eyes?

"There," Jeremy said, nodding forward at one of the larger buildings they'd seen since stepping through the front gate.

It was single-story, but had sections and looked joined together from three separate structures. It occupied a large patch of land near the very center of the compound, and unlike the other buildings they'd walked past so far, had men standing guard outside its front doors and around it. There were two out front and a couple of two-man teams moving along the sides that Keo could see. Likely more, on the other sides, that he couldn't.

Jeremy led them past the conference building without stopping. The guards outside the front doors glanced over, but then away just as quickly. As they walked past, Keo tried to glimpse anything through the windows. Not all the curtains were pulled in, and he got a good look at figures moving around inside, but the angles were wrong and he couldn't make out any of their faces. But something was definitely happening in there, because there were very awake people standing around talking.

Keo picked up his pace to walk alongside Jeremy. "How long have they been in there?"

"Two, maybe three hours," Jeremy said. His voice had dropped to almost a whisper.

He's scared, even if he doesn't show it. Kid's brave, I'll give him that.

"How many are inside?" Keo asked.

"I don't know," Jeremy said.

"Guess."

Jeremy didn't, at least not right away. He thought about the answer before finally replying. "Five to ten."

"Buck and his lieutenants?"

"Yes."

"But Buck is definitely in there?" Rita asked from behind them.

"Yes," Jeremy said.

"Are you one hundred percent sure?" Keo asked.

"I stopped to talk to one of the guards earlier, and he confirmed it. Buck's in there. He's the reason they're all in there."

Keo glanced back at Rita and saw the look of determination on her face. He didn't bother asking her if she was ready or if she could do this. He imagined her response would have been something along the lines of *"Fuck yeah."*

He turned back to Jeremy. "Where's the armory?"

"The armory?" Jeremy asked, his body tensing slightly.

"You guys have an armory, don't you?"

"Of course we do. We have a few of them, actually."

"Where's the closest one?"

"What do you want with it?"

"I would love nothing more than to barge into that little meeting and shoot Buck between the eyes," Keo said. "Maybe even look him in those eyes first before I do it. But it's late, and I'm tired, and I'm guessing blowing the building up should achieve the same results, minus or plus a few extra bodies. What do you think of that plan, Rita?"

"Fuck yeah," the sniper said behind him.

SIXTEEN

Getting into one of Fenton's armories was easy. Too easy. For a moment, Keo almost expected some kind of trap that as soon as he stepped inside men with guns would either shoot him down or capture him. Buck himself might even jump out of the shadows to prove that this entire night was one big joke at Keo's expense.

But it wasn't a trap, and the two armed guards standing outside nodded at Jeremy, who entered through the double front doors of the steel building without having to say a word. Keo and Rita followed closely behind him and got a close-up look at what Buck's people had been hoarding over the years.

Not bad. Not bad at all.

The warehouse was large with an arched high ceiling, and bright lights hummed to life as soon as they entered, revealing row after row of racks holding handguns, rifles, and multiple shelves of ammo. There were sheathed knives and machetes, with light and medium machine guns hanging off the walls.

Some were newer than the M60 Keo had seen watching the front gate, which struck him as odd—why were the guards using older equipment when there were newer models right here?

But he didn't dwell on why the Buckies did things the way they did. The whole place barely made any sense, including why Buck was even picking a fight with Black Tide in the first place. Besides, right now he needed weapons, but not just any weapon. He needed the *right* kind.

"How do they keep track of everything?" Keo asked, his voice echoing slightly off the metal walls around them.

"Keep track?" Jeremy said.

"People don't just come in here and take what they want, do they?"

"Actually, they do. No one's supposed to be in here—in the compound—who doesn't belong. Everything in here is surplus; we don't have nearly enough soldiers to use everything we've stockpiled."

"So you guys were just stocking up?"

"Buck's people were, yeah. They brought most of this stuff over with them when they first showed up in Fenton, but they kept adding to it. There's a lot of stuff just lying around out there."

"I guess we can just take what we want, and no one will notice," Keo said.

"Pretty much," Jeremy nodded.

"What about the guards outside?"

"They won't care. They've seen people come out of this place with plenty of weapons before."

"In the middle of the night?"

Jeremy seemed to think about that question for a bit. "I don't know. I don't think they'll care, but...I don't know."

"I guess we'll find out," Keo said, and began walking through two of the rows.

Rita followed behind him, while Jeremy remained at the door.

"What are we looking for?" Rita asked.

"Something we can take out a building with without having to actually get too close," Keo said.

"What, like a mortar?"

"No. Something more hands-on." Keo glanced back at Jeremy. "Someone told me you guys had shoulder-mounted rockets?"

"I don't know," Jeremy said. "I haven't really looked the place over. Try the back. That's where they keep the big guns."

"I think I found them," Rita said.

Rita was standing in front of a wall of "big guns." There were a dozen or so anti-tank and Swedish-made AT4s, along with some American-made LAWs. But it was the larger and more formable-looking M141s that drew his eyes.

"Oh yeah," Rita said, following where he was looking. "That can definitely take down a building."

"That's what it was designed for," Keo said.

He plucked one of the shoulder-mounted weapons from the wall and got a feel for its weight—sixteen pounds, give or take, and thirty-two inches in carry mode, longer when it was ready to fire. The effective range was somewhere under a thousand meters, but Keo wasn't going to need even most of that. All he required was a clear line of sight to the target.

"How many does it shoot?" Rita asked.

"One," Keo said.

"Just one?"

"One's all you need."

"I guess we could always carry more than one with us."

"No," Keo said. "If we need another shot, we're already screwed." He perched the launcher on his right shoulder and nodded at Rita. "Ditch the rifle and grab a carbine with an M203 and plenty of ammo."

"I don't want to ditch my rifle," Rita said.

"You're going to need the extra firepower. Trust me."

Rita sighed. "Goddammit, Keo, I really like this rifle."

"Black Tide can get you another one."

"But not like this one."

"It's not the gun that matters, Rita, it's the person pulling the trigger."

She smirked. "This coming from a guy who can't live without his MP5SD submachine gun?"

Keo grunted. "Shut up and follow orders, soldier."

"Yes, sir," Rita said, and gave him a mock salute.

Keo walked back up the rows to Jeremy, still waiting at the doors.

The Bucky's eyes widened slightly at the sight of Keo with the M141 on his shoulder. "Jesus. You really are going to try to blow him up."

"Did you think I was kidding?"

"Kind of."

"I wasn't. If I can get the job done from a distance, I'll always take that option."

"Is that thing really going to do the job?"

"The warhead's capable of penetrating two hundred millimeters of concrete. You think the building Buck's in has two hundred millimeters of concrete protecting him?"

"Um, no."

"Then yeah, it'll get the job done." Keo snatched an M4 from one of the racks and tossed it to Jeremy, who just barely caught it. "Grab some ammo."

"Me?" Jeremy said.

"You're in this now, kid. There's no turning back. When Buck's nothing more than a pile of ashes and bones, we need to get the hell out of Dodge."

Jeremy looked down at the rifle. He was holding it as if it were something that could bite him if he wasn't careful.

"Claire will be waiting for us," Keo said.

The young man looked up at the sound of Claire's name, just as Keo had expected.

Like a dog hearing a whistle.

"She told me you were leaving town with us," Keo said. "Is that true?"

Jeremy nodded. "I'm going wherever she's going."

"Then that means this is your last night here, because she's going home with us. So grab a tactical pack and fill it with as much ammo as you can carry. Getting out of here is just one part of it; there's still the woods and everything else inside it to deal with."

"You're talking about ghouls?"

"I'm not talking about Boy Scouts." He turned around as Rita walked up behind him. "Time to ring Claire up and fill her in on the plan."

The armory was just a shade over a hundred meters from the conference building, which meant Keo and Rita didn't have to walk very far backward to reach their target. Not that they went directly there; at least not while the two armory guards were staring after them and had been since they stepped outside the warehouse with the weapons.

If Buck's people ever get their shit together, they might actually be dangerous.

Not that Keo was complaining. He had what he needed, but he couldn't just waltz over to Buck's location and start using it. At least not without attracting a lot of attention. Besides, he needed to give Claire and the others time to get ready anyway.

He followed Jeremy, who was now carrying an M4 rifle and a pack bulging with supplies, away from their target. They walked along the path carved into the ground by hundreds of vehicles before them for about five minutes before turning left into a pitch-black space between two buildings that might have been barracks.

Jeremy stopped and turned around, his breath quickening noticeably. Keo leaned the M14 against the wall of one of the buildings, then stuck his head out from the shadows and glanced over to see if anyone had followed them up the well-lit "road."

No one had, and the two armory guards in the distance had gone back to looking bored outside the warehouse doors.

Keo pulled his head back and found Jeremy waiting behind him. "You sure we can circle back around to the conference building without being seen?"

"All we have to do is avoid the patrols," Jeremy began, but never finished because—

Footsteps were approaching their location.

Keo unslung his MP5SD, Rita doing the same to the

carbine she'd swapped her Mk 14 for, just as two figures moved up the road they had left seconds ago. Two men, white clouds shooting from their lips as they shivered against the cold, walked past them.

Goddamn, I think I almost had a heart attack.

Keo relaxed a little bit as the footsteps slowly faded, but he didn't completely unclutch his submachine gun until he couldn't hear them anymore.

"Okay," Keo said, turning back to Jeremy. "Take us back."

"You sure you wanna be doing this?" Jeremy asked. "Buck's not what you came here for. It was the warehouse, remember?"

"The mission was always fluid. If we knew ahead of time where to find Buck, he would have been the main target."

Keo couldn't be sure if Jeremy believed him—or Rita, next to him, for that matter—because it was just too dark to see much of anything in the alley. He could make out Jeremy nodding, though, before the young man started moving toward the other side of the alleyway.

They followed the Bucky (*Former Bucky now, I guess*), Keo with the M141 once again perched on his shoulder. It wasn't heavy enough to slow him down, but it did take both hands to hold it in place, which meant he couldn't keep at least one hand on the submachine gun at all times. That made him uneasy.

But it wasn't the only thing that kept him alert and looking around. There were so many buildings, so many patrols, and so many chances of being caught before they even got a shot at Buck that he wondered if this wasn't as bad an idea as Jeremy thought. And he was still feeling a little paranoid about how easy everything had been up to now.

Getting into Fenton, then the compound, then the armory...

It's not a trick. Why would it be a trick? It doesn't make any sense. Why let me get this far?

So why was he hyperventilating?

Jesus. Calm down. It's not like this is your first rodeo, pal.

He'd done this before. Too many times to count, even before the world went to shit. It just so happened that back then people were paying him good money to risk his hide. Everything was so much simpler then. There was no cause to bog him down, no right and wrong to limit his options. There was just good ol' fashioned greenbacks.

"See the world. Kill some people. Make some money."

Remember that? Whatever happened to that?

The end of the world, for one.

Then she came into his life. He thought he had gotten away, but oh, was he wrong.

So much for running away being the answer.

⸻

Despite the overwhelming paranoia that he couldn't shake—and in fact kept increasing with every step—about forty-something minutes later, they were close enough to the conference building that Keo felt a little silly. Certainly, if this were a trap, they wouldn't have allowed him to get so close to Buck with a weapon that could blow him to hell with one pull of the trigger.

A sudden burst of optimism that this plan could actually work popped to the surface, but he had to tamp it down. Not now. Not yet. He'd allow himself to indulge when it was over and he was beyond the fence.

Until then...

It had taken forty-something minutes because they had to steer clear of Bucky patrols. Three crossed their paths on the way back, and each time they had to stop and wait for the men to pass. Keo hadn't wanted to risk being spotted by the patrolmen while he was carrying the rocket launcher; the guards at the armory hadn't cared enough to stop them, but all it would take was one overly curious patrolman to ruin a perfectly—at least, up until now—good night.

They had settled in a dark alley between two buildings that looked much too small to be barracks like the last two, but would do the job. Keo went down on one knee and prepared the M141.

"Jeremy, go with Rita," Keo said as he moved the weapon into position.

"Now?" Jeremy said.

"This thing packs one hell of a backblast. You don't want to be anywhere close to me—especially back there—when it fires."

"Oh," Jeremy said, and turned to go.

Rita hesitated. "We really gonna do this?"

"You having second thoughts?" Keo asked.

"No, but I just wanted to make sure that you're sure."

"I'm sure."

"It's not like we can come back from this, you know. Everyone in this place is going to be trying to kill us after you fire that thing."

"They'll have to find out it was us first." Then, "Go. And be ready for anything."

"Just in case, right?"

Keo grinned at the shadows in front of him. "Yeah, just in case."

He listened to Rita and Jeremy retreating behind him until he couldn't hear them anymore. Keo placed his left hand on the second pistol grip in front of the launcher's trigger guard, then squinted through the darkness at his target. This particular model M141 didn't have an extended range sight or a scope of any kind, which was fine with Keo. He'd have to be dumb, blind, and stupid to miss from less than forty meters, since all he had to do was aim straight using the available iron sights and hit *any* part of the building.

Easy peasy. I almost feel sorry for you, Buck.

Almost.

He sucked in a deep breath and watched a patrol—one man and one woman—walking alongside his target, passing by one of four windows on this section of the conference building. It was impossible to miss all four windows because of the bright lights coming from inside. All the activity was clearly focused on this part of the building, which worked out perfectly. The closer he could get the warhead to its intended victim, the better.

A figure walked past one of the windows inside the building. He was too far to tell if the man had white hair and hazel eyes, or if he was in his late forties to early fifties, the way Gaby had described Buck, and Jeremy had confirmed. The man wasn't alone, and two other figures walked behind him, passing the windows before they stopped and began talking.

Keo sucked in a breath and calmed every part of his body. He tried to imagine what Lara would say when she eventually found out what he had done. Not just the whole going-against-her-orders thing—though he was certain she wasn't going to be thrilled about that—but the murdering-Buck-when-she-told-him-not-to thing.

"Sorry, Lara, but I did it for you. I stopped the war before it could get out of control. Before it got really bloody. Trust me, you don't want that blood on your hands. It's hard to wash off. I should know."

Would she buy that explanation? Would she accept that he did it for her, even if it was the truth? Maybe a small part of him was getting back at Buck for Winding Creek, for taking Emma and the others, but it was a very small part.

This was for Lara. She couldn't order him to take out Buck even though she had to know it was the right move. But she couldn't do it because she was Lara—the voice on the radio, the woman who brought order to the chaos. She couldn't be associated with something like this. Because she was right; this was murder, and good people didn't commit or order murders.

It's a good thing I'm not good people.

There would be consequences to this. With Lara, with others—but especially with Lara. He couldn't care less about what others thought of him. But he cared what she thought. God help him, he probably cared too much about what Lara thought.

You've gone soft, pal. Real soft.

He sighed and slowed down his heartbeat, and recalled that brief chat over the radio he'd had with Buck. It seemed like years ago now, but was really just a few weeks back.

"So now that we know each other better, where do we stand?" Keo had asked him.

"I think we both know the answer to that one," Buck had

replied. *"Now, let's see you make good on your promise. You know where to find me."*

Oh, I know where to find you, all right, Keo thought as he slipped his forefinger into the trigger guard of the M141.

"*Flectere si nequeo superos, Acheronta movebo,* mother-fucker," Keo whispered, before he pulled the trigger.

SEVENTEEN

ONE NIGHT AGO

"I don't want you to kill him, Keo. Unless he's standing in front of you, with a gun aimed at you or someone else, and is ready to pull the trigger. Unless one of those things is happening, I don't want you to kill him."

"You've already said that. More than once. I'm not deaf, you know."

"Look me in the eyes and tell me you won't murder Buck if you get the chance."

"I won't murder Buck if I get the chance."

"We have to be better than him. We have to abide by rules. We'll capture him alive and we'll hold him responsible for everything he's done. That's how it has to be, Keo. That's the only way we can do this. Otherwise, we're no better than him. And we *have to be*. Do you understand that? Tell me you understand that."

"I understand."

"I just need to be sure. I'm not sending you out there if I can't trust you, Keo. *Can* I trust you?"

"Yes."

"Are you sure?"

"You want me to sign a form or something? How about a blood oath?"

She stared at him, and he stared back.

Seconds became minutes, which became hours even though it was probably just a few seconds. After all, how could two people possibly stare at each other for *hours* without either one of them blinking?

Seconds. Definitely seconds.

I think.

Lara finally looked away first.

I win! he thought and wanted to laugh, but that probably would have given it away that he'd been lying out of his ass ever since the conversation about Buck started.

Instead, he watched her take out the bottle of painkillers she'd been carrying around in her jacket pocket and shake two of the pills into her palm before swallowing them with the help of some water. She was up and walking and looked better on her feet, but she was still pale around the eyes and lips, and it was clearly easier for her to sit.

"Satisfied?" Keo asked as he went back to reassembling the MP5SD submachine gun after a thorough cleaning. The Heckler & Koch was a hell of a weapon when it worked, which Keo was determined to make sure it did before he took it out into the field.

He leaned over the makeshift workbench and snapped the parts into place, hoping to avoid her eyes. Lara sat across from him and watched him work without saying anything for a moment.

A moment became ten seconds.

Then thirty.

"What about your team?" she finally asked.

"What about them?"

"Are you good with everyone?"

Keo shrugged. "I won't know until we're actually out there. Right now they're just names on a sheet of paper."

"I thought you'd already met them."

"I shook their hands, and we introduced ourselves. It's basically still just names on a paper. I won't know what they're capable of—or not capable of—until I see them in action. Everyone's a tough guy until the bullets start flying."

"I guess you don't have that problem. I mean, everyone knows who you are. The guy who killed Mercer and single-handedly ended his war on the towns. Everyone knows you're the real deal."

"Is that what they're saying?"

"More or less."

"Did you correct them?"

"There's nothing to correct. They're all true."

He *harrumphed*. "As I recall, you did your part to put an end to Mercer's little crusade."

"Not as much as you did. No one did as much as you."

"Which makes your insistence that I don't put Buck out of his misery the first chance I get somewhat baffling."

She sighed. "The situation isn't the same, Keo."

"Isn't it?"

"No."

"Gaby doesn't agree. I bet Danny doesn't, either. Did you talk to him?"

"I did."

"What did he say?"

"The same thing you and Gaby said."

"And yet you're still gung-ho about keeping this asshole alive."

"It's the difference between us being the good guys and them being the bad guys. If we start going around murdering people we think deserve it, we've lost the high ground."

"That's not what the people of Winding Creek will think. The ones still alive, anyway. God knows where Buck's people took them. Did you forget about the women and children they've been taking from the raids?"

"No. I haven't forgotten," she said somberly.

Keo slipped the last piece into the submachine gun and laid it down before folding his hands over the weapon and seeking out the blue of her eyes across the table. "Buck is no better than Mercer. He's out there committing crimes. If there were still a Hague, he'd be standing at the front queue of the International Court of Justice. You know that."

"If the Hague were still a functioning body, they'd want him alive, not executed on the spot without a trial."

"A man like Buck doesn't deserve a trial. Neither did Mercer."

"This situation is different."

He ground his teeth together. "Why are you so sure about that?"

"Because this is what law and order looks like. And if we're going to bring it to what's left of this country, we need to show them we're not above it. We can't go around murdering people, Keo. *You* can't go around murdering people because you think they're guilty."

"I don't think Buck's guilty. I *know* he's guilty."

"It's not your job to decide."

"Isn't it? I decided Mercer was guilty and I sentenced him. And look what happened. You got your very own army, and Texas and the world are better off for it. Tell me I was wrong to kill Mercer."

"I can't."

"Then how can you say it'd be wrong to kill Buck?"

"Because we're in a position now that we weren't in when Mercer was still around. We've done things, brought so many people together. Five years of work. Five excruciating years of hard work. We've sacrificed too much to get this far to just throw it away now."

Keo picked up the H&K and laid it on the chair next to him, then grabbed the Glock and began taking it apart. "Gaby and Danny disagree."

"They're soldiers. Like you."

"We both know that's not true."

"It is true, whether you want to accept it or not. If it weren't for Danny, you'd be the best soldier I have."

"Now you're just being mean."

She smiled. "Only because Danny follows orders."

"Ah." He started cleaning the Glock's parts with a brush. "You know, when you knocked on my door, I wasn't expecting us to pick up arguing about Buck."

"What did you think I was here to do?"

"To wish me luck?"

"I was saving that for tomorrow morning, before you guys leave in the chopper."

"We're leaving pretty early."

"I know. I rarely sleep a lot these days anyway."

"Even with all the pills they have you on?"

"It's going to take more than pills to help me with that. Besides, I also came to give you this."

She took a small bundle wrapped in a slightly oil-stained linen handkerchief out of her jacket pocket. Keo took it, and knew what it was from the shape and size before he even opened it: A knife—ten inches in all, five of that made up of a silver blade.

"A girl named Alice gave it to me about three years ago," Lara said. "It belonged to her father. She inherited it and carried it with her until The Walk Out. After that, she said she didn't need it anymore and it was because of me—because of us—and she gave it to me as a gift."

Keo ran his fingers along the smooth side of the blade. The double edges and point were razor sharp. "How many times have you used this thing?"

"I've never used it."

"Never?"

"That's why it's a good luck charm, Keo."

"The MP5SD is my good luck charm. Wanna know why?"

"I'm sure you're going to tell me."

"Because it never jams and it always works. Now *that's* what I call a good luck charm."

She sighed. "Give it back to me."

"What?"

"Give it back to me," she said, holding out her hand.

"No, you gave it to me," Keo said and put it down on the table next to the submachine gun. "No backsies."

"'No backsies?' What are you, five?"

"I've been called worse." Then, "You could have just given it to Gaby or Rita to give to me. You didn't have to come here in person."

"I could have, but then we'd have missed out on that scintillating conversation about putting a bullet in Buck's brain."

"Definitely wouldn't want to skip out on that."

They exchanged a brief—and maybe just a little bit awkward—smile before Lara stood up, probably more gingerly than she had intended—and walked to the door. "I should go. You need to get all the rest you can for tomorrow."

Keo got up and followed her to the door to make sure she made it there in one try. It was easy to tell she wasn't even 50 percent yet even if she did her best to try to hide it from him. Keo recognized all the signs. God knew he'd seen enough of them on himself.

"What about you?" he asked.

"What about me?"

"You said you don't sleep a lot these days. How much is 'not a lot?'"

She gave him a pursed smile. "Not a lot."

Lara had her hand on the lever when she turned back around to face him, and he was accidentally too close to her when she did. There was a brief moment—a second, maybe two—when he didn't know what to do, and he suspected she didn't, either.

He was about to say something when she slipped her arms around his neck and pulled him close to her and kissed him on the cheek. It was a quick peck, and she let go just as quickly.

"Get in, get out, and don't do anything stupid," she said, and then she was gone.

"Danny said something to me a few years ago when we were in Georgia..."

"What were you guys doing in Georgia?"

"This, that, something in-between."

"Touché."

"He said, 'War does not determine who is right, only who is left.'"

"Danny said that? Our Danny?"

Gaby smiled. "I think it was something Will used to say, that he recalled."

"Will coming up with something like that, I can believe."

"He didn't come up with it. It was a quote from someone else. I'm not sure who or when they said it." She paused. "Anyway, I thought it was interesting."

"Yeah. It's interesting," Keo said, thinking about what Lara had said to him earlier.

"Get in, get out, and don't do anything stupid."

Don't do anything stupid. Right. Easier said than done, Lara.

It was still dark, but the first hints of sunrise had begun to wash across the Gulf of Mexico to their left. The port city of Darby Bay was only now starting to wake up even as the solar-powered lights secured to the lampposts along the streets began shutting off one by one. Keo watched a couple of boats already heading off into the water, the whites of their sails flapping against a chilly wind.

He stood at the edge of the high school rooftop and tried to imagine that the coffee he was drinking tasted better than it really did. Gaby stood next to him, sipping from her own steaming mug with one hand inside her jacket pocket. From up here, they could see almost every part of the city, including the ocean waves to one side and the flat Texas countryside on the other. There were sentries on the other rooftops and in the streets below them, and the guards had been doubled after what had happened to Lara. Except for four stray ghoul incidents in the last week, there hadn't been any further trouble from outside.

As the town came to life around them, the makeshift airstrips were already brightly lit. One spot in particular—the chopper LZs—was a buzz of activity as dark-clad crewmen crowded around a Sikorsky UH-60 helicopter. Soon, Keo would be on that chopper and headed back toward Fenton.

"I should be going out there with you guys," Gaby said after a while.

"Who are you worried about? Us, or Claire?"

"Both." Then, with a slight smile, "But mostly Claire."

"I don't blame you. You practically raised that kid."

"I must have done a pretty shitty job of it for her to think allowing herself to be captured and taken to Fenton was a good idea."

Keo chuckled. "She took initiative. Probably asked herself, 'What would Gaby do?' before she did it."

"Like I said: I should have taught her better."

"She'll be fine. She's still making contact on a daily basis, isn't she?"

"Yes."

"So don't worry. The kid knows what she's doing," Keo added even as he thought, *God, I hope the kid knows what she's doing, or this might be a very short mission.*

"That's the problem," Gaby said. "She's still a kid, but she doesn't know it."

"Sounds familiar..."

"Oh, shut up."

Keo grinned before drinking more of the disgusting coffee. It turned out that it wasn't the cafeteria people that made the thing undrinkable, but just the ingredients they had available. He'd had better tasting swill when he was out in the wilds searching the remains of convenience stores for bagged instant coffee.

"So," Gaby said, "I went to Lara's room earlier. To check up on her."

"Oh yeah?"

"She wasn't there."

"Where was she?"

Gaby sneaked a look in his direction. "I don't know. I was hoping you could tell me."

"How would I know?" Keo said and took another sip, hoping that the steam rising from the mug would hide some of his face from Gaby's squinting eyes.

"Did you guys do it?"

Keo almost spat out the coffee. "What?"

Gaby laughed. "Oh, come on. I was born at night, not *last* night. Did you guys do it or not? Who got to be on top?"

Keo wiped at wet spots on the front of his thermal sweater. "The woman's only a few days removed from being shot, for God's sake. Sex was the last thing on our minds."

"There are plenty of things you can do besides the dirty grind."

"'Dirty grind?'"

"Isn't that what the kids call it these days?"

"I have no idea what the kids call anything these days."

"So, did you guys get all nasty or not?"

"We didn't. We just talked."

"Really?"

"Yes."

"Well, that's boring."

"It was a productive talk," Keo said, remembering the kiss on the cheek at the end. It wouldn't have seemed like much to most people, but it was a large bridging of the gap between the two of them after everything that had happened.

It's a good start.

"I'm just curious..." Gaby was saying.

"I like you, Gaby, but I'm not above throwing you off this rooftop."

Gaby laughed again. "Okay, okay. I'm just happy for you guys, that's all. Even if clothes were kept on."

"Why?"

"Why?"

"Yeah. Why?"

She shrugged. "I don't know. I guess because the both of you have been through a lot. I'm mostly happy for Lara. But a little bit for you."

"Gee, thanks."

"She's been through more."

"So have I."

"But I haven't been there with you when you went through them, so I only have your word for it. I've actually seen all the shit Lara had to slog through to get here and still remain standing."

"Was it really that bad?"

Gaby didn't answer right away, and maybe that was more of an answer than what she eventually said. "She hides it well, but I've been with her for a long time now. Danny and Carly, too. We can see it on her face when she doesn't think we're looking." Gaby reached over and smacked him on the shoulder, so hard that Keo almost pitched forward and off the edge. "So good on you, Keo."

"I'm not sure whether to be embarrassed by this conversation or... No, I'm pretty sure it's mostly embarrassment."

Gaby laughed again, and they watched the Sikorsky getting ready, its crew constantly moving around it like ants from this distance. Around them, the first glimpses of sunlight began washing across the city of Darby Bay.

A new day. A new mission. But an old destination.

Back to Fenton. I'm going back into Fenton.

Now how did I know that was going to happen sooner or later?

"What was that quote again?" Keo asked.

"'War does not determine who is right, only who is left,'" Gaby said. "Is that worth a *daebak?*"

Keo nodded. "*Dae*-definitely-*bak.*"

EIGHTEEN

THOOMPF!

The noise the M141 made as it fired its one and only missile was almost anticlimactic. The resulting backblast as the warhead launched kept Keo from feeling any noticeable recoil, and he remained kneeling for five seconds afterward, watching as the warhead cruised through the night air and slammed into the side of the conference building forty meters away. The detonation occurred instantaneously on contact, and the structure was swallowed up by an eruption of fire and gray and white clouds that pounded the area in a horrific inferno in less time than it took Keo to take a breath.

The blast shook the entire compound for a few seconds, with the only sounds coming from Keo's faster-than-normal heartbeats and the crumbling of masonry in front of him. Thick clouds expanded outward in all directions like a living, breathing fog creature, swallowing up the poor souls with the misfortune to be too close to the blast site.

Keo tossed the shoulder-mounted launcher and stood up,

unslinging the MP5SD as he did so. Doors slammed open from his left and right, and footsteps echoed all around. Men, appearing from seemingly every direction, began running toward the remains of the conference building even as pieces of it came raining down on them. A few fell under the onslaught, but most of them were smart enough to retreat until the hail had settled.

Good luck finding anyone still alive in there, boys.

Keo turned and began moving toward the other side of the alley as voices erupted behind him and the strong, strong first wisps of explosive residue finally reached him.

It smelled like goddamn satisfaction.

A figure appeared in front of him, and Keo stopped and lifted the submachine gun.

"It's me," a familiar voice said. *Rita.*

Keo relaxed. "Jeremy?"

"He's waiting nearby," Rita said, even though he couldn't see anything but her outline in the moonlight. "Jesus, that was one hell of a blast."

"It's one hell of a weapon," Keo said, and picked up his pace until he could slip out from between the buildings and into the open.

They weren't alone, but the closest Bucky was at least twenty meters away and too busy racing toward the source of the explosion behind them. The shouts had gotten louder, the clamor of people trying to make sense of what had happened coming from every direction.

Chickens with their heads cut off. Just like how I like 'em.

It didn't surprise him to see the confusion; after all, these people didn't even have enough sense to keep track of what went in and out of their armories at any given time. But maybe he was expecting too much from a group of killers being led around by a man who had made a deal with the devil.

Lights were blinding into existence from the recently constructed structures around them. The constant flow of loud voices, along with suddenly too-loud-to-miss car engines erupting in the night. There was no one source. It was the entire compound suddenly waking up and shouting and moving at the same time.

"Let's go," Keo said, and turned right and began walking.

Jeremy appeared out of the shadows in front of them, his face covered in sweat despite the chilly air. Keo hoped no one saw him like that—or the way his hands were shaking as he hurried to meet them halfway.

"Stick to the plan," Keo said, just as three figures burst out of an alley between two buildings in front of them.

One of the men saw Keo, and they locked eyes.

"Hey, what's going on?" Keo shouted at the man before the Bucky could say anything.

That did it, and the guy shouted back, "How the fuck should I know!" before racing to catch his two comrades up ahead.

"Clever dog," Rita said, grinning next to Keo as they walked in the opposite direction as the three Buckies.

"Every dog has his day," Keo said.

"God, that was loud," Jeremy was saying. He was walking briskly in front of them, gripping the M4 perhaps a little too tightly. He was still sweating, which Keo could see whenever the former Bucky stepped into a pool of light, of which there was suddenly a lot of in front, behind, and all around them.

What's that old saying? Sweating like a whore in church?

"It's supposed to be," Keo said.

"But I didn't expect it to be *that* loud," Jeremy said.

"Be glad you weren't in that building when it hit," Rita said. "I'm betting it was even louder in there."

I told you I'd get you, Buck. I warned you, didn't I? Don't say I didn't warn you, you piece of shit.

Jeremy made a sharp left turn and left the path they were on, slipping between two buildings that looked like shacks. As they moved between them, Keo thought he heard something growling (?) inside the structure to his right. It almost sounded like an animal, but also slightly...human?

"What is it?" Rita asked when she noticed him looking back.

"Nothing," Keo said. Then, forward at Jeremy, "Slow down, kid. We don't want to be caught running away from the scene of the crime."

"But isn't that what we're doing?" Jeremy said, looking back over his shoulder.

"Yeah, but they don't have to know that. We belong here, remember? People who belong don't run like they're afraid of being caught."

"Okay, okay." The young man nodded, even if Keo didn't believe him for a second.

Stick to the plan, kid. Just stick to the plan.

Keo took a moment to peek back at the plume of gray smoke rising from almost the center of the compound. There was a fire, just barely visible over the roofs of the buildings in the way, but it was the sounds of seemingly the entire Bucky nation moving toward the blast site that made him smile.

A continuous wave of voices, shouts, and running boots echoed from inside of the compound, and flashes of dark-clad figures raced through a sea of lights in front of them. It was becoming harder to find shadows to skulk in, and they had to stop every now and then, but never for too long before they were on the move again.

"You think you got him?" Rita was asking next to him.

"If he was in there, then yeah, I got him," Keo said. "They call those things bunker-bustin' munitions for a reason."

"God, I hope so. I hope this is it—"

"Hey!" a voice shouted, cutting Rita off.

They both turned left at the same time to find a Bucky standing outside a shack staring across at them from about thirty meters away. The man was partially hidden in the darkness, and Keo had walked right past him without realizing it. When he turned around, he easily caught the almost-glowing white *M* on the man's assault vest.

"Don't stop," Keo said to Jeremy, who had slowed down and was about to do just that.

"Where the hell are you going?" the man shouted over.

"Patrol," Keo shouted back.

"Bullshit—" the man began to say, even as he was lifting his rifle.

Keo beat him to it and shot the guard—the first *pfft!* of the suppressed submachine gun was barely audible against all the chaos around them—using the circled *M* as a target. He kept pulling the trigger until the *M* vanished along with the silhouetted body.

"Go," Keo said.

"So we're running now?" Rita asked with a grin.

"Yeah, we're running now," Keo said, grinning back. "Take point."

Rita jogged up ahead toward Jeremy, who had stopped

completely and turned around and was staring at the partially shadowed, crumpled outline of the dead man.

"Come on," Rita said, and grabbed Jeremy's arm and dragged him forward. The Bucky went hesitantly, throwing one—then another—glance over his shoulder toward the dead figure.

Keo jogged after them but stayed far enough back to watch their retreat. Around him, the commotion hadn't lessened for a second. If anything, it was gathering steam, the confusion of war consuming every inch of the place. Which was exactly what Keo wanted. This was by far the best-case scenario. A part of him, though, wondered how long it was going to last.

Captain Optimism, pal. Captain Optimism, remember?

"I knew him," Jeremy was saying to Rita in front of Keo.

"Who?" Rita asked, even though Keo suspected she already knew because he did.

"The man Keo shot. I knew him. I recognized his voice."

"Doesn't matter. Keep moving."

"Doesn't matter?"

"He's dead. Doesn't matter anymore."

"But—"

"Keep moving."

The authoritative tone of Rita's voice did it and Jeremy kept moving, even if that didn't stop him from sending a third glance back at the body, which by now had all but disappeared into the darkness behind them.

Keo focused on the open ground in front of them. The buildings were all but empty, their occupants swarming the blast site near the center of the compound. It was clear sailing to the rendezvous point.

So far, so good, Keo thought, when he heard it.

Car engines.

Approaching their position.

Fast.

Goddammit, Keo thought even as Rita grabbed Jeremy's arm and pulled him out of a pool of light they had been walking across and toward a nearby dark building, the two of them vanishing into the shadows before Keo's eyes.

Keo joined them and went into a slight crouch.

And things were going so well, too.

A jet-black Jeep Wrangler raced by in front of them, two men in the front seat and a third in the back manning a mounted machine gun. Bright spotlights on the roof of the vehicle's cab, flanking the welded MG, lit their way as the vehicle's large tires ground loudly against the gravel under them.

Keo stood up in order to follow the Wrangler's path. It was headed toward the perimeter fence about fifty meters in front of them. The "wall" that separated Buck's authority from the civilians of Fenton was easy to spot, its metal links glinting under the plentiful lights. As soon as the Wrangler reached the fence, it turned right and continued south.

Rita and Jeremy reemerged partially out of the darkness in front of him.

"It's a patrol," Rita said.

Keo nodded. "At least there's just one," he said, when bright spotlights sliced across the shadows in front of them as a second vehicle, this one a white Chevy truck, raced along the length of the fence.

"You were saying?" Rita said.

Keo sighed.

Like the Wrangler, the Chevy had men inside its front

seats, but Keo had difficulty making out the numbers. It was easier to spot the machine gunner in the back. Like the first technical, this one proceeded south along the fencing, leaving behind nothing but clouds of dust in its wake.

"What now, boss?" Rita asked.

"Stick to the plan," Keo said.

He looked across the distance—the *very open* distance—between where they were currently and where they wanted to be: the fence. There was nothing out there to hide them once they left the sanctuary of the generous shadows the building next to them cast. There wasn't a single piece of artificial or natural defilade to hide behind.

And there were a lot of lights. God, there were so many lights out there.

Keo squinted, but he couldn't make out any figures on the other side of the fence. And he should have by now. Claire and Jeremy had agreed on a spot to meet, and they both knew the exact location.

So where was Claire with their rescue posse?

Come on, kid. Where are you?

"We need to go back," Jeremy was saying.

Keo glanced over at him. The former Bucky was sweating less than before, but there were still beads of wetness along his forehead.

"Stick to the plan," Keo said.

"But she's not there," Jeremy said. "I can't see her. Can you?"

"She'll be here. She won't let us down."

"What if she didn't have any choice? What if she couldn't make it? What if—"

"She'll be here," Keo said. He glanced down at his watch. "We just have to give her more time."

"This is too risky," Jeremy said. He was shaking his head as if he was trying to convince himself more than them. "We shouldn't have done this. You shouldn't have changed your mission."

"It's done and over with. *Stick to the plan.*"

"But what—"

The white Chevy was back, shooting up the length of the fence on its way up north, the harsh grind of its oversized tires against the dirt cutting Jeremy off in mid-sentence. Less than ten seconds later the Wrangler also reappeared, and it too raced back toward the front gate.

Thank God for small favors, Keo thought, watching the trucks as they drove past them one by one. He wondered if that was why Claire hadn't shown herself yet. Because she couldn't, with two technicals—that they could see, maybe more on the other side of the front gate—going back and forth along the perimeter fence. Claire was too smart to expose herself until she absolutely had to, and she would assume Keo would do likewise. And she wouldn't have been wrong, because that was exactly what he was doing now.

Keep going, Keo thought, watching as the Chevy disappeared up the length of the fence, with the Wrangler right behind it—

Until it stopped.

*Oh, God*dammit.

The Wrangler had slammed on its brakes and was now idling underneath one of the lampposts next to the fence. That lasted for a few seconds before it backed up and turned around until its bumper almost touched the chain-link fence. The driver and his passenger climbed out while the machine gunner remained at his post behind an M249 with a laser mounted underneath the barrel. The red dot from the light machine gun swept across the ground and the buildings in front of it before moving over in Keo's direction. It raked the path in front of him, missing the three of them by about two feet before jumping off in search of targets elsewhere.

Rita hadn't said a word, but Keo could feel the *"Now what?"* on her face when she looked back at him. He shook his head before glancing over at the fence again. There were still no signs of Claire and the others. But then, there wouldn't be with the Wrangler parked nearby, lit up like some nightmare Christmas tree underneath the lamppost.

"We can't stay here forever," Rita finally said. Or whispered, even though there was no real chance the technical and its occupants could overhear. "Sooner or later, they're going to find that guy you shot. If they haven't found him already."

"Yeah, I know," Keo said.

"We should go back," Jeremy said. "We should go back before it's too late."

It's already too late, kid, Keo thought as he focused on the wall of hurricane fencing in front of them. He wasn't looking at wrought iron or metal, and it wouldn't take much to blast a hole through them with a well-lobbed grenade.

Of course, that would make a hell of a lot of noise, and he didn't think those Buckies near the Wrangler would just let him, Rita, and Jeremy run past them without saying *Hi*.

So close, and yet so, so far away...

"Keo," Rita said. "What do we do?"

"M203," Keo said. "The Wrangler first, then the fence."

"Well, at least I didn't drag this thing along for nothing."

She took a 40mm grenade round out of the pouch around her waist and slipped it into the launcher underneath her M4's barrel. "Ready whenever you are, boss man."

"Can you take out the Jeep from this distance?"

"Only one way to find out."

"Don't forget to account for—" Keo began.

"Shut up and do it," Rita said.

Keo grinned and began walking toward the technical.

He stepped into the light and had managed to cover ten meters before the man standing next to the Wrangler's driver-side door turned around and saw him. Keo had his submachine gun slung and his hands in front of him, palms rubbing against each other to generate heat. It wasn't completely a performance; it was actually that cold.

The Bucky that first spotted him must have said something to the others, because the machine gun in the back swiveled around and Keo grimaced slightly as the red dot underneath the M249 ran across his eyes before lowering to rest on his chest.

Don't miss, Rita! Keo thought even as he continued walking, hands rubbing furiously in front of him, and called out, "Hey, don't shoot, for Christ's sake!"

The Buckies didn't say anything, but the red dot didn't leave Keo's chest, either. It was, ironically, using the circled *M* on Keo's vest as a target.

What's good for the goose is good for the gander, I guess.

Keo kept walking with purpose, without showing any signs of fear. After all, he was wearing the right clothes, which meant he belonged here, so why would he be afraid of other Buckies?

Yeah, that's it. Keep telling yourself that, pal.

He had made up ten more meters on the patrol when the Bucky on the passenger side walked round the front grill of the vehicle. Like his partner, he was armed with an AR rifle, but it wasn't their weapons Keo was focused on. It was the machine gun and the man squinting behind its iron sights in the back. God, he hated those guns, especially when they were pointed at him.

"Don't shoot!" Keo shouted.

"What are you doing here?" one of the Buckies standing around the car shouted back.

"What do you think I'm doing here? I'm on patrol!"

"Where's your partner?"

Partner? Keo thought, then remembered how every patrol he'd seen so far had consisted of at least a two-man team. *Right. Partner.*

"He's taking a leak!" Keo shouted. "I don't know what's taking him so long, though! You'd think he'd get his shit together by now!"

Keo hoped that was enough of a signal.

It was, and barely two seconds after *now* left his lips, there was a soft, echoing *plompt!* from somewhere behind him as Rita finally fired the M203.

The 40mm grenade was sailing over Keo's head when he lunged forward and down onto one knee, about a second before the Wrangler went up in a ball of flames. The last image of the machine gunner was the man craning his neck to see what was flying toward him—and then he was gone.

The explosion also engulfed the Bucky standing in front of the vehicle and blew the second one clear. The man landed nearly five meters away, and to Keo's surprise was picking himself back up almost right away.

Idiot, you should have stayed down, Keo thought before he squeezed off four rounds. He wasn't sure how many hit their target, but enough did that the man collapsed and remained down this time.

Keo vaulted back up to his feet, turned, and shouted at Rita and Jeremy, "Go, go, go!"

They were already running out of the shadows before he got the final *go* out and racing toward the fence. Rita was in the lead, fumbling to reload the M4 between strides, while Jeremy seemed to struggle to catch up to her despite being almost a whole foot taller.

Keo was about to join them when something flickered in the corner of his left eye, and he spun back toward the burning carcass of the Wrangler—and right past it.

The white Chevy was back, its spotlights already dancing across the open ground as it chewed up the distance in the blink of an eye.

*Sonofa*bitch.

Keo had been hoping for a little more time—ten seconds, maybe even twenty—as the other Buckies tried to figure out what was happening along this part of the fence, but whoever was in charge of the other patrol was apparently on the ball.

A competent Bucky. Swell!

Keo began running after Rita and Jeremy, shouting, "Don't stop! Go, go, go!"

He looked past the two fleeing figures at the fence but didn't see what he was hoping to find. There was no Claire or Gholston or Rudolph waiting for them. There were nothing but shadows and outlines of cornstalks in the fields beyond.

Where are you, Claire? Don't let me down, kid!

He wasn't more than two—three?—seconds into his mad

dash to catch up to Rita and Jeremy when he heard the sound he had been dreading:

Brap-brap-brap!
Brap-brap-brap!
Brap-brap-brap!

NINETEEN

The night air instantly went from cold and chilly to hot and scorching with every breath he managed. Of course, the fact that he was *breathing at all* was a good sign. So was the ability to still be running for his life as the *brap-brap-brap!* bellowed and bullets *zip-zip-zipped!* past his head. More than a few vanished into the ground around him, kicking up dirt at his pant legs and waist and chest. Like rain, except falling *up* instead of *down*.

Keo ran, because there was nothing else to do. Only an idiot would stop and try to take on a technical. If the Chevy revving its engines as it streaked toward him (How close was it now? Did it matter? It didn't need to be close for that mounted machine gun to cut him into ribbons.) didn't have an MG in the back, then Keo would have risked it; but it did, and so he didn't.

Run faster! Run faster, you idiot!

He did—or thought he did, anyway. The truth was, he wasn't sure how fast he was going, but it felt like he was

putting everything he had into every stride even as he zig-
zagged to make the machine gunner's job a little harder. He
glimpsed the red laser dot raking the ground to his left and
right out of the corners of his eyes as the man tried to get a
bead on him.

Faster! Faster!

The only bright spot was that while the Chevy and its MG
were intent on reducing Keo to nothing, that left Rita and
Jeremy to make a run for the fence. He kept waiting to hear the
sound of Rita firing the M203 at the fence to make them a hole
to run through, but for some reason it hadn't happened yet.
What was she waiting for?

All thoughts of escape vanished in a blink when he felt the
sting and was knocked off his feet. It was all Keo could to do to
throw both hands, the MP5SD clutched between them, ahead
of him even as he lunged forward and tucked and—*slammed*
into the ground on the back of his neck.

But the back of his neck was better than on his head and
he was rolling, snapping back up to his feet even as he did
his best to *ignore the pain! Ignore the pain!* coming from his
right thigh. He was bleeding, he was sure of it even if he
couldn't afford the second or two it would have taken to
check just how bad the injury was. Thank God for the
adrenaline, or else the pain would have been worse. He still
grimaced and fought back a scream as he shot (*Wrong choice
of words, pal!*) up to his feet and launched right back into a
full sprint.

In front and to the right of him, Rita and Jeremy were still
making a mad dash for the fence. Jeremy was running for all he
was worth and had somehow taken the lead, his taller frame
carrying him ahead of Rita. Keo guessed there was nothing

quite like the fear of impending death to get you running as fast as humanly possible.

Rita was glancing back at Keo, and they locked eyes.

"Do it!" Keo shouted. "Do it!"

Rita turned back around and was aiming the M4 toward the fence when a red dot appeared on the ground in front of him. But it didn't stay there. Instead, the dot began moving, moving, *moving* toward—

Rita and Jeremy.

Oh, Jesus.

Brap-brap-brap!

Rita was suddenly surrounded by bursts of pink clouds. Then the same thing happened to Jeremy, slightly in front of her.

Oh, Jesus!

One second Rita was there, in midstride even as she prepared to fire at the fence, and the next she was gone.

Just like that, Rita Ortega was gone.

And Jeremy, too, but Keo didn't know the young man as well as he did Rita. Hell, he didn't know Rita *that* well, either, but he knew her for a longer time than the turncoat Bucky. That familiarity, no matter how brief, left him with a huge hole in the pit of his stomach, even as Keo stopped running forward and pivoted and went right instead, seeking out the safety of the darkness, because there was nothing in front of him but lights and death.

There, a building—it looked like some kind of warehouse. Moonlight glinted off the structure's steel frame, and it called to him like a siren.

He ran toward it, forcing himself to forget the image of Rita and Jeremy disappearing in puffs of mist, and just run.

Run, run, *run.*

But he couldn't outrun the red dot, and it streaked across the wall in front of him. Keo slid to a stop a few feet from slamming face-first into the building and lunged to his right—

Ping-ping-ping! as bullets bounced off the metallic side of the warehouse. A few slugs came dangerously close to taking off his head on the ricochet. He ducked to lower his profile while still running, racing along the side of the building, hoping and praying to be swallowed up by the shadows so that cursed MG couldn't find him.

But the laser dot followed him and so did the bullets, the continuous *ping-ping-ping!* only occasionally broken up by the roar of the Chevy as it got louder. That meant it was getting closer and soon, very soon, it would catch up to him, because no matter how fast he ran, Keo wasn't going to outrun a truck. No one was *that* fast.

Another sudden stab of pain—this one coming from one of his arms; he couldn't even be sure which one, or how high—knocked him off his feet, and Keo dropped to the ground. This time, he didn't have the wherewithal to stick out his hands and perform another gravity-defying tuck-and-roll maneuver. This time, he twisted in the air before slamming back down to earth on his side with a heavy *oomph!*

Somehow, through all that, he managed to maintain his grip on the submachine gun. He had no idea how; maybe he just knew that his survival in the next few seconds depended on keeping the H&K with him right where it belonged. It was still there, in his hands, when bright lights found him, nearly blinding him in the process.

The truck had located him, but it also gave Keo something to shoot at.

He pulled the trigger at the lights as they grew closer and closer, and didn't stop until both of the incoming Chevy's headlights disappeared in a shower of glass and sparks.

Darkness again!

For him, anyway. The truck was still moving in the light, and Keo focused on its front grill, firing at it until he was completely empty.

The technical slammed on its brakes as smoke shot out from its hood and the driver struggled to see through his bullet-riddled windshield. In the next split second, Keo realized that the machine gunner had stopped shooting for some reason.

What the hell?

Then he saw why: the Bucky in the back of the technical was struggling with the box of ammo that hung underneath his weapon. The MG was either out of bullets or it was jammed.

Either/or's good for me!

The Chevy had stopped thirty meters or so in front of Keo. That was close enough for him to make out one of the Buckies in the front seats—the passenger, who leaned forward and over the dashboard to get a better look at Keo.

They locked eyes for about two heartbeats, though it could have been much shorter—or even longer. Keo couldn't be absolutely sure, because his chest was pounding, sweat pouring down his forehead the way it had Jeremy's earlier, and fire was ravaging the length of both legs and arms. He had no idea how that was possible, but then again, every single one of his senses were overloaded, and he couldn't be sure about anything at the moment except the slightly damp ground underneath him and the cold metal wall of the warehouse behind him.

The MP5SD was impossibly light in his hands when Keo dropped it and drew the Glock. It was easier and faster than trying to reload the submachine gun. At the same time, the Buckies in the front seats kicked open their doors and jumped out of the vehicle.

But Keo ignored them and focused on the man in the truck bed as he scrambled to open the M249's cover in order to either reload or fix the jam. Not that it mattered what he was doing or why, only that he had stopped shooting momentarily.

Momentarily!

He opened up on the machine gunner with the pistol. The first two rounds went high and the man flinched, but didn't stop working. The next round bounced off the hood of the Chevy, and the fourth and fifth shots found their target and the man vanished behind the cab.

A bright light suddenly lit a bullet-riddled section of wall about two feet to the right of Keo's head as one of the Buckies switched on a flashlight. Keo didn't need lights to see the Buckies, because they were standing out in the open.

He shot the man with the flashlight even as the Bucky was racing toward him. The man jerked off his feet and fell on his back. His flashlight went flying out of his hand and landed somewhere nearby.

Pop-pop-pop! as the third Bucky began shooting from the passenger side of the Chevy. Unlike his comrade, who had charged at Keo, this one was smarter and was using the open door as cover.

Keo flattened his chest against the ground as a bullet *zipped!* over his head and *pinged!* off the building behind him. He was hugging the dirt when the entire world shook as something exploded near the Chevy.

Now what?

He looked up and saw the Bucky doing the same thing,

staring wide-eyed across the truck when a second explosion lifted the technical about five inches off the ground as something tore into the five-thousand-something pound vehicle from underneath it. The Bucky disappeared in a rain of fire and shrapnel.

Keo was scrambling to his feet when he heard a familiar voice shouting his name: *"Keo!"*

He spun toward the fence and glimpsed a dark figure on the other side waving wildly in his direction.

Who...?

"Keo!" the figure shouted again.

It was female and very familiar—

Claire? Was that Claire?

"Get your ass over here!" the figure shouted.

Keo grinned and ran—though it was probably a fast hobble, at most—toward the fence, when a large shape appeared next to Claire (or, at least, he assumed that was Claire). Keo opened his mouth to scream a warning, but before he could, there were muzzle flashes and the very loud *brap-brap-brap* of machine-gun fire.

He almost dived headfirst back to the ground, except the bullets weren't coming *at* him but being directed to his left instead. He glanced in that direction even as he ran and saw Buckies coming out of the shadows. They didn't get very far before they were picked off and went down. One, two—a half-dozen!

It didn't take long for ones still standing to get the hint. They turned and fled back toward the buildings for cover. Keo didn't blame them. He'd just endured an MG firing at him, and he knew exactly what kind of pure terror the bastards were feeling right now.

The large figure on the other side of the fence (Was that Rudolph or Gholston, or someone else?) was still shooting, pinning the Buckies down while the smaller figure (Claire?) hurried down the length of the fence and waved for him to follow. Keo obeyed, and it didn't take long before he saw a third shadowed form pulling open a section of the fence not far from where Rita's and Jeremy's bodies still lay.

Rita. Jesus, Rita.

Keo couldn't help but stare at what was left of her, brilliantly illuminated by one of the lampposts. Jeremy lay very close to her, one hand still clutching the M4 he'd never gotten the chance to use. They were dead. Shot to pieces and lying in pools of their own blood. Part of him wanted to run back for Rita's body. After all, they had done it for Chang and Banner, so Rita deserved the same consideration.

Except Keo didn't, because he couldn't. Right now, either Rudolph or Gholston were holding the Buckies back with a constant stream of MG fire, but that wasn't going to last forever.

I'm sorry, Rita. I'm sorry!

He ran toward the opening where Claire—and he was sure it was Claire now; he could see her in the light, even though she was wearing black fatigues and boots—was waiting for him with the other man. It was Gholston, pulling a section of the fence open for him. So the one behind the MG farther up the fence was Rudolph.

"Hurry up!" Claire shouted.

It seemed to take an eternity (*Am I slow or is it just that far?*) before he finally reached them and ducked under and through the jagged slit, ignoring the sudden slivers of pain coming from his arms and legs as the sharp edges of the cut links sliced into his skin through his clothes.

He didn't stop moving for even a second, even after he was on the other side. If anything, Keo thought he had picked up speed, but it was entirely possible that was all in his mind. He was, after all, hurting from a few dozen cuts and bruises and bullet wounds.

The *brap-brap-brap!* finally stopped, and someone shouted, "Rudolph! Let's go!"

It was male, so he assumed it was Gholston.

Keo glanced over his shoulder and saw Claire's eyes up close. She was on his heels, her face locked in a tight grimace as she reached out and grabbed him.

Why was she grabbing him? Oh right, because he was falling and didn't know it.

And why was he falling? Because he had been shot. *Twice.*

"Jesus, Keo, you're bleeding everywhere," Claire said. She was struggling to keep him upright, which meant he was in much more pathetic shape than he thought.

Rudolph appeared on their left side, shouting, "Go now! Chat later!"

It was a good plan, and Keo summoned as much remaining energy as he had available and ran toward, then through the wall of corn that popped up in front of him out of nowhere. Claire was still next to him, both hands around one of his arms to keep him from falling, while Gholston led the way and Rudolph had slowed down until he was behind them.

"Keep going!" he shouted at Keo as they exchanged a glance.

Don't have to tell me twice, Keo thought, but he was too busy trying to fight for every breath to spit the words out. His lungs were burning and both feet were more tree trunks submerged in concrete than legs. Next to him, Claire was breathing just as hard and struggling to remain upright, too.

Well, at least it's not just me!

He didn't ask if she already knew about what had happened to Rita and Jeremy, because there was no point. Claire—along with Gholston and Rudolph—would have seen the bodies next to the fence. It would have been impossible not to.

Keo looked back over his shoulder, not that he could see anything other than corn. A lot of corn. He wished he knew if he'd gotten Buck, if the gamble had paid off. Because if it didn't, then he would have gotten Rita and Jeremy killed for nothing. The turncoat Bucky's death, Keo could live with. It wasn't like he knew the kid that well. Rita, on the other hand, was a good soldier, and Keo thought they could have become friends if given the chance.

There was no chance of that now, because she was dead. Shot down in front of him by that goddamn MG.

I hope you're dead, Buck. I hope you're fucking dead, because if you're not, then all of this will have been for nothing.

Be dead, you sonofabitch. Be covered in a few thousand pounds of rubble right now, your skull smashed in beyond all recognition.

Or just dead. I'll settle for just dead without all the gruesome stuff.

But he wouldn't know. Not yet. And definitely not tonight.

"Almost there!" Gholston shouted from in front of them.

Already? Keo thought when they burst out through the line of cornstalks and into the same open field that he, Rita, and Claire had run across not more than a day ago.

Except this time, it wasn't empty.

This time there were men with rifles standing there, waiting for them.

There was a long line of them, too. Twenty, maybe more, and every single one of them were wearing assault vests with circled *M*'s that almost glowed in the moonlight. They had weapons pointed at Keo, Claire, and Gholston. He had no idea how long they had been there, but they didn't look the least bit shocked to see them.

Flashlights flicked on up and down the row of men. Keo turned his head to keep from being blinded—just as Rudolph, who had been bringing up their rear, finally burst out of the cornfield and into the open.

Rudolph stopped on a dime and did the dumbest thing he could have done, and began lifting the Remington shotgun he was holding in his hands. Keo opened his mouth to scream, but it was too late.

In the next split second, Keo made a decision without realizing he'd done it, and spun around and grabbed Claire, in the process exposing his back to the Buckies. She gasped against him, but it was mostly lost in the thunderous crashing of rifles.

Keo pushed Claire away from him and shouted, *"Run!"*

Claire barreled into the cornstalks, stumbling and fighting to maintain her balance the entire way.

"Run!" Keo shouted again, his voice barely audible against the continued gunfire behind him.

Stalks of corn snapped in half around Claire as she fled, but somehow the teenager managed to stay upright and running until the flickering shadows simply swallowed her up. A second later, men in black charged into the wall of corn after her, their flashlights lighting their way.

Keo stared after them, his breath sledgehammering against his chest. He didn't move. He wasn't even sure if he *could* move, even if he tried.

Slowly, very slowly, it occurred to him that the shooting had stopped.

And he was still alive.

Why was he still alive?

Keo looked down at his feet, where Rudolph's body lay awkwardly crumpled. His black clothing had turned a dark shade of red under the harsh moonlight. He didn't have much of a face anymore, and his right arm had become detached from his body at the shoulder joint.

When he looked to his right, Keo found Gholston's body. Or what remained of it. He was still gripping onto his rifle, his face—at least the part of him that wasn't covered in a thick film of blood—locked in a permanent mask of shock.

But I'm still alive.

Why am I still alive?

Keo was turning to find out the answer when something struck him in the back of the skull and his legs buckled.

"Well, that was nasty," a voice said from behind him.

Keo was on his knees when he heard the voice, and he tried to pick himself up and turn around. He got halfway before something else—a big piece of lumber, maybe—struck him in the back, just under the clavicle, and he gave up on that idea.

"Some people just don't know when they're beat," the same voice said. "You're lucky I told my men what you looked like, or they would have blown your brains out for that stupid stunt."

Keo recognized the voice. He didn't have to see the face to

know who it was. He had heard it only once, and that was over the radio. Voices in real life and on the radio sometimes didn't match, but this one did.

A figure moved around his kneeling form—Keo had learned his lesson and didn't try to get up or move any part of him other than his eyes—and stood in front of him. The white hair seemed to shine in the darkness, but it was the hazel eyes that Keo focused on.

"It's about time we met, don't you think?" the man said.

"And you are?" Keo asked, even though he already knew the answer.

"Marlon J. Jefferson," the man said, sticking out his hand. "But everyone just calls me Buck."

TWENTY

"So your name's Buck, huh?"

"That's what people call me."

"It's a pretty stupid name. I'd have stuck with Marlon myself. Less fishy."

"This coming from a guy named Keo?"

"Hey, I didn't have a choice. That name was given to me. What's your excuse?"

"Fair enough." Buck had his back turned to Keo and was doing something on a bench in front of him. Keo didn't know what that "something" was, but Buck seemed preoccupied with it. "I've found that people respond better to Buck than Marlon. It's a psychological thing. Buck lets them think they can trust me. One of the boys, if you will."

"You said 'lets them think' they can trust you. So you're tricking them."

"I wouldn't put it that way."

"How would you put it?"

"It puts them at ease. That's what I'm all about. Putting people at ease."

That's not what Gaby said, Keo thought, remembering all the things Gaby had told him about the man. One of the words she had used was "intimidating," which wasn't what Keo was feeling at the moment. Of course, it could just be that Buck had only flashed those hazel eyes of his at Keo once when he first entered and hadn't looked at him again since.

"So, it's not because you're an idiot with bad name-choosing skills?" Keo said.

Buck chuckled. "No, it's definitely not that."

"I guess I'll have to take your word for it."

"Up to you. No skin off my nose whether you believe me or not."

Keep him talking, and maybe you'll survive the night. Maybe.

He glanced around him for the fifth time in as many minutes. He felt safe to do so with Buck seemingly disinterested in keeping an eye on him.

They were in a room. Wooden boards on the inside, brick on the outside. Thick enough construction to keep out most of the chilly night but not completely, if the little spurts of cold, tingling sensation along his exposed skin and the scar on one side of his face were any indication. The metal chair they'd put him in before tying his hands behind him and fastening them to the backrest with mud-caked white ropes didn't help. The ropes themselves bit into his skin and were so tight they threatened to draw blood. Or they might have already, but he just couldn't see it. They apparently ran out of rope after that, because they only duct-taped his ankles to both chair legs. Not that he could get out of the duct tape any easier than the rope.

The floor under him was slightly damp dirt, which gave the place a half-finished look.

The corners around him were hidden in shadows, making it difficult to guess the size of the place. It didn't help that the only source of light came from the work bench in front of Buck —a single battery-powered reading lamp with a flexible head that Buck had bent to get the best look at what he was working on.

There was enough light for Keo to see the fresh bandages over his left thigh and right arm, just above the elbow joint. There was numbing from both wounds but no danger of bleeding out. He wasn't in pain, which he owed to whatever was inside the syringe the Bucky who had patched him up had stuck him with. Keo wondered if that was of the Bucky's own accord or orders from Buck himself.

He was still breathing, which was something he couldn't say for Rita, Jeremy, Gholston, and Rudolph. And before them, Banner and Chang. This mission had cost a lot of lives— and it wasn't even a success. He still didn't know a damn thing about the warehouse—what was inside it, what they were using it for—and the only reason he had abandoned it (to kill Buck) was also a big, fat failure.

Definitely a big stinking F on the report card there, pal.

There was nothing inside the room to indicate what it was being used for before they put him in here. Buck himself had entered about thirty minutes after Keo was tied into place; the man was carrying a shiny but dented metal box that he placed on the work bench. Or Keo assumed it was a work bench. It was really just a big table with a lamp on top. Whatever it had been used for before he and Buck arrived, Buck was making very good use of it now.

What the hell is he doing? What was in that box?

Keo couldn't see around Buck's large frame. He was a big man—late forties, his completely white hair almost surfer blond against the bright LED light. Whatever he was doing, it apparently took a lot of concentration.

"Thanks for letting your guy wrap me up," Keo said. "I guess I should be grateful for that."

"You should," Buck said. "I told them to give you something special. After all, we wouldn't want you to fall asleep on me tonight."

"Something special?" Keo thought, but he said, "We definitely wouldn't want that."

"You must be the luckiest bastard I've come across. If only one of my men failed to follow my orders out there, you'd be a pancake on the ground, along with those other two."

"It's a good thing your men are good at following orders."

"Not all of them, but the ones that matter. Thank whatever God you believe in that you're still alive, my friend. The shit you pulled..."

"I can say the same thing about you."

Buck chuckled, but he kept his back turned to Keo.

What the hell is he doing?

There was a strange smell in the air, but Keo couldn't be sure if that was coming from the table or underneath his bandages. The Bucky who had fixed him up had cleaned his wounds and lathered them with ointment before covering them up with gauze. It was excellent field work, and Keo had almost thanked the man when he was done. Almost.

"Where's Claire?" Keo asked.

"You shouldn't worry about her," Buck said. "You should be worrying about yourself."

"I'm good at multitasking. Where's Claire?"

Buck didn't answer him, which made Keo smile. The fact that the man hadn't come right out and told him that Claire was captured—or worst, dead—meant she was still alive and running around out there. There was no reason for Buck to withhold that kind of information, not now.

Claire's status gave him some hope. The night had become a major shitstorm, but at least one of them had made it. He had faith in the teenager's ability to escape Fenton. She was, after all, trained by some of the best survivors Keo knew.

Run, kid. Run far, far away and don't look back.

"What was in the box?" Keo asked.

Buck ignored him and continued working. Keo couldn't hear anything metallic clicking, which he took for a good sign. Preludes to torture, in his experience, usually involved metallic clicking noises. Of course, he didn't think that was what this was; would Buck really do all the dirty (and oftentimes bloody) work himself? Probably not. Especially after he had gone to such great lengths to keep Keo alive.

"So it's the silent treatment, then?" Keo said.

"Not at all. I just don't feel like answering your questions."

"That's rude."

"You're the one who tried to murder me tonight. I'd say that's ruder."

"I had good cause."

"Oh, did you now?"

"You're an asshole."

"Now who's being rude? Besides, being an asshole is a matter of perspective and depends on who you ask."

"It's fact, actually. I would know; I asked around and

everyone agreed: You're an asshole. And assholes deserve killing."

"So you're judge, jury, and executioner?"

"That's correct. Speaking of which, how the fuck are you still alive?"

"Thirty minutes."

"Thirty minutes? What happens in thirty minutes?"

"That's how long after I left the conference building and you blew it up. You were late by thirty minutes."

Thirty minutes. Thirty fucking minutes. Swell.

"Lucky man," Keo said.

"It's fate. I'm not supposed to die tonight. I still have too much to do."

"I don't believe in fate."

"That's your prerogative."

Buck finally finished whatever he had been doing and turned around...and held a double-layer meat sandwich up to his mouth and took a big bite.

A sandwich. A fucking sandwich.

Buck wiped at some mustard stain on his chin with a handkerchief he'd taken out from his pocket as he chewed. "Sorry to eat in front of you, but it's been a long day and even longer night. I haven't had the chance to eat."

"Choke on it," Keo said.

The head Bucky grinned and took another bite. Now that the man had moved slightly to the left, Keo was able to get a better look at the metal box he'd brought in with him. It was a kid's lunchbox with a white dog with big floppy ears on the side. Leftover greens, tomatoes, and slices of something white lay on top of spread-out newspaper. A small see-through squeeze bottle with mustard inside sat nearby. Buck had also put a can of beer on the counter behind him, and he reached back, picked it up, popped it open, and took a large gulp from it.

Keo watched in silence, not quite sure if the sight of Buck enjoying his sandwich and beer was cause for relief or alarm. What had he been expecting? Definitely not a sandwich. And Buck was attacking it like he truly hadn't eaten in days.

"When I heard about what happened, I knew it was you," Buck said, taking another big bite from his carefully crafted sandwich, then wiping at a new mustard stain. "To try something like that takes balls. The kind of balls someone who thought it was a good idea to sneak onto an island in the middle of the ocean and assassinate a man surrounded by an army would have. I just knew it was you."

Mercer. It always goes back to Mercer, doesn't it?

"You were already waiting for me outside the fence," Keo said. "How?"

"I was on my way out of the city when you blew up the conference building. Couldn't just keep going after I got word about what had happened. It was pretty easy to predict where you were headed and which part of the fence you'd come through. Of course, all that shooting helped."

Buck reached back into the lunchbox and took out another beer and snapped the tab open. Keo couldn't help but think that that wasn't what the lunchbox was originally intended to be used for.

"If I'm being honest, I didn't think you'd actually make it out," Buck said. "But God*damn*, son, you actually did!"

I'm not your son, you piece of shit, Keo thought, but he said instead, "So are you gonna offer me one?"

Buck ignored him and drank the beer for a moment before lowering it back down with a satisfied sigh. "Are they dead?"

"Are who dead?"

"You know who."

Loman and Biden...

"Yeah, they're dead," Keo said.

"How?"

"I broke one of their necks. The other one was shot."

"That's too bad. They were good men."

"They were assholes."

"One person's asshole is another's good soldier. You should know a lot about that, Keo." He pursed a forced smile. "It was a long shot anyway, but it was worth a try. Think big, I always say." Then, tilting his head slightly, "I'm assuming she's still alive, if my men are dead?"

Keo stared back at the Bucky. Not just any Bucky. *The* Bucky. "You saying you don't already know?"

"I don't."

Bullshit.

Or was it? How much could he believe the things coming out of Buck's mouth?

Buck must have known what was going through Keo's mind, because he shrugged. "You can believe me or not, it really doesn't matter."

"Why am I still alive?"

"I think you know why."

"You want to be my friend, is that it? Send me a friend request, and I'll think about it."

"You know exactly why you're still alive. Why I've gone to great lengths to keep you that way."

"I'm all out of guesses and I'm tired, so just tell me already."

"He wants you alive."

"He?" Keo thought, but he didn't ask the question. He had a feeling Buck was going to tell him anyway. Wasn't that the whole point of this? To rub his face in his failures?

I guess he's going to be doing a lot of rubbing tonight...

Buck tapped his own temple with his fingers. "He wants to get in here. Deep, deep inside. He talks about you all the time. About how he almost had you in Axton, then again in Cordine City. If I thought he could still get an erection, I'd swear he had the world's most massive hard-on for you."

"He?"

Right. "He."

More like it.

"You talk about *it* like it's still a human being," Keo said.

"He takes offense to being called 'it.' I like to humor him. It keeps things moving smoothly, and it doesn't cost me anything."

"Except your soul."

"You believe in such things, Keo?"

"Don't you?"

"No. And I'm betting you don't, either."

"Goes to show you don't know me that well."

"I know you better than you think."

"You presume. There's a difference."

"Maybe." Then, with a smirk, "Besides, that's some accusation about me selling my soul, coming from the guy who just tried to murder me with a missile."

Keo had to grin at that. "I'm just saying, you lay down with dogs, you wake up with a tail. At least, I think that's how the saying goes."

Buck put the beer down and leaned back against the table. "Face it, people like us don't care about any of that esoteric bullshit. We are what we are. Have been, even before the world went to shit. Before the ghouls, before Mercer; and we'll still be who we are meant to be long after this new iteration of Black Tide is gone and another one replaces it."

"What the hell are you talking about?"

"Haven't you been asking yourself where he is? Where all the ghouls are? Why he isn't already here drilling into that brain of yours?"

Keo didn't say anything. He was almost too afraid to.

But he finally said, "Could be all the BO. I hear they hate it when their victims stink."

"That's not it."

"Are you sure?"

"He's not here because he's busy elsewhere."

Keo narrowed his eyes. "What did you do?"

"Me? I haven't done anything. You saw them, didn't you? At Axton? Cordine City? That was only a small part of what he has at his disposal. Lara's been building an army from the ashes of Black Tide, but so have I, and so has he. That meeting earlier, the one you decided to crash? It was me giving orders on how to proceed after I leave to join him at Darby Bay. The truth is, I'm supposed to be there right now, alongside our mutual friend." He smiled at Keo. "But I just had to come back; I just had to see you up close and tell you, face to face, about how *fucked* you and your friends are."

"Where is it? Where's the fucker?"

"His name is Merrick."

"Merrick? Sounds like a disease."

Buck glanced down at his watch.

"You late for a party?" Keo asked. "Don't let me keep you. I was perfectly content sitting in here all by myself before you showed up."

Buck looked back up. "Merrick and his army should already be arriving at their target right about now. You think all those planes and tanks Black Tide have will make any difference? It doesn't matter if there's one or one hundred Warthogs if there aren't any pilots to fly them. Tonight is the beginning of the end, Keo. It all starts with Darby Bay, and it'll end there, for all intents and purposes. Your friends just won't know it until it's too late."

Wait. Darby Bay? Did he just say Darby Bay?

Buck saw his reaction, and one corner of his mouth tugged upward into a satisfied smile.

"Merrick is attacking Darby Bay," Keo said, and thought, *It's attacking Lara. It's going after Lara.*

"Did you think I was attacking the neighboring towns because I needed their women and supplies?" Buck asked. "I have plenty of both. I knew that sooner or later she'd hear about the raids, about the women and children, and ride to the rescue. That's her job now, isn't it? Saving the world from men like me? It was inevitable. And it was *so* predictable."

Keo laughed. It came out of nowhere, and he surprised even himself.

Buck narrowed his eyes, confusion replacing the smugness that had been all over his face just seconds ago. "What's so funny?"

"That's it?" Keo said when he finally stopped laughing.

"All of this—the raids, the army, the planning—and it all comes down to revenge?"

"What's more primal than revenge? We're primal beasts, when you get right down to it. We've always been. Civilization just hid it, but it never really went away. We fuck and we kill, and when someone crosses us, we demand vengeance. What could be more human?"

"Oh, I could think of plenty of things."

Buck leaned forward, his hazel eyes focusing intently on Keo. "If it were up to me, I'd deal with you myself. Mercer's killer. Oh, the things I could do to you, all the while listening to you beg for mercy."

"Sounds like you've been thinking about this for a while, Buck. Obsessively, you might say. Might want to get some help for that."

"A man can come up with some very creative ways to kill someone in five years."

"So what's stopping you? Or is talking me to death one of those 'creative ways' you came up with?"

Buck chuckled and sat back. "Part of our deal was that he gets you all to himself. You and everyone who was there that day, in Houston. I'll just have to be satisfied with knowing that whatever plans he has for you, it'll be beyond anything I could have come up with. Besides, this isn't about one man, or even one woman. This is about dismantling the new Black Tide, about punishing those traitors who stayed behind. This is about showing them that they made the wrong choice and that it's going to cost them everything."

Keo clenched his teeth, but despite his best efforts, he couldn't come up with a response. His head was too busy spinning, images of Lara fighting off wave after wave of ghouls flooding his mind's eye.

I'm sorry, Lara. I screwed up. I'm sorry...

"I hope you said your good-byes before you left Darby Bay," Buck said, "because that was the last time you're going to see them again. It took five years, but it's here. The night of reckoning."

Buck grinned widely, and Keo imagined a certain blue-eyed ghoul taking over the man's human face.

"You didn't think we'd all forget, did you?" Buck asked. "Well, did you?"

TWENTY-ONE

"Sneak into Fenton. Find out what's in the warehouse. Go back to Lara."

"Go back to Lara..."

It was an easy enough job. Okay, so maybe "easy" wasn't quite the right word; but it was a straightforward task that, while dangerous as hell (then again, what wasn't dangerous as hell these days?), was doable. Very doable. That was why Lara had chosen him to lead the mission: Because he'd done harder things. Way, way harder things. Sneaking onto Black Tide Island, then killing Mercer, for one. Now *that* was hard. Compared to that, this was a cakewalk.

Okay, maybe not really a cakewalk. But definitely easier by a few degrees.

For one, he wasn't alone this time. He had the help of some experienced soldiers.

Like Rita, like Gholston, like Rudolph...

All dead now.

Claire's still alive. So there's that.

Keo clung to that last one. It was the only thing he could do, given his current situation. There wasn't much bright side to everything that had happened, but at least he had the knowledge the teenager had gotten away. Otherwise, Buck would have used it to antagonize him during their long talk, if that weren't the case.

Run, kid. Run as far and as fast as you can, and don't look back.

If only Claire knew what Buck had said, or where he was headed right now, she could have radioed Darby Bay and warned them about what was coming toward them—*if* it wasn't there already.

"You didn't think we'd all forget, did you? Well, did you?"

He sighed out loud to the empty room and watched small white clouds form in front of him. He had been worried about Lara being angry that he had disobeyed orders. Now, he would be happy if she was pissed off and never forgave him, because it would mean she had survived tonight.

Merrick.

That was the creature's name. Keo could have gone an entire lifetime without knowing that little FYI. What the monster called itself didn't mean a damn thing to him, or do him any good right now.

But of course it had to be Merrick. Of course it had to start with an M.

Just like Mabry. Just like Mercer. Just like Marlon J. Jefferson.

And now, Merrick.

What's the deal with all the M's?

There was no one inside the building to answer that question, though he did hear the occasional voices outside the door to his right. Buck had left anywhere from forty minutes to an hour ago. For some reason, Keo found it difficult to concentrate. It didn't help that he couldn't see his watch.

He had glimpsed the silhouettes of guards waiting outside when Buck opened the door to leave. Two that Keo could see, likely more that he couldn't. After what he had done—and maybe a little because of his reputation—Buck would be a fool to leave just two men out there.

Think much of yourself, pal?

Just a tad.

Great. Now try to think of a way out of this.

That was easier said than done, because he couldn't see any way out of here. Not even a sliver. Not even a tiny, itty bitty sliver of hope.

Butkus. That's what you got. Jack shit, and Jack's not answering his phone.

It had grown colder inside the room, and he shivered against the thick rope holding his arms behind him, with the cold metal chair's backrest between them and his back. There was no way he was getting out of the chair. At least, not as long as his limbs were still attached. Even if he could, then what next? The door? What about the men with guns waiting outside?

For some reason, he was still wide awake. He was tired from head to toe, and his muscles ached, and it had to be the middle of the night outside. Well past midnight, actually. So why couldn't he force his body to shut down so he could get some sorely needed rest? Instead, his mind was filled with images of Lara fighting off ghouls and Darby Bay under siege...

"I told them to give you something special. After all, we wouldn't want you to fall asleep on me tonight," Buck had said.

What had they shot into his veins? Whatever it was, it was keeping him wide awake and alert. More strung out than he should be, given everything that had happened and how late it was. And he couldn't stop thinking about Lara, about the hell she could be going through right this very second...

He focused on the metal desk in front of him instead. Buck hadn't done him any favors when he switched off the lamp before leaving. Keo would be sitting in complete darkness, if his night eyes hadn't taken over. He could see enough to know that he wasn't going to find anything to help him out of his bindings, much less out of the building.

There were no rays of sunshine, no yellow brick road out of this one. He had disobeyed Lara's orders and tried to kill Buck, and ended up captured. The entire compound was on high alert, and even if he made it out, he'd have to shoot his way through a few hundred men.

Or a few thousand.

The numbers were irrelevant anyway, since once you reached two zeroes, tacking on an additional third or fourth made no real difference.

He should have stuck to the original plan. Maybe then he would have been on his way back to Darby Bay right now. Or already there, beside Lara when Merrick attacked.

"Tonight is the beginning of the end, Keo. It all starts with Darby Bay, and it'll end there, for all intents and purposes. Your friends just won't know it until it's too late."

He didn't know what was happening at the port town right now. Was Merrick already there? If Buck was to be believed, then the answer was yes. Blue Eyes and that army of undead it had been hiding, building in secret all these years since The Walk Out, would already be at Darby Bay's walls. *If* they weren't already inside it. After so many years of only sporadic ghoul encounters, would the Black Tiders be able to deal with a vast horde the likes of which they hadn't seen in over five years?

"You didn't think you could run from me forever, did you?" Blue Eyes had hissed at him underneath Cordine City. *"This is the end. But it won't be fast. It won't be easy. It'll be long and hard, and it'll hurt. We'll have a lot of fun, you and I. Oh, the wonderful games we'll play."*

He shivered at the memory of its words, at its close proximity and the way those razor-thin lips of the creature's arched to form something that it thought was a smile as it said them.

"If I thought he could still get an erection, I'd swear he had the world's most massive hard-on for you," Buck had said.

Tell me something I don't already know, Buck.

He let out another heavy sigh and watched the cloud form and dissipate in front of him. He was pitying himself, and he knew it. He also knew he couldn't do anything about it, or about much of anything, right now, and it made him angry. Angrier than he'd been in a long time. Maybe even angrier than when he decided to go after Mercer.

All he could do was think about all the things he *couldn't* do as he sat in his prison.

He couldn't go out there to find Claire, to make sure she had gotten away in one piece and wasn't bleeding out somewhere.

He couldn't go find Buck and finish the job he had started.

And most of all, he couldn't run back to Darby Bay and stand beside Lara as the hordes attacked.

He would give anything to see her again, to have her rip into him for disobeying orders. He had it all planned out. Even if she couldn't forgive him, he would leave knowing he had done the right thing. In his mind, at least. But then, Keo's definition of the "right thing" was always a little different (*A little? Try a lot*) than most people's.

Another sigh as he recalled what Buck had said:

"It took five years, but it's here. The night of reckoning. You didn't think we'd all forget, did you? Well, did you?"

Keo let out a scream. It came out of nowhere, and he didn't bother trying to stop it. It was half frustration and half anger... Oh, who was he kidding? It was almost entirely all anger.

Lara.

Darby Bay.

And here he was, stuck in Fenton. Tied up and waiting to die. The helplessness was too much, and he let it out in one massive, primal scream.

He didn't know how long it went on, but it must have been long (and loud) enough that whoever was guarding him heard it and couldn't ignore it, because there was a loud *clack!* as the door opened and a figure appeared in the doorway, backlit by the moonlight in the background.

Keo couldn't make out a face, but it was a man, judging by the broad shoulders, and he had a rifle slung in front of him and two horns sticking up from his head like some kind of bat ears, but smoother and metallic. Night-vision goggles.

"What the hell?" the man said. "You dying or something?"

Keo sucked in a deep breath before forcing a smile at the man. "What was that?"

"What the fuck were you screaming about?"

Keo glimpsed a second figure behind the first, peeking in. He, too, was shrouded in shadows and had an NVG device propped on his forehead.

How many guards did Buck put out there? At least two.

"I'm hungry," Keo said.

"So?" the man said.

"So go get me some food."

"What the fuck for?"

"Which part of 'I'm hungry' didn't you understand?"

"Fuck off," the man said, and slammed the door shut.

Keo stared at it for a moment. For some reason, he was sure that was going to work.

"Hey!" he shouted.

The door remained closed.

"Hey, fuckface!" he shouted again, louder this time—if that was even possible because the first *Hey* had been pretty loud to begin with.

Clack! as the door swung open a second time, and the same outline appeared against the moonlight. "You're really getting on my nerves, dead man. Sit tight and wait there like a good little boy, or I'm going to have to come inside and shove a rag in your mouth."

"Does the rag at least have some food crumbs in it?"

"What?"

"Food crumbs. I told you, I'm hungry."

"And I told you, I don't give a shit."

"Actually you never said that. You said something else, but never 'I don't give a shit.'"

The man didn't respond, either because he was confused or annoyed, or both.

Yeah, probably both.

"I could use some food," Keo said.

"I don't care," the man said.

"What does he want?" a second voice asked from somewhere outside the building.

"He's hungry," the first one said, turning slightly in the direction of his partner, who was invisible to Keo at the moment.

"What did boss man say about feeding him?" the partner asked.

"I don't think he said anything."

"You don't think, or you don't know?"

"What's the difference?"

"There's a huge difference."

"He said I could have some food," Keo said.

"Bullshit," the guard at the door said, looking back at Keo.

"He told me so himself."

"Did he?" the unseen guard asked.

"Of course not," the first one said. "He's lying."

"I'm not," Keo said. "Scout's honor."

"Bullshit, you were in the Scouts," the man said.

"I was. I have a box full of medals and everything."

"Yeah, right." He glanced over at his partner. "Buck didn't say shit about feeding him. But he did say not to go in there for any reason."

A figure appeared over the shoulder of the first one and looked into the room. "Who the hell is he, anyway?"

"The one who blew up the conference building earlier," the first guard said.

"No shit? I thought he'd be dead by now."

"Not yet. But he's going to wish he was—"

The *boom!* of an explosion cut the guard off, and both figures turned their heads toward the source. It had caught them all by surprise, including Keo, who could still feel the trembling under his feet.

What the hell was that?

"What the hell was that?" the first guard asked, echoing Keo's thoughts.

"Sounded like an explosion," the second one said.

"Where'd it come from?"

"I think the front gate—"

Another *boom!* tore through the night, and this time the *brap-brap-brap* of a machine gun responding crackled.

"That's definitely coming from the front gate," the second guard said. He had disappeared out of the open door's view again, and Keo could only hear his voice. "What should we do?"

The first guard remained in sight the entire time. If he was panicking—even a little bit—he was hiding it well. "We're not going anywhere. We have a job to do; that goes for every single one of you."

"We're under attack," a third voice said. A few seconds later, the owner appeared in silhouette outside the door.

Then a fourth joined them. "You hear that? We're under attack."

"I can hear just fine," the first guard said. "We're not going anywhere. Our job is to stay here."

I guess we know who's in charge, Keo thought as the machine gun firing stopped...for about five seconds before it picked right back up again. Except this time there was clearly more than one firing simultaneously.

"Sounds like a party," Keo said.

The leader glanced back into the building at him. "What do you know about it?"

"I know seriously bad news when I hear it. Listen. You hear that?"

"Hear what?"

"Bad news. That's what bad news sounds like. Are you even paying attention to me?"

"You'd be the expert on bad news, wouldn't you?"

"Is that an accusation?"

"Just a statement of fact, from what I hear."

Keo shrugged. Or as much as he could, with his arms bound behind him. "Don't believe everything you hear, son."

"I'm not your son."

"Sorry. I can't see your face, so I don't know what you look like. If you'd step inside a little bit so I can get a closer look..."

A third explosion—followed quickly by a fourth—ripped across the compound, and the ground under Keo's boots shook again, this time for much longer.

"Oh yeah, it's definitely bad news," Keo said.

One of the new arrivals peeked into the room. "What should we do?" the man asked. "We're under attack. We can't just stand around here doing nothing."

"Stay the fuck put," the first guard said. "No one's going anywhere. Do your jobs."

"We're under attack," another voice said. It was the second one, who remained out of view. "That changes everything."

"It doesn't change shit," the leader said. "Buck gave us an order. Whatever's happening over there isn't our problem." He pointed into the building at Keo. "Our job is him. Let the others take care of the rest."

"Sounds like your friends are going to need all the help they can get," Keo said.

"Shut the fuck up," the leader said before he slammed the

door shut and Keo found himself alone inside a dark building again.

He no longer had a view of the outside world, but he could still hear it.

The *brap-brap-brap* of machine guns firing nonstop now, while the *pop-pop-pop* of small arms answered. They went back and forth, a constant stream of gunfire and the occasional explosions, as if someone were lobbing grenades into the compound.

Someone? It was more like a lot of *someones*, considering how much chaos he was listening to at the moment.

The question was: Who was attacking the compound, and was he going to have to kill them to get the hell out of this place and back to Lara, too?

TWENTY-TWO

His right arm, where he was shot, was starting to tingle. His left thigh, where he had also been shot, was starting to join in on the fun. He continued telling himself that both wounds could have been much worse if either bullet had gone an inch or two in the wrong direction. He wished he could ignore them, but whatever Buck's medics had given him wouldn't allow him to. But at least the pain was of the tingling variety and not the *"Oh my fucking God, I've been shot and I'm about to die"* type.

Thank God for that—and the World War III that was raging outside the building at the moment, because they allowed his mind to stop obsessing about what Lara was going through right this second in Darby Bay.

Gotta get out of here. Gotta get to Lara.

Gotta get to Lara...

It was the beginning of the end everywhere it seemed, and he was stuck in a lousy building waiting to die.

"You saw them, didn't you? At Axton? Cordine City? That

was only a small part of what he has at his disposal. Lara's been building an army from the ashes of Black Tide, but so have I, and so has he."

How many Black Tiders did Lara have with her to fight against that? A few hundred, most of them support personnel. Fighter pilots for the Warthogs, but no tank crews because those guys were busy elsewhere. She had a hundred soldiers at the most—men and women who could be counted on to actually *fight*—and a lot of civilians. The townspeople wouldn't be of much help. Five years of relative normalcy since The Walk Out had made a lot of people lower their guards. Even he had fallen victim to complacency until that mess at Winding Creek.

There was Gaby. Lara would have Gaby. The kid was tough, and still limping or not, when the attack began, she would become invaluable.

But who else?

Who *else*?

Jesus. He had to get to Darby Bay. He had to get to Lara. He couldn't warn her anymore—that ship had sailed—but he could stand by her side while Merrick attacked.

Goddammit!

He looked over at the door as a ferocious round of *pop-pop-pop* crackled outside. The shooting hadn't stopped for longer than a few seconds since it began over ten minutes ago. (Fifteen minutes? Thirty? Was he losing track of time again?) The back and forth raged on along with the occasional *booms* of things exploding.

Grenades. Those are grenades.

And what else?

The *brap-brap-brap* of machine-gun fire was easy to pick

out from the constant torrent of what sounded like firecrackers popping endlessly. Then there were the screams. Keo was pretty sure he could hear screams, along with voices shouting commands. People were dying out there, and he wasn't sure if that was something that was good for him.

The enemy of my enemy is my friend, right?

Unless the enemy of his enemy also wanted him dead, then not so much. What were the chances of that? Given his luck tonight, pretty damn good.

Keo had tried to get his guards' attention again, but they were either ignoring him or they were gone. How possible was the latter? Unlikely, given how adamant the leader had been about everyone holding their ground. Four men, as far as Keo knew, possibly more that hadn't spoken up when the fighting began.

Not that four or more (or less) did him any good in his current situation. The ropes only seemed to get tighter the more he struggled against them, and he couldn't even move his legs even a little bit. There was nothing left for him to do but sit and wait, and listen.

"Fuck," he whispered out loud to the empty room.

Then, louder: "Fuck."

Then, even louder: *"FUCK—"*

Except the *"-ck"* half of the word was lost in an ear-splitting *BOOM!* from his left side and Keo instinctively dove forward, taking the chair with him, and hit the dirt floor on his face and chest—grunting as he ate some damp earth—as one side of the wall exploded inward.

Raindrops fell around him, except these raindrops were made of brick and mortar and chunks of splintered wood. He braced himself against the assault as debris pelted his arms and legs and back, but the ones that landed on the back of his skull and exposed neck weren't quite so easy to just shake off.

Fuck, fuck, fuck!

Keo rolled over onto his side when the pummeling finally stopped. His arms strained against the backrest of the chair, and he let out a series of coughs as smoke and soot filled up the room. His chest heaved, but at least all the new rounds of pain helped him to momentarily ignore the bumps he was sure had just appeared across the back of his skull.

Slowly, very slowly, the clouds began to thin out, and he was able to see the remains of the wall—a gaping jagged opening that revealed a battlefield on the other side.

Now it's a party!

Buildings were on fire, white plumes of smoke shooting out of windows and raging flames lighting up the night sky. Figures raced back and forth across the opening, but if any of them noticed Keo staring out at them, no one bothered to stop and make sure he didn't try to get out. *If* they even knew who he was to begin with. *If* they even noticed the makeshift hole in the wall in the first place.

That's right, move along! Nothing to see here!

It was chaos outside, the constant clatters of gunfire easier to pinpoint now that he didn't have a wall separating him from the battle. Most of the shooting was coming from where he knew the perimeter fence to be, which further convinced him that someone and their friends were attacking the compound head-on.

The enemy of my enemy is my friend, right?

God, I hope so...

The sudden roar of engines as a technical zoomed past the building, the machine gunner in the back—his face hidden behind a balaclava—holding onto his weapon for dear life as the vehicle drove at dangerous speeds. The man in the back might have glanced in Keo's direction for the split second he was visible, and Keo waited to hear brakes as the truck came back to check on him, but that never happened.

He turned to look at the door behind him. It was still closed. If his guards knew what had happened—and they surely would have, given how loud the explosion that had taken out the wall had been—they weren't responding to it. The only explanation for why they hadn't checked on him yet was because there was no one out there.

Was that possible? Had his guards actually taken off after all?

Captain Optimism, pal!

He lay on his side for a minute, trying to figure out what to do next. He had limited options, but at least no one had come in to check on him yet, and if the constant blur of black-clad Buckies racing across the open wall—and nary a single soul stopping to glance in his direction save for maybe—*maybe*—the machine gunner earlier—that wasn't going to happen for a while. At least until someone finally got curious enough.

Right now, Keo was hoping not to meet Mr. Curious.

He concentrated on his binds, on how to get out of them. Could he even get out of them? He'd be damned if the ropes didn't feel even tighter since his swan dive. Keo spat out some dirt, then worked saliva around his mouth to get rid of the taste. It was disgusting, but at least it wasn't concrete. Now *that* would have really hurt.

His head continued to throb from however many chunks of the wall had bounced off his skull in the aftermath of the explosion. That was okay, because he didn't feel any blood back there. The operative word being *feel*. But he would have if he were bleeding, right?

Maybe...

He concentrated instead on what he could control, which was very little. But there were a few, like—

A shadowed figure climbed through the hole in the wall, gloved hands grabbing the jagged opening—and loosening some bricks in the process—for stability as they stepped through and into the building.

Aw, hell.

The newcomer was wearing all black—cargo pants, boots, and a long-sleeved sweater with a black assault vest featuring the dreaded circled *M* over one of the ammo pouches. Mr. Curious was wearing a gun belt, and the long barrel of a rifle jutted out from behind his shoulder.

You had to get curious, didn't you? Didn't you?

Keo stared, because he didn't know what else to do as the figure walked over, crunching debris under its boots. Mr. Curious stopped next to him and looked down. The face was covered by a balaclava, but there was something familiar about those blue eyes...

"If only I had a camera," the figure said.

Keo grinned at the sound of the voice. "You're alive."

"Lucky for you," the figure said as it pulled off the balaclava, revealing blonde hair and an oval-shaped face underneath.

Claire!

"Yeah, that's me," Keo said. "Lucky Keo. Good to see you, kid."

"You too."

The teenager glanced over her shoulder and out the hole

in the wall, when a ferocious torrent of rifle fire rang out. This one sounded a lot closer than the others, and Claire must have realized that, too.

"I think they're finally in the compound," Claire said as she turned back to Keo and took a knife out from behind her back.

"Who is 'they?'" Keo asked as Claire crouched and moved closer to cut him from the chair.

"I don't know." She sliced his legs free first, then started on his arms.

"Black Tide?"

"I don't think so. I couldn't reach anyone on the radio. If they were Black Tiders, they would have answered."

"Did you radio Darby Bay?"

"I tried."

"'Tried?'"

"No one answered."

"Shit."

"What?" Claire said, standing up and putting the knife away. "You know something, don't you?"

Keo stood up and rubbed his wrists. Both arms were stiff, and it took some doing to get his legs to stop weakening as he straightened them out. "They're under attack. Have been for a few hours now, as far as I know."

"Shit," Claire said.

"What I said."

Keo walked over to the hole in the wall just as another technical zoomed by. Like the last one, this one never bothered to slow down. Neither did the three black-clad figures running alongside it, as if they were using it as a shield against something.

"It's been like that for almost an hour now," Claire said.

"An hour?" Keo said, looking back at her.

"Yeah. Why?"

He shook his head. Damn it. What did Buck's people give him? He was definitely having great difficulty keeping track of time.

"They gave me something," Keo said as he moved away from the opening to hide himself in the shadows.

Claire hurried over to stand next to him. "What?"

"I don't know. But it's doing *something* to me."

"I guess that explains your eyes."

"What's wrong with my eyes?"

"They're huge, Keo."

"Huge, how?"

"The size of marbles. You didn't know?"

"It's kind of hard to see my own eyeballs, kid." He sighed. "You didn't come here empty-handed, did you?"

"Merry Christmas," Claire said as she handed him a weapon hanging behind her back. It was a Heckler & Koch UMP with a foldable buttstock, and it was too light in his hands. "I know it's not an MP5SD, but hey, same family, right?"

"Close enough."

Claire reached into her pocket and took out a spare magazine. "It's all I could get from the dead guy I took it off."

Keo put the spare into his back pocket. "Are you alone?"

"The Seven Dwarves are waiting for us outside. You can call me Snow White."

Keo grunted. "Could have just said yes."

Claire grinned. "Yes. I'm alone."

"Any ideas who the other guys are?"

The teenager shook her head. "Not a clue. I thought it was prudent to avoid them, too. They didn't seem to be taking any prisoners. I took advantage of the confusion they were creating to come back in here and get you out."

"How'd you get inside?"

"Are you kidding me? The fence is gone."

"Gone?"

"All those explosions you heard at the beginning? They took out most of the perimeter fencing. I just walked in. It helped that I was dressed properly. When I was in the compound, anyway. I could have been shot before then, but the attack was just getting started at the time."

Keo could barely make out her dark wardrobe in the shadows, but it was impossible to miss the white *M* on her vest. "Where'd you get that?"

"Jeremy," Claire said, and frowned slightly. "I knew where he kept his things."

"I'm sorry about the kid, Claire."

"He was a good guy. He was just trying to do what was right."

"I know," Keo said. "You made it through the cornfields all right?"

"Better than you," Claire said, staring at his bandaged thigh and arm. "You going to make it?"

"Yeah. They fixed me up and gave me that...whatever it was they gave me. It's helping with the pain."

"Why did they do that?"

"Buck's orders. I got the impression he wanted me as wide awake as possible so he could crow about how much of a fuckup I am tonight. Then he left."

"Are you sure he's gone?"

"Yes. Why?"

"I saw a large force leave the compound earlier. About an hour before the fighting began."

"Buck. He's going to join the attack on Darby Bay. How large of a force did you see?"

"Dozens of technicals, even more men on horseback, and trucks. Those big trucks that can haul ten, twenty men in the back." She paused, then, "They're attacking Darby Bay? Right now?"

Keo nodded. "We have to get to Lara, kid. We have to get to our friends *fast*."

"Maybe that's why no one answered my radio calls. They're...occupied right now."

Claire's face became somber, and Keo wondered if his looked the same, because he was pretty sure he was thinking the same thing she was.

Their friends, fighting for their lives, and they couldn't do a damn thing about it.

Gotta get to Darby Bay. Gotta get to Darby Bay fast.

"What—" Claire began when a blast tore through some buildings at least fifty meters from their position, visible outside the hole in the wall. It was so much stronger than all the previous ones that both he and Claire could feel the aftershocks for seconds afterward.

"The big ones are getting closer," Claire said.

"Big ones?" Keo said.

"They've been lobbing grenade rounds and rockets into the compound, but that was something else. Something bigger."

"What kind of rockets are they using?"

"What?"

"The rocket launchers. What kind are they using out there?"

"How should I know? Do I look like Danny?"

"Fortunately, no." He paused for a moment. "Did you see them? The attackers?"

"I saw some of them while I was hiding, looking for a way in. They were getting into positions to attack, but I didn't recognize any of them."

"How were they dressed?"

"They weren't wearing uniforms. A lot of black fatigues and black faces."

"Camo?"

"Yeah. They're not in any hurry, but there's a lot of them."

"How many is a lot?"

"Enough to give Buck's people a fight, and without the force that left earlier…" She shook her head. "I don't care how many Buckies are here and how many guns they have in their armories; they're going to lose sooner or later, Keo."

More men with circled *M*'s on their assault vests ran past them even as the *pop-pop-pop* of rifles firing nearby pounded the air. In the distance, smaller explosions occurred, like a series of trucks backfiring.

"How did you know where to find me, anyway?" Keo asked.

"I didn't," Claire said. "I was nearby looking for you when one of those rockets hit the side of your building. I took a chance and peeked in, and there you were."

"Wait. A rocket hit my wall?"

"What did you think it was?"

"I guess I didn't really know."

"They're firing everything they have into the compound.

Something that looked like a cruise missile almost took my head off."

"That explains all the buildings on fire," Keo said, when another technical flashed by outside the hole. This one also kept going, along with the figures running alongside it—

But not all of them.

One of the black-clad men slowed down, then stopped completely before turning toward the opening.

Mr. Curious Part 2. Swell.

Keo had a good view of the man from his position, standing in the shadows, but he didn't think the Bucky could see him. The man had, though, easily spotted the metal chair and ropes that Keo had recently escaped from lying unattended in the middle of the room.

Claire had seen the Bucky, too, and tensed a few inches to Keo's left, while her right hand tightened around the pistol grip underneath her AR's barrel. Keo looked over at her and shook his head. She narrowed her eyes back questioningly, but before he could attempt to answer, the Bucky stepped through the opening to Keo's right.

Keo turned, switched up his grip on the UMP, and smashed the unfolded buttstock into the side of the man's head. The Bucky staggered sideways but didn't go down. Keo didn't expect him to, either, given how light the buttstock was, so he was fully prepared to follow the swaying form and hit the man again, this time getting him square in the forehead.

The Bucky dropped to his knees, still clinging to his AK-47, and he was looking up to see who had struck him when Keo gave up on using the submachine gun as a blunting instrument and just used his fist instead. He punched the young man twice, both times in the face—breaking his nose with the second strike—and the man collapsed to the dirt floor and lay still.

Keo grabbed the Bucky by the arms and pulled him away from the opening and out of view of anyone else passing by. The fighting continued to rage outside, and a few more buildings had gone up in flames while Keo was sliding back into the shadows.

He crouched next to the unconscious man and removed his vest while Claire stood guard.

"If Buck's attacking Darby Bay, we have to get to our friends," Claire said. "We have to get out of here, Keo."

"I know," Keo said. "Trust me, kid, I know."

Another series of explosions, followed by the sounds of falling buildings, rocked the night. One of those *booms* landed close enough to their position that chunks of the ceiling loosened and pelted the floor around their boots.

"What did you see out there?" Keo asked.

"There are guys with guns everywhere. I was lucky to get this far unnoticed, even luckier to stumble across you. I don't think we can leave the same way I got in. Not unless we want to fight our way through *two* armies."

Keo stood up and nodded. "All right. If we can't go out the front, we'll leave through the back."

"What about those guys with guns I mentioned?"

"If we have to, we'll kill everyone that gets in our way," Keo said. "One way or another, we're getting back to Darby Bay."

TWENTY-THREE

If it sounded like World War III was raging across the compound from the comforts of his little prison, with only a hole in the wall to witness the events from, it was much worse and even more frenetic once he was outside.

Which was exactly how Keo liked it.

Especially since he and Claire were going to use the chaos to escape. The only way out was running from the front lines. That, though, came with its own problems, since it wouldn't have looked natural for two "Buckies" to be fleeing the fight while everyone else was running toward it.

To make sure they didn't completely stand out, Keo and Claire stuck to the shadows as much as they could, and when they couldn't, they went with the flow until they didn't have to anymore. It was easy enough; all they had to do was run a little slower toward the front lines than everyone else, and once they were in the rear of the pack, detach themselves and slip back into the night.

Each time they pulled the move, no one noticed; everyone

was simply too busy, too frantic to get to the fight, either because they wanted to or they didn't have any choice. Keo recognized the whirlwind of confusion in the eyes of the ones he saw. War did that to you; the sounds and adrenaline overwhelmed your senses and got your heart beating overtime, and you weren't sure whether to run or hide.

It was easy for Keo to think that he wasn't looking at Buck's main force. These had to be the Fenton people who joined up, or new recruits. Keo didn't see a Greengrass among them leading them. It made him wonder if Buck had abandoned Fenton hours ago with his real force, the *real* Mercerians.

Keo and Claire pulled the same stunt—running with the Buckies until they could sneak off—five times before they finally made it to the back of the compound and were close enough to the lake to see its calm, glistening surface, with the battle taking place at their backs.

And there, to their right, was the warehouse.

It looked smaller in person than it had seemed in the pictures, but the moonlight and heavy shadows probably had a little something to do with that. The guard towers that surrounded its four points stood out along with the men watching from behind their walls and the few that he could see walking the grounds. Unlike the guards outside Keo's prison, these hadn't abandoned their posts yet.

"It's a good thing your men are good at following orders," he had said to Buck.

"Not all of them, but the ones that matter," the man had replied.

Keo guessed these guys mattered, along with whatever was inside the warehouse they were guarding.

What the hell is in that warehouse? What are you hiding, Buck?

But that wasn't something he could solve tonight. Besides, the warehouse had gone down his list of priorities. At the very top was *Get back to Darby Bay as soon as you can or die trying*, and below that was...everything else.

Gotta get back to Darby Bay. Gotta get back to Lara...

Keo looked back at the rest of the compound. Instead of slowing down, the gunfire seemed to be getting even more intense as the battle dragged on. He had a feeling it hadn't even reached its peak yet; that was still to come.

The flames that had engulfed some of the buildings were flaring up high enough into the sky—while constantly being fed by all the fresh, wooden constructions around them—that Keo thought it could be seen for miles. Buck's people were simultaneously trying to fight back the attack, defend their positions, and contain the fires from spreading. They were, as far as Keo could tell, coming up horribly lacking at all three jobs.

All in all, it was a perfect recipe for a late-night escape.

He refocused on the lake in front of them. It was called Lake Mansfield, and it separated the rear of the compound from the woods on the other side. According to the reports he'd read, the lake circled nearly half of Fenton—almost all of its west side and half of its southern tip. There were nothing but walls of black trees on the other end, which looked deceptively closer in the darkness, but Keo knew from the recons that it was about two football fields of open water between here and there.

"Is your leg okay?" Claire asked.

The question surprised him, mostly because he had been

concentrating so hard on how to get across Lakes Mansfield that he had momentarily forgotten she was even standing next to him in the darkness, the two of them squeezed in between a pair of equipment sheds.

Keo nodded. "I don't know what they gave me, but I can barely feel it."

That wasn't entirely true; there was still tingling, but the pain had mostly numbed over. He had noticed it while they were "going with the flow" earlier as they made their way to the shoreline.

Keo looked back at Claire. "You can swim, right?"

"Of course I can swim," Claire said.

"I mean, you can *really* swim," he said, nodding over at the lake.

She stared at the water and didn't answer right away. If he had to guess, she was trying to measure the distance between the shoreline and the woods.

"Two hundred meters, give or take," Keo said.

"Two hundred..."

"Meters."

"That's pretty...long."

"Yeah, it is. Can you swim it?"

"I'm not sure," Claire said, shaking her head. "I mean, I can swim. We all had to learn back at the island during basic, but two hundred meters..." She sighed. "I don't think I can swim that far, Keo. Not in this kind of weather, anyway," she added, shivering slightly. "Can you do it?"

"Two hundred meters is no cakewalk. Even for me." He looked toward the marina on their left. "We'll find another way across."

"Boats?" Claire said.

He nodded, eyeing the crafts moored to a series of docks. They were easily visible with the lampposts nearby. Motor-powered boats, about two dozen or so of them, and any one would work to get them where they needed to be, which was as far away from the compound as possible. The problem was the five men Keo had counted walking back and forth along the bank of the lake.

"How many?" he asked.

"I count six," Claire said.

"Six?"

"Yeah. How many did you see?"

"Five."

"I saw six. There's probably more."

"I'm pretty sure there's more."

Keo looked down at the UMP in his hands. He didn't like the weight of it. That told him he didn't have a full magazine already loaded. The spare in his back pocket put his mind slightly at ease—as long as he didn't go around spraying the submachine gun on full-auto, anyway.

Just in case, he made sure the fire selector was on semiauto before asking Claire, "How are you for ammo?"

"I haven't had to shoot anyone, so I still have a full mag. Plus two spares in my vest."

"So ninety rounds?"

"Yeah, I think so." Then, "You wanna trade?"

Keo grinned. "I think that's probably for the best."

He took her AR and immediately liked the heavier weight. The ACOG scope mounted on top with the illuminated reticle didn't hurt either. If he had his choice, he wouldn't sacrifice the maneuverability of a submachine gun for a longer weapon, but then again he was used to making his living up close and personal. This wasn't going to be one of those times, though.

Claire took the UMP from him along with the spare. She took out the two magazines from her vest's pouch, and he slipped them behind his back instead of in his vest for easier reach.

"How are we gonna do this?" Claire asked.

"See that white fifteen-footer?" Keo asked, pointing at one of the boats. It barely moved on the surface of the calm Lake Mansfield water and was the first one in line. Fifty meters, give or take, from their position.

"Yes," Claire said.

"That's the one we'll go for. You know how to drive a boat?"

"Is it like driving a car?"

"Closer to a motorcycle. You crank the lever next to the steering wheel to throttle forward, and back to reverse."

"Where's the brake?"

"The reverse is the brake."

"Oh." Then, "What if there isn't any gas in those engines?"

Hunh. Didn't think of that.

"Keo?" Claire said when he didn't answer quickly enough.

Maybe we'll get lucky, he thought but didn't think that would go over well with the teenager, so he said instead, "It should have gas. They probably use those boats pretty often to patrol the area during the day. We wouldn't need a lot to get across."

He thought he sounded pretty convincing, but Claire didn't completely buy it.

"Should, huh?" the kid said.

Keo grinned. "Yeah. Should. Think positive."

"You Captain Optimism all of a sudden?" she said, smiling back.

"That's me. Now, are you ready?"

"No, but let's do it anyway."

"That's my girl."

He glanced over his shoulder to listen to the back-and-forth clatter of gunfire and explosions from the active side of the compound. There were a couple of *booms!* that made the sheds to both sides of them tremble slightly, and Keo thought, *Someone's having a blast with those rocket launchers. Or grenades. Or maybe both.*

"The white boat," Keo said, turning back around. "Go straight for the white boat."

"Got it," Claire said. "The white boat."

"Go," he said, and he was already moving before the word was completely out of his mouth.

Keo lifted the carbine as he jogged out of the shadows and forward, angling toward the fifteen-footer. He pointed the weapon at the closest Bucky as the man stood underneath a lamppost, his own rifle clutched in front of him as he stared off toward the fighting. It didn't take long for the man to glimpse Keo and Claire out of the corner of his eye, and he began turning, raising his rifle as he did so.

The red, glowing reticle lined up against the guard's chest, and Keo squeezed the trigger—once, twice—and the body was falling even as he felt a blast of wind as Claire raced past him on his left.

Faster, kid, faster! he wanted to shout, but held off. Claire was probably unnerved enough that she didn't need him shouting something stupid like that after her. She was probably running as fast as she could already.

Keo swiveled the AR slightly while still moving, maintaining his pace toward the docks as best he could even as he searched for the other two patrols he'd seen earlier.

There, running toward the fallen man. Two figures.

Keo fired, knocking the man up front off his feet. Keo had only managed one shot before the man fell, so he didn't know if the Bucky was going to stay down or not. Not that he had the second or two it would have taken to pull a double tap and make sure, because the second guard slid to a stop and looked over in his direction. Keo shot him, too, and this time he was able to pull the trigger twice, hitting the man each time in the chest and watching him slump lifelessly to the ground, the shadows swallowing him up like some living beast.

He turned to his left even as his fourth shot echoed and became lost in the continuous *pop-pop-pop* of other rifle fire coming from the other side of the compound. While he was pretty sure his own gunshots wouldn't pull any extra attention from those fighting at the perimeter, it would be a different story with Buckies in the immediate area. Especially the ones along the shoreline.

And he was right, as three figures appeared in the lights to his left and began firing—*at Claire.*

The teenager was halfway to the boats when she threw herself down to the ground. Keo hadn't realized she had gotten so far ahead. The only reason the guards were shooting at her and not him was because he was still moving in the shadows while she was running in the light and giving them a perfect target to shoot at.

Then Claire was back up on her hands and knees and crawling. Fast crawling. She was clearly wounded, though he wasn't close enough to see how badly or where she'd been shot. But she wasn't down and out, and that was all that mattered.

Keep moving, kid. Keep moving!

Keo flicked the fire selector on his AR to full-auto and unloaded on the three guards. He used up the remains of the magazine in one pull, which was a hell of a waste, but seeing two of the Buckies go down while the third turned in his direction made it worth it.

He was still in the shadows, which made it difficult for the guard to locate him. That, though, didn't stop the man from firing in his direction anyway. A couple of rounds came close —the *zip!* of the 5.56 an inch from his forehead, making Keo go down on one knee even as he reloaded, worked the charging handle, and fired a quick burst that dropped the third guard.

Keo was on his feet and running again a second later.

So was Claire, who had scrambled up from the ground and was running—no, *hobbling*—toward the dock. She looked hurt, but he couldn't see where. The fact that she was moving awkwardly probably meant a leg wound.

But she was *still moving.*

Keo ran after her, shouting, "The white boat, kid! The white boat!"

Claire didn't bother looking back at him or answering as she hopped onto the dock and ran straight for the rope that tied the white fifteen-footer in place. She was still working on it when gunshots rang out, and Claire either fell or lunged to the wooden floor to dodge them.

Four more Buckies were racing out of the darkness along the shoreline to Keo's right. They were still too far away—over sixty meters—when they began shooting, firing in three-round bursts that chipped away at the dock and *pinged!* off some of the boats moored in place.

Keo returned fire, knowing the chances of hitting them weren't very good. He was running and so were they, and he wasn't *that* good of a shot. But firing in bursts made the guards stop their forward momentum and turn and flee back in the other direction.

Or two of them did, while the other two dived for cover behind a wooden shack. Keo stitched the side of the building with a series of shots but never unloaded everything he had. As soon as he stopped providing covering fire for Claire, the guards would immediately resume shooting at her, and he couldn't allow that.

Claire, thank God, was already back on her feet and pulling at the rope. By the time she tossed the line into the boat, Keo was almost at the dock himself while still firing toward the shack.

"Fire it up!" Keo shouted, while thinking, *And let's hope there's some gas in the tank, or this is going to be a pretty short escape!*

He was waiting to hear the sound of the two motors roaring to life even as he kept squeezing off shot after shot at the guards. He glimpsed a head or two peeking out from behind cover, waiting for him to stop shooting so they could return fire. Whoever they were, they weren't willing to risk their lives being heroes.

That's it, boys. Play it safe. Just like that!

But he couldn't hear the motors.

Not after five seconds.

Not after ten...

Come on, kid. Fire up those motors! Let's hear them!

Instead, he heard Claire shouting, "Keo!"

What now?

He glanced back while still shooting down the shoreline. He wasn't really aiming for any specific target now, just listening to the satisfying echoes of the rounds hitting the side of the building.

"There's no key!" Claire shouted.

He stared at her for a second.

There's no...

Two seconds.

...key?

The words rang inside his head.

"There's no key!"

What does she mean, there's no key?

Where is the key?

"There's no key!" Claire shouted again.

There's no key.

There's no key!

He wanted to laugh his ass off. They had been worried about having gas for the boat's engines, but neither one of them had considered the possibility that the Buckies wouldn't leave the keys in the ignition when the crafts weren't in use. After all, why would they? The keys would instead be in one of the buildings behind them, or maybe even in that shack the two guards—four now, that the two that had fled earlier had found enough courage to run back to rejoin their comrades—were hiding behind.

He glanced up and down the dock, looking for a box that could potentially hold keys. It wasn't uncommon for marinas to have locked boxes with the keys inside, especially in places where there were few security issues.

Except he didn't see anything that even remotely looked like a key box.

Well, fuck me!

"Keo!" Claire shouted.

He was pretty sure he actually laughed out loud that time, but if he did, it was instantly lost in the suddenly ferocious *pop-pop-pop* of rifles as the Buckies unloaded on the dock. The teenager ducked behind the fifteen-footer's console, but there was no place for Keo to hide.

He wasn't sure when he got the bright idea, but it was already in his head when he tossed the empty AR instead of reloading it, spun around, and jumped into the boat behind Claire.

The teenager glanced frantically back at him even as bullets slammed into the hull of the craft and even more chipped at the wooden walkway in front of them. She opened her mouth wide to shout something when he grabbed her shoulders—

—and threw her overboard.

TWENTY-FOUR

There was blood in the water. Literally. Claire was bleeding from a graze along her right thigh, but it wasn't bad enough that he had to worry about it. At least it wasn't nearly as bad as his wounds, but thankfully Buck's medic knew what he was doing, and whatever the man had injected Keo with, it was still running through his system and keeping him wide awake. Not that fighting to keep from drowning in the very cold Lake Mansfield water wasn't already helping with that.

The thin tendrils of blood highlighted by the generous splash of moonlight, like mirages circling him and Claire, were distracting, but the bullets *zip-zip-zipping* into the water around them were worse. The rounds looked as if they were moving in slow motion, but they were still going to hurt (a lot) if they hit either him or the teenager. The school of white bass that had scattered when they plunged into the water were swimming away as fast as possible, but one of them didn't move fast enough, and a bullet skewered it through the head.

The poor fish turned sideways before beginning to float up to the surface.

As soon as he went under, Keo immediately grabbed Claire's struggling form and began pulling her away from the boat. The bright white hull of the fifteen-footer gave him a perfect target to swim away from. He moved his legs with practiced ease, years of swimming on, under, and above the often-times antagonistic waves up and down the coastline of San Diego coming to the forefront instinctively.

Keo didn't panic. He was beyond that. Too many days and nights alone in the cold and warm and every other temperature in-between helped him to rise above any notions of panic. It wasn't the same for Claire, but Keo was ready for that, too, and he held onto her as she fought against him, both legs kicking frantically as bullet after bullet sank into the water in front of her, like living creatures chasing her.

He wasted five seconds reaching behind him and pulling out the spare magazine in his back pocket, then did the same to the UMP spare Claire had put into her pouch. He also pulled the Glock out of her hip holster and let it sink into the bottom of the lake. Keo would have lightened their load even further but just didn't have the precious seconds that would have taken.

He didn't blame the teenager for being freaked out by the combination of being shot *while* she was sinking. Even though he wished she would calm down just a little bit, he understood why she wasn't—or couldn't. Most people weren't accustomed to being underwater, which was why most people couldn't swim to—literally, in some cases—save their lives. So in that respect, Claire wasn't unique.

Even so, her constantly twitching form made his job

multiple times harder than it should have been, and it was becoming a chore to keep his mind tuned to his internal clock. The last thing he wanted was for Claire to black out before drowning. That meant he had to maintain his steady progress moving them away from the boat while counting down the seconds before he had to take her back up.

From experience, Keo knew he could hold his breath for up to three minutes, sometimes longer under optimal conditions. The key word there, of course, was "optimal." Swimming while dragging a one hundred and twenty-something pound woman fighting him every inch of the way wasn't ideal, but he figured he could probably manage two minutes and change. Of course, he wasn't going to be able to prove that theory, because there was no way Claire was going to last that long.

Or even half that.

One minute. One minute, tops. Can't risk more than that, or she'll drown.

And Gaby would kick my ass if I let that happen.

They were under for ten seconds when he began moving them away from the dock and away from the bullets.

Twenty seconds after that, Claire's resistance lessened noticeably, but he couldn't be sure if that was because she was dead or—

No, not dead, he thought when she turned her head to look over her shoulder at him. She was holding her breath, and her eyes were wide. Her cheeks were already ballooning...

Shit. She's going to black out.

He began moving up toward the surface and—

They broke through, the sound of Claire gasping desperately for fresh breath the signal he needed that he'd gotten her up in time. He held onto her while using the brief respite to get a better grip and slid both hands farther underneath her armpits.

"Keo!" Claire gasped, but if she had more to say, it was interrupted by the *pop-pop-pop!* of gunfire and bullets *splack-spack-spacking!* into the lake's surface around them. Keo was less worried about the ones falling short and hitting the water and more concerned with the rounds *zipping!* past his and Claire's head.

It didn't take a lot of looking around to see the Buckies. They were charging up the shoreline, racing toward the dock where he and Claire had just jumped from. There were more than four of them now—six in all—and they were running full speed. The only reason they hadn't hit their targets yet was precisely because they were running full speed and shooting at the same time. That was the good news.

The bad news was that he hadn't managed to drag Claire very far from the fifteen-footer, still moored in place. They'd put barely fifteen meters between them and the dock.

I'm slowing down in my old age!

"Take a deep breath!" he shouted.

Claire nodded and did, just before he pulled them both back down under the surface.

Once they were surrounded by cold (*freezing!*) water again, the cracks of rifles faded into the background. Unfortunately, he couldn't ignore the bullets punching into the swirling space around them like knives cutting through jelly. The sight was almost surreal, if they weren't *getting so damn close.*

Keo immediately began swimming again, but without his arms to work with, it was slow going. He took them down deeper than before so they wouldn't be too visible from the surface. The morning was coming up on them fast, but there was still plenty of darkness that it wouldn't be easy to spot them from land with enough murky water between him and the shooters.

Or he hoped, anyway.

Captain Optimism. Amirite?

Claire had stopped struggling in his arms, so that helped tremendously. She did appear to be slightly alarmed when they began sinking, but she must have realized what he was doing and stopped after a while.

Smart kid.

Slowly, the whiteness of the fifteen-footer's hull was swallowed up by the blackness, which was exactly what Keo was hoping to see. The bullets were coming at them from more random locations now, sure signs that the shooters couldn't see them—or were having trouble—and were just firing into the lake with no clear targets.

Ten seconds...

Twenty...

Around the thirty-second mark post-reentry, Claire began moving in front of him again.

At around forty seconds, her legs began kicking.

Shit. She needs more air!

Keo looked up, locked on the flickering shape of the moon in the sky, and took them back up.

Claire sucking in air and the constant streams of small arms and machine-gun fire from the raging war crashed against Keo's ears the second they broke through the surface for the second time.

Keo glanced around, trying to relocate the Buckies—

Almost fifty meters away, spread out on the same dock

with the white boat. A couple had flashlights, one with a flashlight underneath his rifle's barrel, and they were scouring the lake.

But the Buckies hadn't seen them yet, so he didn't take Claire back down so quickly.

As he watched, one of the black-clad figures ran back up the dock and jumped into one of the moored boats—a big red twenty-footer. A few seconds later, the craft's twin motors roared to life.

I guess he found where they kept the keys!

Claire glanced back at him, her body shaking badly against his. She didn't look ready at all, but Keo asked anyway, "Ready?"

"No!" she said back, barely able to get the word out with her teeth chattering so badly.

"Take a breath."

"God, Keo..."

"One, two, *three*."

She stiffened as he stopped moving his legs and let them both sink back into the water.

Even as they dropped and dropped, Keo did the calculations in his head.

They were fifty meters (*Give or take*) from the dock, which meant they had managed a quarter of the distance to the other side of the lake. That wasn't good. He'd hoped for better time, but having to drag Claire along for the ride had slowed him down. Of course, he could have easily made the trees if he dumped the teenager, but that was a nonstarter.

Besides, both Lara and Gaby would take turns killing me.

If they're even still alive...

He pushed the negative thoughts away (*Captain Optimist,*

pal! It's Super Captain Optimism Time!), and resumed swimming, using the beams of light visible from above him as an indicator of which direction to move *away* from.

He could hear it—the boat's motors as it began moving across the lake. It wasn't anywhere close to being on top of them yet, which meant the Buckies still didn't know their exact location. He could feel the waves moving against them as the twenty-footer splashed across the lake, but waves were better than bullets.

Claire remained calm in front of him and was even starting to help by kicking with her legs. Or she probably thought she was helping anyway, but the teenager had terrible form and wasn't really doing much to assist him. He couldn't tell her that, though, and used her activity instead to keep track of her status. As long as her legs were moving, she was doing fine; the sooner they slowed or stopped completely, he'd have to take them back up again.

And with the boat up there, skimming the water looking for them...

He wasn't looking forward to that. Not one bit.

Claire was able to hold her breath for much longer this time. It still wasn't the two minutes he would have been ecstatic with, but it was closer to the one minute he had already decided to settle for.

At around thirty seconds, her kicking started to slow.

At forty, they had all but stopped, and her body tightened noticeably in his arms.

Keo knew the signals and started moving back up to the surface, the constant refrain of, *Please be far away, boat, please be far away!* going round and round inside his head as he rose higher and higher.

They broke through Lake Mansfield for the third time.

Oh hell, Keo thought when he saw the big red boat less than thirty meters to the left of them.

The craft was pointed west toward the tree line on the other side of the lake, and there were four men in the back, all with flashlights, and they were skipping beams across the water's surface when—

One struck Keo in the face and almost blinded him.

"There!" one of the Buckies screamed.

Keo tightened his grip around Claire's body and was about to drop them like stones back into the water when there was the hellacious *brap-brap-brap!* of machine-gun fire. The thought, *Wait. Where is that coming from?* ran through his head, because he hadn't seen an MG anywhere on the boat. As far as he knew, the Buckies were only carrying rifles.

So where were the gunshots coming from?

He was still wondering that when tracer rounds flashed over the boat and struck the water around them.

Someone was shooting at the boat!

Keo turned slightly, tracking the incoming bullets—like hundreds of individual white ropes being flung across the lake —back to the wall of trees on the other side of Lake Mansfield. That should have been enough to distract the men in the boat from Keo and Claire, and it did, except for one determined asshole who pointed his rifle in their direction and opened fire.

Keo pulled Claire under just as the water around them rippled against a fresh wave of bullets. He took them down and down, eyes focusing on the red belly of the boat the entire time as it began to turn, turn—until it stopped turning and began exploding.

No, not exploding. Its hull was coming undone as bullets

punched into it, ripping it apart in front of Keo's eyes. The rifle fire that had been directed at him and Claire ceased at the same time a body broke through the surface and sank like a stone, along with the rifle the man had been clutching onto, in front of them.

Then a second body, this one dropping feet first into the lake, just before a ball of fire engulfed the remains of the boat.

The fuel tank. The incoming MG tracer rounds had enough of an incendiary effect that they could easily ignite a flammable source.

Like a boat's gas tank...

Keo grinned and began swimming away from the burning boat and toward the other side of the lake.

Ten seconds...

Twenty...

They were making good time now, thanks to Claire helping out by no longer fighting him every inch of the way. Keo guessed seeing the Bucky boat go up in flames had a little something to do with how calm she had become. He was able to carry them for nearly fifty seconds straight until her body signaled that her air was running out again.

There was still plenty of moonlight in the nighttime sky to greet them when they broke through the surface for the fourth time. Keo was able to locate the burning twenty-foot boat in the distance, parts of it still on fire as it began to sink into the water, the lake dousing the flames as soon as it came into contact with the burning sections of the craft. He could barely make out the docks in the distance, which signaled they had made excellent progress across the lake. Which left them with...

He glanced toward the tree line and was surprised at how

far they'd come. They were now closer to the other side than to the compound. He was catching his breath, trying to decide how to respond to this new development, when a flashlight blinked on between some of the trees.

Then it turned off, before coming back on.

Then off and on again...

It was a signal, one directed at *them*.

"You see that?" Claire asked, turning her head to look at him. Her hair was matted around her wet face, her lips and teeth trembling so badly that he was afraid she might accidentally bite her own tongue. With all the swimming he was doing and trying not to drown the both of them, he had forgotten just how freezing the lake was.

Nothing like the prospect of immediate death to keep your mind off hypothermia!

"Yeah," Keo said.

"What should we do?"

"Well, they've already seen us. And they just destroyed that boat. They could do the same to us, but instead they're... waving us over?"

"Are you sure about that?" she asked, every word stuttering from the cold.

"I don't think we have any choice. It's either them or, you know."

"Since you put it that way..."

"Hold on," Keo said, and began swimming toward the shoreline.

This time he didn't have to take them both under the surface, so they made better progress. Also, Claire's kicking did more good up here.

"Keo," Claire said after a few seconds of swimming.

"Yeah?"

"You're a hell of a good swimmer, you know that?"

He grinned. "Thanks, kid. If I let you go, can you swim on your own?"

"Keo, I don't think I can move my arms right now. I can barely feel my legs."

"In that case, just relax."

"Now that I can do," Claire said, though she didn't stop kicking.

Good enough.

He glanced over his shoulder a couple of times even after the flashlight had turned off. He knew where he was going and could see the trees getting brighter as the night continued to fade and morning began to creep into its place, little by little.

In front of him, on the other side of Lake Mansfield, the fighting hadn't stopped for a second, the *pop-pop-pop* coming across the length of the lake like endless ropes of firecrackers. It was harder now to see the burning buildings or pinpoint where the battle was most intense. Gunfire seemed to come from every end of Buck's former command center. There were the occasional explosions, but most of it was small arms and machine guns.

Have at it, boys. Have at it to your heart's content.

And there, the island with the warehouse, looking small. It wasn't anywhere close to their position, and though it was likely within shooting distance of the people who had destroyed the Bucky twenty-footer, no one had fired at it and vice versa. He could barely make out the guard towers, never mind the men in them.

What are you hiding in that warehouse, Buck? What secrets don't you want us to know?

"Keo," Claire said, her voice bringing him back to the freezing lake water.

"Yeah?"

She was looking behind her, back toward the trees, and Keo followed her gaze.

In the growing morning dusk, there were men back there, watching them approach. They wore black fatigues and some had black camo on their faces.

"They look like the same ones attacking Fenton," Claire said.

"That's good to know."

"Is it?"

"'The enemy of my enemy is my friend.'"

"You hope."

Yeah, that too, Keo thought as he turned around so he could more easily drag Claire and swim at the same time.

On the plus side, no one was shooting at them yet.

That, he concluded, was good enough, for now.

TWENTY-FIVE

They were pulled out of Lake Mansfield by a half-dozen men wearing black clothing—not quite fatigues or BDUs, but close enough—and dark face paint. Neither Keo nor Claire had any weapons to give up, so it made for an uneventful "capture." The men didn't say anything and led them away from the shoreline and into the woods before they even had the chance to dry out.

Keo took a second or two to glance back at the compound across the lake as they were taken away. Unlike the calm water that separated him from Buck's base, there was nothing tranquil about what was taking place on the other side. The fighting raged on under the ever-expanding cloak of morning sunlight, though it wasn't quite as helter skelter as it had been during the night. He sensed a stalemate on the horizon.

Claire was shivering from the long swim, and one of their captors was nice enough to take off his thick winter jacket and give it to her. The teenager smiled and thanked him, and got back a shy smile from behind a face covered in black and green camo.

The others weren't quite as nice, but they weren't assholes, either. Instead, they marched Keo and Claire through the trees that, like the rest of the wooded area, were coming to life. Animals and men alike were coming out of their slumber and moving around. Keo glimpsed figures around them, armed men and a few women, going back and forth from the shoreline.

There were two men in front of Keo and Claire and two more behind them, including the shy kid who had given Claire his jacket. Keo's instincts were to try to get some information, but like the teenager next to him, he was suddenly very cold from their arduous trek across Lake Mansfield to do very much except control his shivering and keep his teeth from chattering too loudly. Unfortunately, he wasn't nearly as attractive (or female) as Claire, and no one offered their winter gear to him. There was some benefit to trying not to freeze to death, though; he could barely feel the aches and pains from all his bruises and wounds. Claire hobbled noticeably next to him, and when their captors noticed, they slowed down their pace.

The long walk—about two hundred meters or so from the shoreline—gave him and Claire the opportunity to dry out. He was still dripping lake water, though not nearly as heavily as before, by the time they reached the makeshift command post. There were two to three dozen tents spread out inside a clearing, with guards on the perimeter and patrols around the area. Men on horseback moved back and forth, but Keo couldn't see any vehicles. Which made sense if the compound's attackers had been sneaking into position all night last night before launching their surprise strike. A car engine would definitely give away their approach.

Even all the way back here, Keo could still hear the *pop-pop-pop* of gunfire coming all the way from Fenton. Things were clearly slowing down to a series of sporadic back and forth, though, and nothing like the full-on attack he'd been hearing all night.

Their captors led them through the CP and into a tent near the middle that looked identical to all the others except for the guards standing outside. There were three men already inside, standing around a cheap plastic portable table with a map of the area spread out between them. They looked up when Keo and Claire were brought in.

"This them?" one of the men asked. Keo had never seen the speaker before; he was older than the other two in the tent with him by about twenty years. He was in his fifties, wearing similar black clothing to the others, except his didn't have a single dot of dirt on them.

Someone hasn't gotten his hands dirty yet.

Keo zeroed in on one of the men standing next to the leader. Thirties, dark hair, with equally dark eyes that widened almost comically at the sight of Keo.

"Fancy meeting you here," Keo said.

The man smirked back at him. "What the hell are you doing all the way out here?"

Keo took a moment to squeeze some leftover water from his shirt. "I thought it was a perfect morning for a swim. What does it look like?"

"You know him?" the older man asked.

"His name's Keo," Nolan said. Keo recognized him instantly from Cordine City—or what was left of the place after Merrick had gotten through with it. Nolan was dressed the same as the others, with a rifle slung over his shoulder, but his "uniform" looked a little more worn than the older man's.

There were no signs of Cassandra, the woman who had been at Nolan's side back in Cordine City. Instead, the third man in the tent was a redhead with a goatee and not very much on top. He was in his thirties and he kept silent; even so, Keo recognized the signs.

Now that's a dangerous man. Might want to keep a close eye on him...

"I know that name, don't I?" the older man was saying as he eyeballed Keo.

"Probably," Nolan said. "Ol' Keo's been around, from what I hear."

"Here, there, everywhere in-between," Keo said. He glanced back at the two armed men who had led them into the tent. "We good, Nolan?"

"Yeah, we're good," Nolan said. He nodded at the guards, who exited. "Keo, this is Copenhagen."

"Copenhagen?" Claire said.

"That's right," the older man said. He walked the short distance over and shook Claire's, then Keo's hand. "Let me guess: All that commotion last night—that was you two?"

"Guilty as charged," Keo said, and thought, *Copenhagen. I guess he's not dead after all.* "What are you guys doing here?"

"What does it look like?" Nolan said. "We're taking Fenton."

Not today, you're not, Keo thought, but he didn't think that was going to help his cause, so he said instead, "So what is this? Some kind of alliance?"

"That's exactly what this is," Nolan said. "We didn't feel

like waiting for Black Tide to make their move. Buck needed to be stopped. *Now*."

"So you guys joined forces?"

"Not just us. There are people from about ten towns here. Most of them already know what these Mercerian assholes are capable of. They've seen the damage up close. We're going to put a stop to them now, whether Black Tide approves or not."

"They don't know you're here."

Nolan shook his head. "We don't need their permission. Or hers."

He didn't say who *her* was, and Keo guessed he didn't really have to. Everyone knew.

"We're going to take Fenton, then put Buck on trial for his crimes," Copenhagen said. "He has a lot to answer for."

Like taking Fenton away from you? Keo thought, but again, he didn't think that kind of straightforward talk was going to help his cause.

He said, "Have you talked to Black Tide lately?"

"Not for a while," Nolan said. "Why?"

"I need to make contact with them," Keo said, even as he thought, *If they're still out there. God, please let them still be out there...*

He got a change of clothes and fresh venison from one of the campfires, and one of Copenhagen's medics took a look before redressing his wounds. He pocketed some painkillers before leaving the camp with a long-range radio, anxious to reach Darby Bay. The city was close enough to his current position that they should have answered, but they didn't. He tried Black Tide Island itself, but it too failed to respond.

Keo spent the next thirty minutes trying anyway, repeating his calls and switching back and forth. When that still didn't work, he attempted every Black Tide emergency channel he knew, hoping that maybe there was someone—*anyone*—out there who would answer. He needed information. He needed to know what was happening in Darby Bay. He needed to know *something*.

But he got nothing, and the frustration grew. He spent more time chewing and filling his belly with warm soup than he did getting any closer to reaching Lara or anyone from Black Tide. He couldn't stop and didn't. When sitting around using the radio got to be too much, he got up and moved around. He was now wearing a gun belt with a pistol in a holster, which was like a pass to roam in and around the CP.

Claire found him pacing in the woods a few meters from the main campsite. She had changed into warm clothes, and like him, got her wound dressed. She stood by listening to him fruitlessly trying to make contact with *someone* over the radio. Every now and then she would glance over in the direction of Fenton as cracks of gunfire continued throughout the morning.

When Keo finally put the receiver back into the radio's cradle, Claire asked, "I don't understand. Where is everybody? Even if Darby Bay..." She stopped short before continuing. "Someone should be out there. *Someone* should have answered."

Keo shook his head. She wasn't saying anything he hadn't thought to himself a hundred times in the last hour. Someone should have answered one of the channels. It was impossible for Buck and Merrick to have taken out every single arm of

Black Tide in one night. Lara's people were heavily spread out over multiple states, for God's sake.

So where the hell was everyone?

"This doesn't make any sense," Claire was saying. "The island should be safe, no matter what's happening in Darby Bay or anywhere else. And if the island's safe, then Jane should be answering your calls."

The kid wasn't wrong. Jane was in charge of Black Tide's radios. The woman practically lived in the communications room on the island, and the fact that she hadn't answered any of Keo's attempts spoke volumes.

Keo kicked the radio in frustration and watched it slam into a tree and shatter.

"We need to go," he said. "We need to be halfway to Darby Bay by now."

"You want a horse?" Nolan asked.

"Two, actually," Keo said. "One for me, and one for Claire. Unless you have a car sitting around that you're not using?"

Nolan shook his head. "We used horses and boots to get here. It was the only way to make sure Fenton didn't hear us coming."

"Did you get him?" Claire asked. "Buck?"

"We don't know. And we won't know until we take the compound."

"Which isn't going to be today," Copenhagen said.

They were back inside the main tent, with Nolan and Copenhagen. The third man with the red goatee wasn't there this time. They could still hear small arms crackling in the distant sky, but they were far and few now. According to Copenhagen, his men had taken the perimeter around the base but hadn't been able to make any further headway inside. The Buckies were too dug in and had too much fire-power, and Copenhagen had elected to hold off on another full-frontal assault now that they no longer had surprise on their side.

"They're not going anywhere, and neither are we," Copenhagen said. "It might take a day or a week, but they're not getting out of that place. That army is dead; it just doesn't know it yet."

"What about the city?" Claire asked. "The civilians?"

"They're hanging back. I know most of those people; they were never that enthusiastic about Buck's arrival, and from the intel I've been gathering before last night, that hasn't changed. So they won't get in the way."

"If anything, they're helping our forces with food, water, and shelter," Nolan said. "I have to admit, I didn't see that coming."

"He's not in there, you know," Keo said.

"Who?" Nolan asked.

"Buck."

Nolan and Copenhagen exchanged a look, before Copenhagen said, "And you know this how?"

"He left last night. That large caravan you saw taking off that still hasn't come back? That was him. He was on his way to Darby Bay. He's there right now, and I doubt very much he cares what you do with Fenton. He was always just using the city as an FOB for something bigger."

"Black Tide," Nolan said.

Keo nodded. "Yeah. This was never about Cordine City or

Fenton or any of the other towns he massacred. This was always about Black Tide."

"Shit."

"So I need horses. The fastest ones you have, and supplies to get me to Darby Bay."

"And what is it you'll do when you get there?" Copenhagen asked. "If you're right, and Buck is already there with an army?"

Kill everyone if they've harmed her, Keo thought, but he said, "I'll figure it out on the way over. So? Can you spare those horses or not?"

"Yeah," Nolan said. "I'll tell them to bring you two."

"Thanks," Keo said, and turned to go with Claire. He stopped at the tent flap and looked back at Copenhagen. "What was in the warehouse?"

"The warehouse?" Copenhagen said.

"The one on the island."

Copenhagen shook his head. "I don't know. The last time I was in Fenton, that building was under construction. I don't know what's inside or what Buck's been using it for. Whatever it is, it couldn't have been that important."

"What makes you say that?" Claire asked.

"Because if Buck did take off last night, he left whatever was inside the warehouse behind."

"Unless he took it with him," Keo said.

***

A horse was a horse, but not when its name was Horse. Keo recognized it instantly, along with the large man sitting in its saddle as they trotted through the camp toward him.

Keo grinned and waved them down. "Jesus. You're still alive."

"Why wouldn't I be?" the big man, Wally, said as he jumped down. "Oh, you weren't talking to me, were you?"

Keo ignored him and walked over to the big thoroughbred. The animal lifted his head and let out a loud whinny.

"I guess he remembers you, too," Wally said.

"Of course he does," Keo said. "We've been through a lot together."

"You two know each other?" Claire asked.

"We met in Cordine City," Wally said. "Wait. You're talking about me and Keo here, right?"

Claire smiled. "Who did you think I was talking about?"

"The horse."

"The horse?"

"Yeah. His horse."

"That's your horse?" Claire said to Keo. "When did you get a horse?"

"Long story," Keo said. Then to Wally, "Thanks for taking good care of him, Wally, but I need him again."

"Hey, he was always just a loaner anyway," Wally said. "Where you running off to?"

"Darby Bay."

"What's in Darby Bay?"

"I'll find out when I get there," Keo said. "Can you get Claire another horse? Something that can keep up with Horse here?"

"Wait. You named your horse, Horse?" Claire asked.

"You say that like it's an odd thing to do."

"Well, it is."

"Everyone thinks it's odd except you, Keo," Wally said. He nodded at Claire. "Follow me, kid," and led her away.

The teenager followed the big Cordine City man, but not before glancing over her shoulder at Keo as if to say, *You really named your horse, Horse?*

Keo smiled back at her before turning his full attention to Horse. The animal had already lost interest in their reunion and was grazing on a heavy patch of green on the ground.

"Got a long road ahead of us, boy," Keo said as he rubbed down the animal's silky smooth mane. "I'm gonna need you to be fast. Faster than you were in Axton. Faster than you were in Cordine City. *Really* fast. Can you do that?"

As if in response, Horse lifted his head and whinnied before going back to his lunch.

"Gotta fly, boy, gotta fly like the wind," Keo whispered. "Gotta get to Lara. Gotta get to Lara before it's too late..."

Made in the USA
Middletown, DE
22 March 2018